D0201162

Hogarth Shakespeare

Shylock Is My Name

THE MERCHANT OF VENICE RETOLD

Howard Jacobson

London   New York

Copyright © 2016 by Howard Jacobson

All rights reserved.
Published in the United States by Hogarth, an imprint of the Crown Publishing Group, a division of Penguin Random House LLC, New York.
www.crownpublishing.com

HOGARTH is a trademark of the Random House Group Limited, and the H colophon is a trademark of Penguin Random House LLC.

Simultaneously published in Great Britain by Hogarth UK, a division of Random House Group Limited, a Penguin Random House company, London.

Library of Congress Cataloging-in-Publication Data is available upon request.

ISBN 978-0-8041-4132-1
eBook ISBN 978-0-8041-4133-8

Printed in the United States of America

Jacket design by Christopher Brand
Jacket photography by Rodney Smith

10 9 8 7 6 5 4 3 2 1

First United States Edition

To the memory of Wilbur Sanders

How it is, that over many years of friendship

and teaching Shakespeare together we never

discussed The Merchant of Venice, *I cannot*

explain. It is a matter of deep regret to me that

we cannot discuss it now.

PORTIA: Which is the merchant here, and which the Jew?

DUKE: Antonio and old Shylock, both stand forth.

PORTIA: Is your name Shylock?

SHYLOCK: Shylock is my name.

Shylock Is My Name

ONE

It is one of those better-to-be-dead-than-alive days you get in the north of England in February, the space between the land and sky a mere letter box of squeezed light, the sky itself unfathomably banal. A stage unsuited to tragedy, even here where the dead lie quietly. There are two men in the cemetery, occupied in duties of the heart. They don't look up. In these parts you must wage war against the weather if you don't want farce to claim you.

Signs of just such a struggle are etched on the face of the first of the mourners, a man of middle age and uncertain bearing, who sometimes walks with his head held arrogantly high, and at others stoops as though hoping not to be seen. His mouth, too, is twitchy and misleading, his lips one moment twisted into a sneer, the next fallen softly open, as vulnerable to bruising as summer fruit. He is Simon Strulovitch—a rich, furious, easily hurt philanthropist with on-again off-again enthusiasms, a distinguished collection of twentieth-century Anglo-Jewish art and old Bibles, a passion for Shakespeare (whose genius and swashbuckling Sephardi looks he once thought could only be explained by the

playwright's ancestors having changed their name from Shapiro, but now he isn't sure), honorary doctorates from universities in London, Manchester and Tel Aviv (the one from
Tel Aviv is something else he isn't sure about) and a daughter
going off the rails. He is here to inspect the stone that has
recently been erected at the head of his mother's grave, now
that the twelve months of mourning for her has elapsed. He
hasn't mourned her conscientiously during that period—too
busy buying and lending art, too busy with his foundations
and endowments, or "benefacting," as his mother called it
with a mixture of pride and concern (she didn't want him
killing himself giving money away), too busy settling scores
in his head, too busy with his daughter—but he intends to
make amends. There is always time to be a better son.

Or a better father. Could it be that it's his daughter he's
really getting ready to mourn? These things run in families.
His father had briefly mourned him. *"You are dead to me!"*
And why? Because of his bride's religion. Yet his father wasn't
in the slightest bit religious.

"Better you were dead at my feet . . ."

Would that really have been better?

We can't get enough of dying, he thinks, shuffling between the unheralded headstones. "We"—an idea of belonging to which he sometimes subscribes and sometimes
doesn't. We arrive, lucky to be alive, carrying our belongings
on a stick, and immediately look for somewhere to bury the
children who betray us.

Perhaps because of all the anger that precedes all the
burying, the place lacks the consolation of beauty. In his student days, when there was no word "we" in his vocabulary,
Strulovitch wrote a paper on Stanley Spencer's *The Resur-
rection, Cookham,* admiring the tumult of Spencer's graves,

bulging with eager life, the dead in a hurry for what comes next. But this isn't a country churchyard in Berkshire; this is a cemetery of the Messiahless in Gatley, South Manchester, where there is no next. It all finishes here.

There is a lingering of snow on the ground, turning a dirty black where it nestles into the granite of the graves. It will be there until early summer, if summer ever comes.

The second person, here long before Strulovitch arrived, tenderly addressing the occupant of a grave whose headstone is worn to nothing, is Shylock, also an infuriated and tempestuous Jew, though his fury tends more to the sardonic than the mercurial, and the tempest subsides when he is able to enjoy the company of his wife Leah, buried deep beneath the snow. He is less divided in himself than Strulovitch but, perhaps for that very reason, more divisive. No two people feel the same about him. Even those who unreservedly despise him, despise him with different degrees of unreservation. He has money worries that Strulovitch doesn't, collects neither art nor Bibles, and finds it difficult to be charitable where people are not charitable to him, which some would say takes something from the soul of charity. About his daughter, the least said the better.

He is not an occasional mourner like Strulovitch. He cannot leave and think of something else. Because he is not a forgetful or a forgiving man, there never was or will be something else.

Strulovitch, pausing in his reflections, feels Shylock's presence before he sees him—a blow to the back of the neck, as though someone in the cemetery has been irreverent enough to throw a snowball.

The words "My dearest Leah," dropped like blessings into the icy grave, reach Strulovitch's ears. There will be many

Leahs here. Strulovitch's mother was a Leah. But this Leah attracts an imperishable piteousness to her name that is unmistakable to Strulovitch, student of husbandly sorrow and fatherly wrath. Leah who bought Shylock a courtship ring. Leah, mother to Jessica who stole that ring to buy a monkey. Jessica the pattern of perfidy. Not for a wilderness of monkeys would Shylock have parted with that ring.

Strulovitch neither.

So "we" does mean something to Strulovitch after all. The faith Jessica violates is *his* faith.

Such, anyway, are the only clues to recognition Strulovitch needs. He is hard-headed about it. Of course Shylock is here, among the dead. When hasn't he been?

Eleven years old, precociously moustached, too clever by half, he was shopping with his mother in a department store when she saw Hitler buying aftershave.

"Quick, Simon!" she ordered him. "Run and get a policeman, I'll stay here and make sure he doesn't get away."

But no policeman would believe that Hitler was in the store and eventually he escaped Strulovitch's mother's scrutiny.

Strulovitch hadn't believed that Hitler was in the store either. Back home he made a joke of it to his father.

"Don't cheek your mother," his father told him. "If she said she saw Hitler, she saw Hitler. Your Aunty Annie ran into Stalin on Stockport market last year, and when I was your age I saw Moses rowing on Heaton Park Lake."

"Couldn't have been," Strulovitch said. "Moses would just have parted the waters."

For which smart remark he was sent to his room.

"Unless it was Noah," Strulovitch shouted from the top of the stairs.

"And for that," his father said, "you're not getting anything to eat."

Later, his mother sneaked a sandwich up to him, as Rebekah would have done for Jacob.

The older Strulovitch understands the Jewish imagination better—why it sets no limits to chronology or topography, why it cannot ever trust the past to the past, and why his mother probably did see Hitler. He is no Talmudist but he occasionally reads a page in a small, private-press anthology of the best bits. The thing about the Talmud is that it allows a bolshie contrarian like him to argue face to face with other bolshie contrarians long dead.

You think *what*, Rabbah bar Nahmani? Well fuck you!

So is there a hereafter after all? What's your view, Rabbi?

To Strulovitch, Rabbah bar Nahmani, shaking off his cerements, gives the finger back.

Long ago is now and somewhere else is here.

How it is that Leah should be buried among the dead of Gatley is a question only a fool would risk Shylock's displeasure by asking. The specifics of interment—the whens, the wheres—are supremely unimportant to him. She is under the ground, that is enough. Alive, she had been everywhere to him. Dead—he long ago determined—she will be the same. Wheeling with the planet. An eternal presence, never far from him, wherever he treads.

Strulovitch, alert and avid, tensed like a minor instrument into affinity with a greater, watches without being seen to watch. He will stand here all day if he has to. From

Shylock's demeanour—the way he inclines his head, nods, looks away, but never looks *at* anything, sees sideways like a snake—he is able to deduce that the conversation with Leah is engrossing and devoted, oblivious to external event, and no longer painful—a fond but brisk, even matter-of-fact, two-way affair. Shylock listens as much as he speaks, pondering the things she says, though he must have heard her say them many times before. He has a paperback in one hand, rolled up like a legal document or a gangster's wad of banknotes, and every now and then he opens it brusquely, as though he intends to rip out a page, and reads to her in a low voice, covering his mouth in the way a person who is too private to make a show of mirth will stifle a laugh. If that is laughter, Strulovitch thinks, it's laughter that has had a long way to travel—brain laughter. A phrase of Kafka's (what's one more unhappy son in this battlefield of them?) returns to him: *laughter that has no lungs behind it.* Like Kafka's own, maybe. Mine too?—Strulovitch wonders. Laughter that lies too deep for lungs? As for the jokes, if they are jokes, they are strictly private. Just possibly, unseemly.

He is at home here as I am not, Strulovitch thinks. At home among the gravestones. At home in a marriage.

Strulovitch is pierced by the difference between Shylock's situation and his. His own marital record is poor. He and his first wife made a little hell of their life together. Was that because she'd been a Christian? ("*Gai in drerd!*" his father said when he learnt his son was marrying out. "Go to hell!" Not just any hell but the fieriest circle, where marriers-out go. And on the night before the wedding he left an even less ambiguous phone message: "You are dead to me.") His second marriage, to a daughter of Abraham this time, for which reason his father rescinded his curse and called him Lazarus on the phone, was brought to an abrupt, numbing halt—a suspension of all feeling, akin to waiting for news you hope will never come—when his wife suffered a stroke on their daughter's fourteenth birthday, losing the better part of language and memory, and when he, as a consequence, shut down the husband part of his heart.

Marriage! You lose your father or you lose your wife.

He is no stranger to self-pity. Leah is more alive to Shylock than poor Kay is to me, he thinks, feeling the cold for the first time that day.

He notes, observing Shylock, that there is a muscular tightness in his back and neck. This calls to mind a character in one of his favourite comics of years ago, a boxer, or was he a wrestler, who was always drawn with wavy lines around him, to suggest a force field. How would I be drawn, Strulovitch wonders. What marks could denote what I'm feeling?

"Imagine that," Shylock says to Leah.

"Imagine what, my love?"

"Shylock-envy."

Such a lovely laugh she has.

Shylock is dressed in a long black coat, the hem of which he appears concerned to keep out of the snow, and sits, inclined forward—but not so far as to crease his coat—on a folding stool of the kind Home Counties opera-lovers take to Glyndebourne. Strulovitch cannot decide what statement his hat is making. Were he to have asked, Shylock would have told him it was to keep his head warm. But it's a fedora—the mark of a man conscious of his appearance. A dandy's hat, worn with a hint of frolicsome menace belied by the absence of any mark or memory of frolic on his face.

Strulovitch's clothes are the more abstemious, his art-collector's coat flowing like a surplice, the collar of his snowy white shirt buttoned to the throat without a tie in the style of contemporary quattrocento. Shylock, with his air of dangerous inaffability, is less ethereal and could be taken for a banker or a lawyer. Just possibly he could be a Godfather.

Strulovitch is glad he came to pay his respects to his mother's remains and wonders whether the graveside conversation he is witness to is his reward. Is this what you get for being a good son? He should have tried it sooner in that case. Unless something else explains it. Does one simply see what one is fit to see? In which case there's no point going looking: you have to let it come to you. He entertains a passing fancy that Shakespeare, whose ancestors just might—to be on the safe side—have changed their name from Shapiro, also allowed Shylock to come to him. Walking home from the theatre, seeing ghosts and writing in his tablets, he looks outside himself just long enough to espy Antonio spitting at that abominated thing, a Jew.

"How now! A Jew! Is that you cousin?" Shakespeare asks.

This is *Judenfrei* Elizabethan England. Hence his surprise.

"Shush," says the Jew.

"Shylock!" exclaims Shakespeare, heedlessly. "My cousin Shylock or I'm a Christian!"

Shapiro, Shakespeare, Shylock. A family association.

Strulovitch feels sad to be excluded. Only a shame his name doesn't have a *shush* in it.

It is evident to Strulovitch, anyway, that receptivity is the thing, and that those who go looking are on a fool's errand. He knows of a picturesque Jewish cemetery on the Lido di

Venezia—once abandoned but latterly restored in line with the new European spirit of reparation—a cypress-guarded place of melancholy gloom and sudden shafts of cruel light, to which a fevered righter of wrongs of his acquaintance has made countless pilgrimages, certain that since Shylock would not have been seen dead among the ice-cream-licking tourists in the Venice ghetto, he must find him here, broken and embittered, gliding between the ruined tombstones, muttering the prayer for his several dead. But no luck. The great German poet Heine—a man every bit as unwilling to use the "we" word as Strulovitch, and the next day every bit as much in love with it—went on an identically sentimental "dream-hunt," again without success.

But the Shylock hunting—with so much unresolved and still to be redeemed—never stops. Simon Strulovitch's trembling Jew-mad Christian wife, Ophelia-Jane, pointed him out, hobbling down the Rialto steps, carrying a fake Louis Vuitton bag stuffed with fake Dunhill watches, as they were dining by the Grand Canal. They were on their honeymoon and Ophelia-Jane wanted to do something Jewishly nice for her new husband. (He hadn't told her that his father had verbally buried him on the eve of their wedding. He would never tell her that.) "Look, Si!" she'd said, tugging his sleeve. A gesture that annoyed him because of the care he lavished on his clothes. Which might have been why he took an eternity following the direction of her finger and when at last he looked saw nothing.

It was in the hope of a second visitation that she took him there on every remaining night of their honeymoon. "*Oy gevalto*, we're back on the Rialto," he complained finally. She put her face in her hands. She thought him ungrateful and unserious. Five days into their marriage she already hated his

folksy Yiddishisms. They took from the grandeur she wanted
for them both. Venice had been her idea. Reconnect him. She
could just as easily have suggested Cordoba. She had married him to get close to the tragic experience of the Hebrews,
the tribulations of a noble Ladino race, and all he could do
was *oy gevalto* her back to some malodorous Balto-Slavic
shtetl peopled by potato-faced bumpkins who shrugged their
shoulders.

She thought her heart would stop. "Tell me I haven't
gone and married a footler-schmootler," she pleaded as they
wandered back to their hotel. He could feel her quivering by
his side, like a five-masted sailing ship. "Tell me you're not a
funny-man."

They had reached the Campo Santa Maria Formosa,
where he paused and drew her to him. He could have told her
that the church was founded in 1492, the year the Jews were
expelled from Spain. Kiss me to make up for it, darling, he
could have said. Kiss me to show you're sorry. And she would
have done it, imagining him leaving Toledo with his entou-
rage, praying at the Ibn Shoshan Synagogue for the last time,
erect in bearing, refusing to compromise his faith. Yes, on the
fine, persecuted brow of her black-bearded hidalgo husband
she would have planted a lipstick star. "Go forth, my lord,
be brave, and may the God of Abraham and Moses go with
you. I will follow you with the children in due course." But
he told her no such thing and gave her no such opportunity.
Instead, aggressively playing the fool, he breathed herrings,
dumplings, borscht, into her anxious little face, the fatalism
of villages unvisited by light or learning, the broken-backed
superstitions of shmendricks called Moishe and Mendel.
"Chaim Yankel, ribbon salesman," he said, knowing how little
such a name would amuse her, "complains to the buyer at

Harrods that he never orders ribbon from him. 'All right, all right,' says the buyer, 'send me sufficient ribbon to stretch from the tip of your nose to the tip of your penis.' A fortnight later a thousand boxes of ribbon turn up at Harrods' receiving centre. 'What the hell do you think you're playing at?' the buyer screams at Chaim Yankel down the phone. 'I said enough ribbon to reach from the tip of your nose to the tip of your penis, and you send me a thousand miles of it.' 'The tip of my penis,' says Chaim Yankel, 'is in Poland.'"

She stared at him in disbelieving horror. She was shorter than he was, finely constructed, exquisite in her almost boyish delicacy. Her eyes, just a little too big for her face, were shadowy pools of hurt perplexity. Anyone would think, he thought, looking deep into them, that I have just told her someone close to us has died.

"You see," he said relenting, "you've nothing to worry about, I'm not a funny-man."

"Enough," she pleaded.

"Enough Poland?"

"Shut up about Poland!"

"My people, Ophelia . . ."

"Your people are from Manchester. Isn't that bad enough for you?"

"The joke wouldn't work if I resituated the punchline to Manchester."

"The joke already doesn't work. None of your jokes work."

"What about the one where the doctor tells Moishe Greenberg to stop masturbating?"

The Campo Santa Maria Formosa must have been witness to many sighs, but few so dolorous as Ophelia-Jane's. "I beg you," she said, almost folding herself in half. "On my bended knees, I implore you—no more jokes about your *thing*."

She shook the word from her as though it were an impor-
tunate advance from a foul-smelling stranger.

"A foolish thing is but a toy," was all he could think of
saying.

"Then it's time you stopped playing with it." Strulovitch
showed her his hands.

"Metaphorically, Simon!"

She wanted to cry.

He too.

She traduced him. He, playing? How could she not know
by now that he had not an ounce of play in his body?

And his *thing* . . . why did she call it that?

And on their honeymoon, to make things worse.

It was a site of sorrows, not a thing. The object of countless comic stories for the reason that it wasn't comic in the
least. He quoted Beaumarchais to her. "I hasten to laugh at
everything for fear I might be obliged to weep at it."

"You? Weep! When did you last weep?"

"I am weeping now. Jews jest, Ophelia-Jane, because they
are not amused."

"Then I'd have made a good Jew," she said, "because neither am I."

When mothers see what's been done to their baby boys the
milk turns sour in their breasts. The young Strulovitch, sla-
loming through the world's religions, was told this at a garden
party given by a great-great-grand-nephew of Cardinal New-
man in Oxford. His informant was a Baha'i psychiatrist called
Eugenia Carloff whose field of specialism was circumcision
trauma within the family.

"*All* mothers?" he asked.

A sufficient number of them of your persuasion, she told

him, to explain the way they mollycoddle their sons thereafter. They have a double guilt to expiate. Allowing blood to be spilled and withholding milk.

"Withholding milk? Are you kidding?"

Strulovitch was sure he'd been breastfed. Sometimes he feels as though he's being breastfed still.

"All men of your persuasion think they were copiously suckled," Eugenia Carloff told him.

"Are you telling me I wasn't?" he said.

She looked him up and down. "I can't say definitively, but my guess is no, actually, you weren't."

"Do I look undernourished?"

"Hardly."

Deprived then?"

"Not deprived, denied."

"It was my father who did that."

"Ah," Eugenia Carloff said, tapping her nose, "there is no end to what those executioners we call fathers do. First they maim their boy children then they torment them."

Sounds right, Strulovitch thought. On the other hand, his father liked amusing him with anecdotes and rude jokes. And sometimes ruffled his hair absent-mindedly when they were out walking. He mentioned that to Eugenia Carloff who shook her head. "They never love you. Not really. They remain excluded from the eternal nativity play of guilt and recompense which they initiated, forever sidelined and angry, trying to make amends in rough affection and funny stories. This is the bitter nexus that binds them."

"That binds the father and the son?"

"That binds men of your persuasion, the penis and the joke."

I'm not a man of any persuasion, he wanted to tell

Eugenia Carloff. I have yet to be persuaded. Instead he asked her out.

She laughed wildly. "Do you think I want to get into all that?" she said. "Do you think I'm mad?"

Poor Ophelia-Jane, who must have been mad, did all in her power in the few years they were together to make their marriage work. But in the end he was too much for her. He agreed with her in his heart. He upset and even frightened people. It was the acrid jeering that did it. The death-revel ironies. Did he or didn't he belong? Was he or wasn't he funny? His own mortal indecision for which everyone who knew him— Ophelia-Jane more than any of them—had to pay.

"You could just have loved me, you know," she said sadly on the day they agreed to divorce. "I was willing to do anything to make you happy. You could just have enjoyed our life together."

He enfolded her in his arms one final time and told her he was sorry. "It's just who we are," he said.

"*We!*"

It was the last word she said before she walked out on him.

There was one small consolation. They had been virtually children when they married and they were still virtually children when they parted.

They could be done with each other and still have plenty of life left with which to start again. And they hadn't had children of their own—the cause of all human discontent.

But the divorce itself was wormwood to them both. And in the end she couldn't help herself. Though she believed Jews to have been grievously maligned, when the final papers were delivered to be signed she still stigmatised them, through the person of her husband, in the usual way. "Happy now you've extracted your pound of flesh?" she rang him to ask.

The accusation hurt him deeply. Though not yet wildly wealthy, he was the one who had brought money to the marriage. And what he didn't spend on her went, even in these early years, on causes to which she had given her blessing and which would always bear her name. He believed the settlement was more than generous to her. And he knew that in her heart she thought so too. But there it was—the ancient stain. She hadn't been able to help herself. So the stain was on her as well.

The phone became a viper in his hand. Not in anger but in horror, he let it fall to the floor.

He wrote to her the next day to say that henceforth they were to speak to each other only through their solicitors.

But even after he remarried he carried a torch for her. Despite the pound-of-flesh allusion? He wondered about that. Despite it or because of it?

A watched kettle never boils, but Shylock watched by Strulovitch rattles like a seething pot. It's not noise that distracts him but anxiety, disquiet, neurasthenic perturbation. On this occasion, Strulovitch's. Conscious of him, Shylock fractionally shifts his position on his Glyndebourne stool and twitches his ears. He could be an Egyptian cat god.

"What's to be done with us?" he asks Leah.

"Us?"

"Our people. We are beyond help."

"Nobody's beyond help. Show compassion."

"I shouldn't have to feel it as compassion. I should feel it as loyalty."

"Then show loyalty."

"I endeavour to, but they try my patience."

"My love, you have no patience."

"Nor do they. Especially for themselves. They have more time for those who hate them."

"Hush," she says.

The tragedy is that she can't stroke his neck and make the wavy lines go away.

When Leah was big with child she would call Shylock to her and get him to put his hand on her belly. Feel the kicking. He loved the idea that the little person in there couldn't wait to join them.

Jessica, my child.

Now it was Leah who made her presence felt. The gentlest of nudges, as though some burrowing creature were at work in the ground beneath him. "Well said, old mole," he thinks. He knew what she was nudging him about. One of the traits of his character she had always disliked was his social cruelty. He teased people. Riddled them. Kept them waiting. Made them come to him. And he was doing the same with Strulovitch, not letting on he knew he was there, testing his endurance. Hence her prod, reminding him of his obligations.

Only when Shylock turned did Strulovitch see that his cheeks and chin were stubbled—not so much a beard as a gnarling of the flesh. Nothing about his face admitted softness, but the company of his wife had called light into his features and the remains of a querulous amusement lingered in the cruel creases around the eyes he showed to Strulovitch. "Ah!" he said, closing the paperback from which he'd been reading, rolling it up again and putting it with some deliberation in the inside pocket of his coat, "Just the man."

Two

There lived once in a big old house equidistant from Mottram St. Andrew, Alderley Edge and Wilmslow—at the very heart of what is still known to estate agents as the Golden Triangle—a dope-smoking media don who disapproved of dope and media, heir to a pharmaceutical fortune who favoured the redistribution of all wealth but his own, a utopist who mistrusted the principle of social amelioration, a lover of Gregorian chant who fantasised about being a rock legend, a whimsical conservationist who bought his sons fast cars with which they tore up the very country roads he wanted conserving. If he sounds like many people it's because many people were wrapped up in him. But he was just one man, a single fretting bundle of idealistic envy. "Sometimes," he told his students at the business school in Stockport of which he was the dean, "even the fortunate and gifted can feel their lives are mortgaged to a perplexing sadness."

"You don't say," his students said behind his back.

For Peter Shalcross MBE, one day had become the same as every other. A live morning radio interview on any subject, an afternoon lecture to his students on Mercantilism and Alienation—on alternate weeks he changed the title to Money and Estrangement—and then the drive home in the early evening to the heart of the Golden Triangle where a neat Scotch and scarlet smoking jacket awaited him, and where he could fulminate in comfort against the faux manses and manor houses of which the Strulovitches and their kind had taken possession. Every evening at the same time he fulminated, saying the same things and feeling the same burning sensation in his chest. But habit took nothing from the fervour of his animus. Only someone who enjoyed the benefits of great wealth himself could have been made so angry by the great wealth of others—the difference being that he hadn't had to earn his, the fact of which also made him obscurely angry.

"Can you smell anything?" he would ask visitors, throwing open the doors to his grounds, and when they had exhausted the possibilities—someone burning off leaves in the next county, horse manure, faulty plumbing, dust from the Sahara—he would rub the tips of his fingers together and say, "No none of those, what I smell is more like lucre . . . The filthy sort."

Though he was concerned about the effect that the propinquity of lucre might have on the air quality, the hedgerows and his only daughter, Anna Livia Plurabelle Cleopatra A Thing Of Beauty Is A Joy Forever Christine—Christine being the name of the flighty society model he had ill-advisedly married and whose influence on him extended all the way down to his candy-striped socks and fashionably pointed, high crepe-soled shoes—Shalcross was known to boast to his academic colleagues about the millionaire pop stars and footballers who were his neighbours. This was not to be confused with hypocrisy. A man can boast and still deplore.

"If you wanted a pop-idol life, Christine, you should have run off with a pop idol," he told his wife the night the Cheshire constabulary raided the anything-goes party she'd thrown for Plurabelle's sixteenth birthday. In fact he was the one who should have run off with a pop idol. Or better still, *been* a pop idol.

It wasn't the amyl nitrite that brought the police out, it was the amplified music. And it was a rhythm guitarist, residing half a mile away, who'd alerted them. He couldn't hear himself practise, he'd complained. Even the noisy were entitled to peace. It was their human right.

After thinking about it for a week, Christine Shalcross did precisely as her husband suggested, though running off in this instance meant no more than moving to the other side of the paddock, where pop idols proliferated like peonies. "For all that I'll be able to keep a close eye on her from here," she told her husband, "I'd still prefer you to bring Plurabelle up. A girl needs a father's example and she loves you more than she loves me. You have that in common with her."

Estranged from himself, humiliated by his wife, disappointed in his sons who had gone to work for banks which had the indecency to fail, depressed by the cynicism of his students, appalled by the social deterioration of the Golden Triangle and expecting to die early, anyway, as his parents and grandparents had, Shalcross left instructions with his solicitors for the care of Plurabelle. "Taking into account the size of her fortune and the sweetness of her nature, Plury will be at the mercy of every moneybags and bloodsucker that comes along," he told his lawyers. "Find listed below a number of ordeals of character to which every aspirant to her bed must be submitted. Any who hope to approach her by some other route should know that my family's reach is long and extends to low places as well as high."

Having deposited these detailed stipulations, he went into the garden of the Old Belfry—his belfry, of course, was genuinely old—laid himself out beneath the second most ancient oak tree in Cheshire, stuffed tissues up his nostrils against the stench of filthy lucre, took an overdose of the pills for which his family had been overcharging grossly for half a century, and expired.

Richly left and richly independent, Plurabelle shed copious tears—for she had inherited the sadness gene from her father—and allowed a decent interval of time to elapse before summoning the courage to read her father's test, presented to her in a long Manila envelope, like a Last Will and Testament, by his solicitors. A gap year, she called this decent interval of time. A period in which to travel, meditate, meet interesting people, have a breast enlargement and work done on her face.

At the fulfilment of which, looking simultaneously younger and older than her years and ever so slightly Asiatic, she sliced into the envelope with a letter opener made of the horn of one of the rhinos she intermittently marched through the centre of Manchester to preserve. Unable to see how being able to identify the three biggest lies of the twentieth century, or to name the fifty richest "foreign" families in the United Kingdom, or to suggest a viable scheme for assassinating Tony Blair, would yield her the ideal partner, she put her father's test in the bin and devised trials more likely to yield the sort of man she thought she wanted. On her twenty-first birthday she attended a swinger's party in Alderley Edge, having taken the sensible precaution of ascertaining first that her mother would not be there. She went wearing a Formula One driver's suit and goggles and jiggling the keys to each of her cars—a Volkswagen Beetle, a BMW Alpina, and a Porsche Carrera. These, once she had secured the attention of the majority of the guests, she threw into an ice bucket and went outside to wait in the Beetle. That fights broke out over the BMW and the Porsche but no one followed her to the Volkswagen didn't entirely surprise her, given that this was Cheshire, but she felt she'd learned an invaluable lesson. Deceived by ornament and the glitter of appearance, men were incapable of seeing substance let alone valuing it. She became a lesbian for a year, received instruction in holy orders from a nun who had once done secretarial work for her father, tried her hand at modelling, journalism, photography and kinetic sculpture, had her breasts reduced, and settled finally for running a restaurant—though she had no cookery skills—in what had been the stables of the Old Belfry.

She called the restaurant Utopia and envisaged it as the centrepiece of that experiment in idealistic living her father had often talked to her about but never got round to putting into practice. Guests would be invited to stay the night, or even the weekend, go on treasure hunts, play croquet, fall in and out of love, treat one another beautifully, avail themselves of therapies of various kinds from Ayurvedic massage to marriage guidance—Plurabelle herself excelled at mediating between stressed partners, having practised for many years on her parents—inveigh against wealth, though only the wealthy could afford to attend, and of course enjoy food that bespoke honest endeavour combined with profligacy. Cottage pie washed down with Krug Clos d'Ambonnay. Or white Alba truffle with tap water. Eventually, she told a reporter from *Cheshire Life*, she would put her own ornamental virginity on the menu but as yet had not devised a method for distinguishing the right buyer from the wrong.

Though highly photogenic in the gamin style, with a retroussé nose, a Daisy Duck mouth, golden tresses, a throaty voice that brought to mind a bee buzzing in a windowpane in late summer, and a Scandinavian weather girl's figure, Plurabelle Shalcross had her father's fascinated mistrust of the media. No, she wouldn't make a television programme about her Utopia weekends, but then again, if it were to be a series, maybe she would. To the idea of bartering her virginity on screen she brought the same complex of scruple and consent, with both finally winning out. Better, surely, from the point of view of audience interest, to keep the question of her finding the right man forever in suspense. Week in, week out, she could set new challenges and, week in, week out, suitors would fail them. Thus she laughed, cried, frolicked, cooked badly and, as episode followed episode, adjudicated—not just between lovers prepared to joust to win her, but between the affairs of others among her guests. Soon, imperceptibly, her programmes came to be about judgement as much as food and love. A new series entitled *The Kitchen Counsellor* became an overnight success. Couples, friends, even lifelong enemies, would bring their disputes to Plurabelle's table where, as she served them delectable dishes prepared behind the scenes by someone else, she would deliver verdicts held to be binding at least in the sense that all parties had agreed to abide by them in their release forms.

Not only was this a cheaper option than going to law or even arbitration, it gave combatants a taste of passing fame and, still more alluringly, Plurabelle's incomparable sagacity.

Who cared, after that, whether they had won their argument or lost it!

For those for whom fame was less important than vindication, Plurabelle, flushed with success, initiated a live interactive Webchat facility called Bicker. Here, the contentious would submit their grievances to the arbitration of the British public. "I can't be the one who decides everything," Plurabelle told her friends. But the British public turned out to be too vitriolic an arbitrator even for its own taste, the site consumed itself in rage, and Plurabelle was once again the person who—in the humane spirit of it not mattering whether anything was decided or not—decided everything.

Life was a game and Anna Livia Plurabelle Cleopatra A Thing Of Beauty Is A Joy Forever Wiser Than Solomon Christine its master of ceremonies.

Oh, but sadness is a curse.

Plurabelle's mother told her it was natural in a girl who had recently lost a father. But Plurabelle sought a deeper cause. Or maybe a more superficial cause. A different cause, anyway.

Her mother couldn't help her with that. "Philosophy exceeds my maternal brief," she said. "Why don't you go to sadness classes in Wilmslow?"

"Because I don't need to be taught it. I need to get rid of it."

"That's what they do there," her mother said. "I put it wrong. It's like Alcoholics Anonymous only for sad rich people."

"Will I have to stand up and say, 'Hello, my name is Anna Livia Plurabelle Cleopatra A Thing Of Beauty Is A

Joy Forever Christine, I have a personal fortune in excess of twenty million pounds and I am a saddist'? Because if I do I'm not going."

Her mother shrugged. In her view what her daughter needed was a lover. When you have a lover there's no time to be sad.

Plurabelle went anyway, despite her initial reluctance. It's possible that she too secretly hoped to find a lover there. Though God knows she didn't need any more sadness around her. In order not to be recognised she wore a headscarf that made her look as though she had toothache. Most of the others were in disguise too. We are sad because we're famous, Plurabelle thought. But the convenor told the gathering not to look for reasons right away, not to attribute it to ambition or stress or the spirit of competition and envy prevailing in the Golden Triangle. They were sad because they were sad. The only important thing was not to be in denial.

Over coffee, after the first session, she discussed this idea of not looking for a reason for their sadness with an older, elegant man whom she'd noticed at the meeting, sitting somewhat apart and staring ahead of him as though the sorrows of ordinary mortals were not to be compared to his. He introduced himself, in a manner that was part apologetic and part disdainful, as D'Anton, and close up seemed to her to be sad because he was homosexual (or at least not definitively heterosexual), for which, as she understood it, they were also not to look for reasons. They talked at length in a serious vein, after which she asked him to one of her Utopia house parties. It was up to him whether he wanted to be filmed or not. Bring someone, if you like, she told him. But he arrived alone, bearing an enormous glass paperweight in the centre of which was a teardrop. "That's beautiful," she said, "but you shouldn't have." He made light of the gift. Among the objets d'art he made a living from importing, he explained, were glass paperweights. This one came from a small village in Japan where they'd been blowing glass since the fourteenth century and no one knew how to do anything else. She wondered if the teardrop was human or animal. They say it's the teardrop of whoever beholds it, he told her. Whereupon they both cried a little and held on to each other as though they meant never to let go.

Soon D'Anton became a regular visitor, sometimes staying after the rest of the weekend guests had gone home. They found comfort in each other's melancholy. "You must think it's ridiculous me living in all this splendour and still being sad," she said.

"Not at all," he answered, shaking his head. "I import beautiful objects from Japan, Grenada, Malibu, Mauritius and Bali, and have a home in each, and yet I am sad in all of them."

"Bali is one place I haven't yet been to," Plurabelle said. "What's it like?"

"Sad."

Plurabelle shook her head in sympathy. "I can imagine," she said. Then, after a moment's contemplation, she asked him, "Do you think it's because we have too much?"

"We?"

"Us. You and I. People of our sort. The advantaged."

"But *are* we the advantaged?" D'Anton asked. "For the love of money is the root of all evil: which while some coveted after, they have erred from the faith, and pierced themselves through with many sorrows."

"That's so beautiful," Plurabelle said. "And so true. It makes me want to cry. Paulo Coelho often makes me want to cry."

"A greater man than Paulo Coelho said that," D'Anton surprised her by saying. She didn't know there was a greater man than Paulo Coelho.

"Nelson Mandela?"

"St. Paul."

"So would we be less pierced with sorrows if we gave all we have to the poor?"

He didn't know but said he sometimes asked himself whether the sadness problem, for him anyway, wasn't money but modernity. "Do you never feel," he asked her, "that you are too modern?"

Plurabelle liked that idea. "*Too modern*—yes, you're right," she said. "Too modern. I have often felt that, yes I have, though until now I didn't know I'd felt it. Too modern—yes, of course." Then she had a thought. "But that doesn't explain," she said, "why Aborigines and American Indians always look sad on the Discovery Channel. They can hardly be called modern."

"No, but that's a different kind of sadness, isn't it. The cause of their sadness is that they have been made abject. It's been done to them. They are sad because they're victims."

Plurabelle remembered seeing photographs of South American tribesmen in colour supplements. They looked thousands of years old. Maoris too. And Pygmies. And Pashtun tribesmen. Why were they all sad, she wondered.

"Again, they have been exploited and made abject."

"And Jews? They're old."

He was less comfortable about Jews. But offered to put his mind, or at least St. Paul's mind (for he was a confirmed

Paulinist), to their sadness. "I'd say they are made abject by their own will," he declared at last. "They are neither modern nor victims. They have chosen to look the way they do."

"Why have they done that?"

"Whether it's a flaw or a stratagem I cannot say, but they have always put themselves at the centre of every drama, human or theological. I think of it as a political sadness. The glue of self-pity is very strong. As is emotional blackmail."

Plurabelle furrowed her lovely brow. She wanted this conversation never to stop, testing as it was. "So they don't count, is what you're saying?"

"In my view they don't, no."

Plurabelle's expression was suddenly relieved of its customary dejection. "Oh yes they do," she laughed. "That's *all* they do. They just sit and count . . . and count . . . and count . . ."

She was so pleased by this that she skipped like a little girl.

"I hope you don't think I mean anything unpleasant," she remembered to say.

D'Anton assured her that he didn't.

She clapped her small hands in relief.

He thought how pretty she was when she was skittish. Inflamed around the mouth, as though she had a perpetual cold sore, and disconcertingly wide-eyed, which made it difficult for her to look straight ahead, but that could be said of all the women in the Golden Triangle. And she had a girlish expectancy which they didn't. A desire for happiness shot through with an expectancy that she would never find it. He almost wished he could feel romantically about her.

She thought the same about him. Such a pity.

But the absence of romantic feeling made it possible for them to talk freely to each other, or at least for her to talk freely to him. She told him, with clever illustrative imitations of their mannerisms, about the would-be lovers who came and went in her real life, as opposed to those who were found for her by the production company to appear with her on television. Oh God, they wearied her, each thinking that the way to reach her was to spoil her or to flatter her, this one bringing her a Hermès Birkin bag the colour of the lipstick he'd been told she always wore, that one bearing a Guerlain lipstick case made of Swarovski crystals and a solitary diamond, the lipstick itself the colour of what researchers had told him was her favourite handbag. Did they think she was an object to be won by empty words and cash? She even showed him the handbag and the lipstick. What did he think?

He said he thought she should wear them together.

She told him that she'd come to that same conclusion herself.

They both laughed.

"But this isn't who I am," she said.

They both laughed again.

He became installed in her house, like a steward or confessor. When he wasn't popping over to Japan to look at paperweights he didn't seem to have much to do. "I pay people," he explained. There was a prematurely retired air about him. On occasions, she would have friends around to listen to him talk about the exquisite things he imported and about beauty in general. In no time at all he was indispensable to her—handsome, sad, chivalric, unavailable, and somehow uncontaminated. It was as though he made clean every space he walked through, just by walking through it.

THREE

How long will a man lie i' th' earth ere he rot?
And a woman? Will she not rot even sooner?
Shylock, broken-hearted, beloved husband of
Leah, feared so. The skin so much finer, the bones so much
more fragile.

It was in order to delay the process, to keep her alive
to herself as well as to him, that he visited her grave every
morning, taking her violets or forget-me-nots, talking to her,
listening to her, exactly as he had when she'd lived. He break-
fasted in her company, a flask of Turkish coffee—she loved
the smell of coffee—and a cheese panino wrapped in a linen
handkerchief. He wasn't careful to avoid crumbs falling on to
her. It was almost like feeding her. And he did feed her, in
another sense, selective gossip about the goings-on of their
friends, sustaining her with news of Jessica. The latter more
selective still: only the best things, how womanly she was
becoming, how like her mother. Some mornings, when he
thought it advisable to spare her the details of his business
affairs altogether—the catastrophe in waiting, the threat
of destitution hanging over him—he read to her. Not about

Jacob and his sheep, nor about Laban and Hagar and the prophet Daniel. Those references he reserved for the Gentiles, knowing how troubling they found Bible stories issuing from the mouth of a Jew. Their actual reading, and they had read together most evenings, was much wider. They too could quote Virgil and Ovid, knew who Scylla and Charybdis were, and discussed Pythagoras' philosophy of the soul. To prevent Leah from freezing over he read Petrarch to her, and Boccaccio. Also, as time went by, Philip Sidney's *Arcadia*, Thomas Nashe's *The Unfortunate Traveller*, as well as Edmund Spenser's "Epithalamion." Eventually he would progress to Dr. Johnson, Wordsworth, Dickens, Dostoevsky, the great novelists of the fag-end of the Austro-Hungarian Empire, and ditto of the American. It was important he kept Leah informed and didn't allow her to grow bored. She too had always had a taste for the lyrical, the sarcastic, and some days even the preposterous. "Read me the comedy about the person who's made to think he's vermin," she'd say. "Do you mean *Metamorphosis*?" "No, my love, *Mein Kampf*." And they would laugh together like demons.

To those in his community who thought his devotion morbid he argued that the opposite was the case, that it was only Leah's company that kept him from falling into that dejection of spirits that was such a common affliction of the times and to which he had more reason than most to be susceptible. This one unaccountably sad, that one inexplicably weary—well, he had his own thoughts about the roots of so much fashionable moping, but for him, and he could speak for no one else, life would have been unbearable had he allowed himself to forget, even for the smallest particle of time, the woman he had loved from the moment he first saw her. You made your vows and you stuck to them. There had been no one else and there would be no one else. If that made him heavy company sometimes, so be it. Who decreed that life was to be one long rowdy masquerade (punctuated with those little pets of melancholy indulged by a crowd who made a religion of their feelings)?

And if this mourning without end put intolerable pressure on his daughter Jessica?

He denied that he was in mourning. Quite the contrary. Spending so much of his time with Leah meant there was no reason to mourn. He was celebrating his marriage, not lamenting it. Where was the sackcloth? Where the ashes? Didn't he go to the cemetery every morning as spruce as a bridegroom?

But this, as he knew well, was ultimately an evasion. Jessica was, as he told Leah proudly, growing up. Sometimes when he passed her on the stairs he even mistook her for his wife. She had the right to be the giver and the recipient of just such an adoration as her parents had enjoyed, and were still—no doubt unnaturally to her—enjoying. It was her turn.

He would look away when this matter was raised. Even when he raised it with himself he would look away, into another corner of his conscience. *Her turn*! What father wanted to think of his daughter enjoying *her turn*?

And with whom?

She should, by the logic of their society, have been safe. The daughter of a repugnant Jew!—why, with such blood in her veins the problem should have been to find her suitors, not protect her from them. Who wanted what appertained to Shylock? Yet just as they would take his money, no matter what they thought of him, so they would take his daughter. Did commerce wash the obloquy away? Did desire?

Or was the obloquy the very thing that added savour to

what they desired and borrowed or, where they couldn't borrow, stole?

His daughter was a fine-looking girl. She would assuredly have attracted admirers on her own behalf in a less envious and grasping society, where every man not already married to a rich wife was on the make. He intended no disrespect to her by suspecting the motives of those who wooed her. Quite the opposite: it was because he loved her and saw—often much to his embarrassment—what others saw in her, that he stood guard over her happiness. It was his appreciation of her, as much as anything else, that made him clumsy. A mother would have known better how to do it, but Jessica had no mother. Yes, she deserved to be wooed. But a Jewess was a commodity, the times were acquisitive, and these people were collectors.

Well, the moral confusion was theirs, not his. It went with their religion and they were welcome to stew in it. But his contempt for the prevarications of Christians who professed one thing and did another didn't help him when it came to working out what to say to Leah. He couldn't tell her that Jessica had left. That she had become a turncoat, a liar and a thief. Least of all could he tell her what it was that Jessica had stolen.

It was an agony to him—keener than any knife-wound— to be keeping secrets from his wife, whatever the damp was doing to her flesh. It felt like a betrayal of the heart.

And still she doesn't know.

A mercy, Shylock believes. A mercy she got away when she did.

———

Simon Strulovitch's daughter had not got away. Not yet. Unless you call college getting away. Otherwise, he was similarly situated. He too fretted about the value placed on her as an exotic, feared the strength of the avidity she inspired, and the effect of the flattery on her. Added to this was his reputation as a wealthy connoisseur, a donor to elitist institutions and, for no reason other than that he'd visited Israel and given artworks to some of its universities, a Zionist—all in all a reputation he was vain enough to see as an inducement beyond Beatrice's charms. It wasn't theft he feared—Beatrice did not have the key to his vaults—it was the view of him as a bogeyman on all counts that she was bound to encounter at college, and the added value which that view of him lent her as a prize. She was worth turning, that was what it came to. The histories of terrorism and brigandage, of revolution and sedition, bulged with the apostate daughters of rich men with unacceptable convictions. A girl who would sleep with her father's enemies was of a succulence beyond description, plunder that exceeded in value even Simon Strulovitch's rubies and turquoises.

Strulovitch resembled Shylock in another way as well. He, too, was denied the opportunity to raise the matter with the girl's mother.

The stroke she suffered on Beatrice's fourteenth birthday felt too horribly symbolic to be any such thing. It was the cruellest misfortune, no more. Fate stuck out his hand and idly struck. It could have been any woman on any day. Hold on to that, Strulovitch told himself. Embrace the arbitrary. Otherwise the blaming would start and of blaming there is no end.

Little by little Kay had recovered words—not actual utterances but the will to move her lips and shape a silent sound, and this was enough to make him feel that someone he knew was still in there. They never approached—in dumbshow or any other way—what had befallen her. She lived in bed now—her own bed—needed to be helped to bathe and eat, and couldn't always make herself intelligible—beyond that, the pretence went, things were as they'd always been. About Beatrice he was careful to say little, and about his fears for her he said nothing at all. He was reluctant to put any pressures on her. Let Kay decide what subjects she wanted to approach by whatever means were available to her. Beatrice's presence cheered her, but she seemed to wish to see her only on her own, as though they were separate families, individual spokes of a wheel that had fallen off.

Strulovitch looked past her when he was in her presence. Beyond her, as in a broken mirror, he sometimes saw the wife he'd known but it felt like an infidelity to smile across the room at her. Better, in the presence of a ruined memory to remember nothing oneself. So they sat silently together, he in a chair by her bed, holding her hand, she looking into nothing, the two of them possessed of no before, and certainly no after, in a perfect harmony of unbeing. So unalive to sensation they could have been the first man and woman, waiting to be breathed into, poised for creation to begin.

Strulovitch had never been more thankful for the fortune built on car-parts he had inherited. His relations with his father were repaired. The burial had been only temporary: with his divorce from Ophelia-Jane Smythson came reconciliation, and with his marriage to Kay Kominsky came an inundation of fatherly love strong enough to knock him off his feet. A marriage in instead of a marriage out: it seemed that that was all his father—a man in every other way a heathen—had ever lived for. Keep it in the family. Just that. Fine by Strulovitch. He was re-inherited. And now that Kay was ill he understood how important it was to have money. You needed to be rich. Assuredly he appeared richer than one needed to be—which was why he gave so much away, endowing lectureships, providing music rooms and extending libraries, helping to buy works of art that would otherwise leave the country—yet you needed to be nearly as rich as he was just to live. By which he meant to reside in a house big enough to show art and shelve books, to travel in comfort, to have suits made by Italian tailors, to have a chauffeur, to send one's daughter to be schooled, and to afford round-the-clock care for one's wife. He had his own working definition of poverty as well as wealth. Whoever couldn't afford to make provision for carers and nurses, whether they were necessary now or would be necessary in the future, was dirt poor. To avoid falling into the hands of the state was reason in itself for making money. One worked and earned in order not to die disgracefully. You take my life when you do take the means whereby I live . . . and the means whereby I hope to die as well.

And then, of course—talking of dying—there was the money needed to escape in a hurry when the hour came, scooping what was left of his family into his arms and never stopping to look back. Even the Jewishly on-again off-again Strulovitch was never Jewishly off-again when it came to believing this: safety was not to be taken for granted, the danger hour always came around.

In the meantime, knowing each morning that his wife would be washed, that his daughter would be educated, and that his money would be there when he needed it for bribing officials at borders, or just for carers of his own, left him free to pursue his interests. And pursuing his interests kept him from bewailing the ruins of his wife. There was a great deal to be said, Strulovitch believed, for keeping busy, the other word for which—as Beatrice's teachers were surely telling her with relish—was capitalism.

But he didn't revel in wealth. He revelled—in so far as he could be called a reveller at all—in the world he could see. I already am spiritual, he would have said to anyone who tried to remind him of all that wasn't worldly—I am spiritual to the degree that I think the material world is infused with the divine.

And love?

He didn't understand how anyone could love what wasn't visible.

This didn't mean he didn't love his daughter when he didn't see her. But then when didn't he see her? Worry is a way of keeping an image close and safe, and from the moment of his wife's stroke—no, further back than that—he had worried about his daughter constantly.

They had waited a long time for their only child—a wait more agonising for Kay, who spoke conventionally of hearing her clock ticking and dreaded running out of time altogether. He hadn't especially wanted children and suspected other men of exaggerating when they said their hearts burst at the sight of their first child, but his own heart did exactly that. Partly this was on behalf of Kay. A vicarious joy compounded by relief and terror—for to want something as much as she had was surely an invitation to disappointment or worse. Doubly fragile and precious is that child whose conception relies on miracle. And there was the usual selfishness, too. When he looked at the baby Beatrice he saw himself projected into the future. But he gave in momentarily to the "clouds of glory" experience as well, imagining her as an emissary from God, fancying that her eyes were still closed against the brightness of the effulgence she had witnessed before coming here. And that in its turn raised the question of which God that was, and what message Beatrice was bringing from Him. Was this a religious moment for Strulovitch? He didn't think so. He didn't do religion. He didn't pray. He didn't bind his arm or cover his head. Devotionally he did so little he might as well have been a pagan. And the moment itself, however one described it, didn't last long enough to effect a transformation. But he would have admitted, if pressed, that the God whose glory he imagined his baby daughter squinting against was the Jewish God not the Christian, a being too serious and majestic ever to have taken human form. Nothing more. The beginning and the end of Strulovitch's seeing into the heart of things, but it was enough to determine the course of his preferences for Beatrice once and for all. She should have a Jewish husband, not because he looked down on non-Jews, or wanted his Jewish line to continue, but because her life had started seriously, in a sort of pain of remembered solemnity and anticipated grief that could not be thrown away on merely arbitrary affection and wilfulness—on whim or spite or capricious apostasy, or even haphazard love, however deeply felt—but owed, and was owed in return, an obligation of honour and loyalty, no matter that he was damned if he knew loyalty to what. Something that wasn't just hers to determine—was that it? A covenant. Something that would have found tangible expression in circumcision had she been a boy. Something in the nature of an oath of allegiance, never mind that she was not in any position, as someone born only an hour before, to swear it on her own behalf. And wasn't that the reason why he, as her father, was obliged by all he understood as holy, to swear it for her?

"*Swear.*"

He swore.

Swore to keep the covenant.

Not without looking about him to see if anyone was watching—in particular Kay, for whom this moment of supreme motherly love was complete as it was, and who wouldn't have wanted it scarred with whatever it was that had taken possession of her husband: superstition, fanaticism, tribalism, a seriousness too great for mortal flesh to bear—but he swore nonetheless.

FOUR

D'Anton performed a secondary function for Plurabelle in that he was well and variously connected
and could extend her circle to people she would not
in the normal course of things encounter, no matter that many
were her neighbours. The models and actresses, bankers, rappers, star footballers and breakfast TV astrologers—the obvious ones—she could find herself. And when she didn't, they
found her. But cricketers and rugby players, accountants,
architects, designers, life coaches and even the odd free-
talking bishop (for D'Anton's family had Church connections
that went far back)—such B-listers, who were not entirely
without glamour, she was soon relying on D'Anton to provide. He knew people of this sort because they paid him to
fill their houses with beauty and sometimes even hunt out
specific paintings for them. "Anything you can get me from
the Sistine Chapel," was one request. "A painting of gay men
screaming at one another in the lavatory by that guy they say
wrote Shakespeare," was another. Plurabelle marvelled at the
breadth and variety of his connections.

Sometimes he rolled his eyes in her direction when he

brought them to her parties, as though to say they were unaccountable for by him, not of his doing or acquaintance, and she would do well to have security staff keep watch on them.

Once he introduced her to Mehdi Mehdi, a French Algerian ventriloquist who was in hiding from the French and Algerian police on account of the Nazi ideology his dummy espoused, though he persuasively argued, in D'Anton's view, that as a ventriloquist he had neither person nor ideology of his own and employed his dummy to comment critically (though it wasn't strictly speaking his business to be a critic either) on the ideology in question. When quizzed by journalists as to the fondness he appeared to feel for his dummy, and indeed the fondness it inspired, he offered no reply in his own voice but left it to the doll to say that if the unintended consequence of his fame was that half the youth in France was giving Nazi salutes that was better than their making the Star of David.

Plurabelle was astonished to learn that half the youth of France had been making the Star of David.

D'Anton waved away her concern. "He's amusing," he said, "in a vindictive and perhaps even mendacious way, but he's essentially sound and good value to have at a party."

Plurabelle understood the distinction and told D'Anton to bring him and his dummy along. She was pleased to discover they were both good dancers. But for his being wanted by the police she would have had him, or at least his puppet, on *The Kitchen Counsellor* in argument with a rabbi.

A rabbi, ideally, who was also a ventriloquist, so that their dolls could have gone at it hammer and tongs.

What it was about him that appealed particularly to sportsmen neither she nor D'Anton could have said, but his puppet's hallmark Nazi salute was soon being copied in France by footballers who had been to see his act in underground cabarets in Marseilles, and in Cheshire by footballers who thought it chic to do what the French did, though of these Gratan Howsome—the latest of D'Anton's invitees—was the only professional so far actually to perform it on the field of play.

"He's the godson of a very dear friend of mine, now deceased," D'Anton explained, when Plurabelle expressed surprise at the affection there seemed to be between the two men. She had a fondness for tattoos and piercings herself, and liked men who padded around you like a dog and turned up with a different haircut every time you met them, but she wouldn't have imagined any of this would appeal to D'Anton. It seemed, however, that their goodwill—and something even stronger than that—was of long duration. "It's complicated," D'Anton told her, "as explanations of deep but apparently incongruous affections often are. I inherited an obligation I would go so far as to call sacred from a friend who had inherited it from a friend of his. If I say that poor Gratan is something of a football in all this I don't want you to think I'm being flippant. He is, in all but name, an orphan. In a manner of speaking I stand in watch and ward over him."

"He would seem to me to have more people watching over his welfare than most orphans," Plurabelle said with an irritation that surprised herself.

Could she have been jealous of Gratan for enjoying a protection she had come to see as hers alone?

"Then I have not explained myself well enough. His mother left him. His father maltreated him. He was abused by an uncle. But for the intervention of Federico and then Slavco there's no knowing what would have become of him. I must continue where they left off."

"You make it sound like a chore."

"Not a bit of it. The obligation I've inherited I undertake

willingly. What else are we for if we do not answer when the helpless call? Especially if, by so doing, we go on remembering friends who have been taken from us. In Gratan I see something of the gentle temperament of those who cared for him, no matter that he might sometimes strike some people as a bit of a brute. In fact, he has a physical vulnerability rare in a footballer. And a sweet nature for all his reputation as a womaniser."

"And his reputation as a Nazi?"

D'Anton laughed and shook his head. "Oh, that's only recent," he said. "Since his coming here and meeting Mehdi Mehdi, in fact. He has a twitchy arm, that's all. I think the world of him."

According to Gratan himself, the salute was a misunderstanding. Given that other players (no names) were performing it surreptitiously, pretending they were scratching their ear or taunting the opposition with rabbit signs, there was, in his view, a necessity to bring it out into the open. He wasn't a racist in general—when had he been booked for taunting a black or Asian player?—and he could prove categorically that he wasn't an anti-Semite. Name a single occasion on which he'd been booked for fouling a Jewish player. And at least one of his wives—he wasn't sure offhand which—had been a bit Jewish.

"He has a thing for Jewish women," D'Anton told Plurabelle. "He thinks they're hot. There's no accounting for taste."

"Does he have one at the moment?"

D'Anton thought about it. "Not that I know of."

"Then we should try to find him one. We owe that to your friends."

Some time after D'Anton's installation—say eighteen months—Plurabelle fell in love. Not with D'Anton and certainly not with Gratan or the wanted Algerian ventriloquist or his dummy, but with a person she saw first—feet first, as it happened—underneath the chassis of her Volkswagen Beetle. Her Porsche Carrera had needed servicing, but the mechanic who'd been sent (the garage went to her, she didn't go to it) decided he would much rather recline a while under the Beetle, a car that was rarely seen in the Golden Triangle whereas Porsche Carreras were ten a penny.

Informed by her house manager that the gentleman, who in plain truth didn't much look like a mechanic to him, hadn't given the Porsche a second look but had made a beeline for the Beetle, Plurabelle squealed with the consciousness of her good fortune. Found him—found him at last!—a man not to be deceived by ornament. If he were to turn out to be even marginally well favoured when he rolled himself out from underneath the meanest of her cars, she would give herself to him on the spot. No matter that the spot was a gravel drive.

She ran inside to wash off her make-up. Fifteen minutes later, wearing her oldest clothes, she returned to the gravel drive. "Let me see you," she called out, clapping her hands. A woman used to being obeyed. But who also wanted someone to obey.

And when he did, inch by inch appear, smudged with engine oil and more than a little bashful to be seen not in overalls but in his shirtsleeves—Plurabelle noted that he hadn't even rolled them up—he presented as pretty a picture of innocent manliness as ever delighted a maiden's eyes . . .

To the mind of a cynic the word "opportunistic" might have occurred sooner than "innocent." He who would win the heart of an heiress known to be wary of flattery from men with a marked taste for the meretricious must surely, if he has a brain in his head, choose to please her by preferring what is plain over what is gaudy. Those chumps who fell at the first hurdle, blinded by sparkle, deserved to be sent packing. Wherein did they suppose lay the test of their mettle if all that was required of them was to be predictably loquacious on the subject of glitter? And why hadn't a woman who could be won by such banalities been won a hundred times already?

Some such calculation would have saved many a suitor expense and bother.

Against the charge of opportunism, however, must be laid the intriguing fact that this heiress wasn't at home when the gentleman slid underneath her Volkswagen, wasn't at home and wasn't expected to be home any time soon, leaving open the question of how he knew she would find him there unless he intended never to move until she appeared. A calculation, or absence of calculation—they can amount to the same thing—which while it might not save him from the charge of contrivance does bespeak wholeheartedness. So either way he had qualities to recommend him to Plurabelle.

That it was his friend D'Anton (his dear, dear friend D'Anton) who tipped him the wink—a couple of winks, to be precise—a) to the fact that Plurabelle's heart was unoccupied, and b) as to the means to occupy it—did him no disservice, either, once it was discovered, for to be a dear, dear friend of D'Anton was an endorsement of his character in itself. Though when Plurabelle was apprised of all there was to be apprised of she wondered less that D'Anton was so sad. For who, once they had seen him, could not love Barnaby?

Or Barney as she called him in her heart at once, and then later in the company of everybody but the servants.

Had she been more certain of the codes that governed

the pastoral ideal she meant to live by, she would have considered clasping both D'Anton and Barney to her bosom and seeing what transpired. Sleeping with two or more men was not unheard of in the Golden Triangle, and she had more than once slept with two women in the aftermath of her first disillusionment with the other sex. But while she had no fear of losing Barney to D'Anton, who didn't own a Volkswagen Beetle for him to tinker under, she did worry how the former would view such unconventionality on her part. Just because he didn't idealise wealth, or see purity in gold, didn't mean he didn't idealise and see purity in her.

D'Anton the same, if from a different perspective.

One night, at a local restaurant, she asked the two men how they met. They gave conflicting answers. Barney said he didn't remember. D'Anton said he would never forget. They met, D'Anton recounted, by the pig roast at an agricultural fair in Alsager. D'Anton was not a big pig-eater himself but he was escorting a visiting Japanese glass-blower, whose favourite dish happened to be pork. This was the third festive event in Cheshire he'd taken Takumo to and his guest had made straight for the pig roast at every one of them. Barnaby seemed just to be sauntering, neither curious nor incurious, neither hungry nor not. The day was warm, he was idle, and agriculture was in his veins. He was wearing an oatmeal coloured suit, loose-fitting like a hay bag, his hair the colour and texture of the straw D'Anton imagined spilling from it. Cloud-filtered light cast the glow of late summer on Barnaby's face, making him resemble the Hireling Shepherd in William Holman Hunt's painting of that name. Plurabelle knew the painting, she was quick to say—it hung in the Manchester Art Gallery. Often she had stood before it in a sort of rapture, imagining herself to be the shepherdess. Her interruption appeared to distress D'Anton, perhaps for the reason, Plurabelle reasoned, that in his picture there was no shepherdess.

Barney laughed a shepherd's laugh. "I don't recall any such fair and I have never owned such a suit," he said.

"You wore an off-white linen shirt under it," D'Anton went on. "It had a button missing."

"Never owned one of those either."

"And you were carrying a straw panama."

"Not me guv'nor."

"So what's your version?" Plurabelle asked him, aroused by the mention of the missing button.

He shook his head. "D'Anton was just somehow always there or thereabouts," he said. "You might as well ask me when I first saw the sky."

D'Anton's expression brought to Plurabelle's mind another painting by William Holman Hunt. *The Light of the World*. Jesus with the moon behind him like a halo, knocking on a door with no expectation of its being opened, his lips pursed almost pettishly, his eyes downcast, a lonely, self-pitying man—"Behold I stand at the door and knock; if any man hear my voice, and open the door, I will come in to him, and will sup with him, and he with me"—all the while knowing that the door will remain unanswered.

There seems to be something about all this being rejected that D'Anton quite likes, Plurabelle thought. Could it be that he hopes Barney won't give him whatever it is he wants?

Or was it she who was hoping Barney wouldn't give him whatever it was he wanted?

FIVE

I have to take this," Strulovitch said, reaching for his phone.

"It's your daughter, of course you do," Shylock told him.

"How do you know it's my daughter?"

"I recognise the ring," Shylock said.

The two men were strolling with a forced companionability out of the cemetery towards the car park. Strulovitch had invited Shylock home—get out of the cold, have a bath, drink Scotch, stay the night—and Shylock had accepted with a rough alacrity that surprised and flattered Strulovitch. Despite his wealth and influence, Strulovitch was a man of modest origins and expected his invitations to be turned down. People surely had better things to do with their time than spend it with him. "Good, good, very good," he'd said, with something too like a bow. And Shylock—a man vexed in the matter of giving and receiving hospitality himself—had patted his shoulder. It was as though—without strong instincts for such a thing on either side—they felt they needed to accelerate the process of friendship.

Quite why, Strulovitch would have been unable to say.

He was not a man who made friends easily with other men. A mother, a wife, a daughter—these were the loadstones of his life. Possibly, then, he missed what he had never had. As for Shylock—Strulovitch would not have dared ask what *he* missed.

He liked it that Shylock took his arm, even though the grip was fierce. The gesture made him feel European. He hoped an observer would have taken them for professors of fine art at the University of Bologna, discussing how to improve the architecture of Jewish cemeteries.

"It's evident you spoil her," Shylock said, when Strulovitch rang off.

Strulovitch detected emotion in the other man's voice. How could it be otherwise? But which emotion—sorrow, envy, bitterness?

Did each of them envy the other?

Or was it just his own fatherly pride and sentimentality he was listening to?

"Her mother is too sick a woman to care for her as a mother should," he said. "The responsibility for her falls to me. It's not something for which I'm suited."

"Is any man?" Shylock interposed.

"Without a wife—probably not. So yes, I spoil her—spoil and deprive her in equal measure."

"That too I understand."

"I praise her and then I castigate her. What I give with my left hand I take with my right. It's all indulgence followed by exasperation followed by remorse. I feel as though I'm confined in a small space with her—impeding her movements one minute, too intimately aware of her presence the next. And then I punish her for feeling what I feel. I can't find any equilibrium in my love for her."

Shylock tightened his grip on Strulovitch's arm. Through the taut fingers Strulovitch could feel memory vibrating.

"Your words are daggers," Shylock said. "But so they would be to any father. It's an invariable law that fathers love their daughters immoderately."

He made it sound like a terrible duty enjoined by a God who'd done no better bringing up his own children. An exaction of affection more than a bestowal of it. To be loved by Shylock, Strulovitch saw, would be an arduous experience. But his words consoled as well as frightened him. So he wasn't the only one. The universe decreed that fathers should love their daughters not wisely but too well. And that daughters should hate them for it.

"I want to let her alone but I can't," he said. "I fear for her. I wish she would go to sleep and wake up ten years older. A daughter studying at college is a living torture. She comes home addled."

Shylock could barely wait for him to finish. "You think it would be any different if she never left the house? A daughter doesn't have to have an education to be taught how to hate her father. She can learn rebellion through an open window. It's in the nature of a daughter."

"It's in the nature of an open window."

"It's in the nature of nature."

"Then I am not for nature."

Shylock made a noise in the back of his throat that sounded like a laugh dying. "I wish you luck with that," he said, slowing their pace and looking beyond Strulovitch as though to be sure nature wasn't following them. "We've been battling nature a long time. How many jungle Jews do you know?"

Offhand, Strulovitch could only think of Johnny Weissmuller.

Shylock slapped the air, as if he meant to swat away a fly. "Him I can't comment on, but Tarzan, let me tell you, wasn't one of us. We don't hang out with apes. It's the gibbering of primates or it's the law. We chose the law. You read Stefan Zweig? Of course you do. There's a story that when he was a young man he used to expose himself to women by the monkey house in the Schönbrunn Zoo in Vienna. So why did he choose the monkey house? To deride the sexual imperative to which he was enslaved. I am no better than a monkey, he was saying. He grew out of it. That's the whole story of the Jews. We grew out of it. You have to draw a line under where you've been. Christians like to think they've drawn a line under us."

"We aren't monkeys."

"In their eyes we are. Apes, curs, wolves."

"That's nothing more than invective. Their real argument with us is that we drew the line too strictly under nature."

"Their argument with us is whatever will serve their purpose at any given moment. They don't know what it is they can't abide, only that they can't. I am more precise when it comes to what I can't abide about them. We lack charity, they say, but when I ran out on to the streets calling for Jessica children jeered at my distress. No *charitable* Christian parent dragged them home and admonished them for their cruelty."

Christ, Strulovitch thought admiringly, he doesn't lack outrage or intransigence, or come to that celerity, my new friend.

Then again, though he didn't mean to be critical so early in their acquaintance, wasn't it reported that Shylock ran out on to those very streets calling at the same time for his ducats? Strulovitch knew never to trust what was reported, but what if, in this instance, it were true?

He wanted to be fair. It was, after all, as an object of

material worth that Shylock's daughter had been stolen. But you can't—can you?—put everything down to the prevailing mercantilism of your society. Strulovitch lived in a wealth-crazed world himself; he hoped, however, that he knew the difference between his daughter and his bank account. Yet this, too, he understood—that in the outrage of loss, objects and people lose their delineation. The robbed commonly speak of violation, feeling the theft of things as keenly as an attack on their person. He couldn't say he would feel the same, neither could he say he wouldn't. But he wondered if he cut a similar figure as a father. Obsessed. Wolf-like. En-raged into possessive befuddlement. Was it just as arduous to be loved by him? Was he just as laughable a father in the cruel eyes of Christians?

"I can read what you're thinking," Shylock said. "All very well drawing a line under where we've been, but how do you draw a line under where your daughter wants to go? The an-swer is you can't."

Both men paused and looked down into the cold grey sludge they'd been sploshing through. They could have been back in the cemetery, hanging their heads in sorrow over the graves that contained people they loved.

They resumed a normal speed for a minute or two, until Shylock slowed them down again. "You know," he said, as though they'd been discussing such things for weeks, and only this minute had a new thought come to him, "it wasn't just to spite me that Jessica bought the monkey . . ." They were at a standstill now, close to the chapel with its Star of David over the door. It was in here that the young rabbi of-ficiating at Strulovitch's mother's burial had mispronounced her name and Strulovitch had vowed never again to attend an event, solemn or light, at which a rabbi officiated.

"So why did she buy the monkey?"

"Excuse me, we wash our hands here," Shylock said. Strulovitch stood his ground, perhaps a little too obdurately. Shylock went over to the washbasins at the rear of the building and poured water over his hands from a tin cup. Strulovitch knew the meaning of the custom. With water did you wash away the foul impurities of death. It made sense whether you were religious or not. But to Strulovitch it still smacked of fanaticism.

He had the grace to laugh at himself—Strulovitch the moderate.

Shylock picked up the conversation where they'd left it. "You were asking me why Jessica bought the monkey . . ."

"Yes."

"To disavow the Jew in herself. I do well not to say 'cursed be her name.'"

You are dead to me.

Dead at my foot.

"A lost daughter doesn't have to be a dead daughter," Strulovitch said. Wasn't he a lost son who'd been found again?

Shylock dug his fingers into Strulovitch's arm. "May you never come to understand the wrongness of those words. The loss I suffered I wouldn't wish on my enemies."

Strulovitch rode the rebuke. But he knew Shylock was lying. He *would* wish such a loss on his enemies.

He felt he'd joined his dad's old club. The Rot-in-Hell Jewish Fathers' Society. Much as he welcomed and was flattered by Shylock's companionship, he wondered how much of this naked wrathfulness he could take. Back in the days when she had words, Kay would accuse him of bringing ancient theological disputation into the house. Ironical that he wanted to say to Shylock what she had said to him. Lighten up, Shylock.

They walked the rest of the short distance to Strulovitch's hearse-like black Mercedes in silence. "Ah! I'm surprised," Shylock commented when he saw it.

A black chauffeur was holding the door open for them. Strulovitch handed him Shylock's Glyndebourne stool. "In the boot, Brendan," he said.

To Shylock he said, "Surprised by what? That I have a driver?"

"That you have a German car."

"I thought you believe we have to draw a line."

"That's another sort of line."

"A line's a line. We must let bygones be bygones."

"I'm surprised you believe that."

"I don't."

And so, sitting side by side in the back seat of the unexpected Mercedes, they'd dropped into the usual pattern of conversation between fathers on the pains of bringing up a family, especially fathers on whom the burden of bringing up a daughter had exclusively fallen.

"This may surprise you," Shylock said, "but I half expect to hear from my too dear daughter every hour. I buried her in my heart the day she left, but a daughter doesn't stay buried. Even a daughter that steals her father's most precious possession . . . apart, that is, from herself."

Strulovitch felt it behoved him not to present himself too alacritously as an equal in distress. Beatrice was giving him trouble but she hadn't yet bunked off through a window with a thieving lout. "You haven't heard anything so far then?" was the best he could think of saying.

Then he heard how ludicrous it sounded. *So far!*

"I say I half expect," Shylock went on, staring beyond him as he spoke, looking but not looking at the Cheshire countryside, "but I confess there's no volition in it. That's simply a description of the state I've been left in. I am in expectation because that's what follows when nothing does. But hope is idle because the story ends where the story ends. She could be on her way to me today, she could be knocking at my door this hour, but that's a disallowable supposition. Today is always yesterday. There's no Act Six. For me there wasn't even an Act Five. But at least no resolution means no final rejection. Anything could be. There's no knowing. Wounding doubt wounds not as fatally as wounding certainty. I am toyed with but I breathe."

"So there is no looking forward?"

"None."

"Are you telling me you don't ever wonder how she is?"

"I wouldn't be human if I didn't wonder that. Some days I think I only want her to be happy. Some days I don't. But it's vain. There is no 'is.' Her story, too, stopped when it stopped. She and the vile layabout she ran off with—and for all I know their monkey—inherit my wealth, but they won't ever see it. That's some consolation. But I can't help myself. I imagine her remorse. I am ashamed to say I pray for her to suffer agonies of remorse. I picture it. I see her ravaged face. But that's to ask for something that can't eventuate—might never have been, and certainly won't ever be now."

Strulovitch shook his head. "There must have been the seeds of remorse in her actions even as she took them. Who can set out on any journey without at the same time wishing they'd stayed at home? She must at times have looked back longingly."

"Those are Old Testament misgivings."

"Well who's to say Jessica didn't give in to them the minute she left the house?"

"The minute she left the house she bought a monkey."

"That's a sort of looking back."

"Yes, but not a looking back to me. The monkey once and for all made her not my daughter. She found living in a Jewish house something worse than prison. But yes, yes, it's always possible she didn't like what she had become when she became it and experienced, if not remorse exactly, then something like the regret you speak of, if only for her dear mother's sake. But I mustn't give in to fancy. She grew to hate me and I dare say her mother too for dying. It's crossed my mind to wonder whether the manner of her leaving was meant to mimic the manner of her mother's—for she died abruptly, my beloved Leah. As was done to Jessica, in her perception, so Jessica did. Certainly the manner in which she eloped was cruel to the highest degree. Cruel, disdainful and blasphemous. Had she wished to show me how badly she'd fared without a mother, or a father who could better play the mother—how inconsiderate she'd grown under my tutelage and example, how brutal even—she could not have made a better job of it. My hope now is that the ill treatment she's receiving makes her see things differently, though I will never know if it does or doesn't. But this is not what a father should want—for his daughter to suffer so that she should understand how much suffering she has caused. I should wish her happiness, should I not?"

"You should. But now you are asking too much of yourself. No father can completely want his daughter to be happy."

Shylock sucked air in through his teeth. "That's harsh philosophy."

"No, it's harsh psychology."

Shylock eyed Strulovitch stealthily, as a snake might. I have shocked him, Strulovitch thought. Good. I have shocked myself.

He asked Brendan to open the car windows briefly. He wanted to feel an invigorating air blow in off the fields, even if it was only Cheshire out there. It is civilised to accept the violence of our natures, he thought. It is justice that makes us human, not forgiveness. We are things of blood, not things of milk.

Then he asked for the windows to be closed again.

"I am complimented to be thought too harsh by you," he said.

"You shouldn't be," Shylock said. "It does no good to confirm Christians in their suspicions that we are lost to loving-kindness."

Strulovitch took the liberty of tapping Shylock's knee. He nodded in the direction of the chauffeur. Was Shylock up to date enough to know that a black man could be a Christian? Strulovitch hoped his expression told the story and served to warn him. In front of a Christian of whatever colour we should not talk slightingly of Christians.

Shylock apologised. "I am not accustomed," he said under his breath, "to minding my ps and qs. I am used to abusing in the spirit I'm abused. The times have grown nice."

"Appearances," Strulovitch said in a whisper, "can be deceptive."

SIX

The chauffeur drove them—somewhat surlily, Strulovitch thought—to the Strulovitch home in Mottram St. Andrew, the eastern apex of Cheshire's Golden Triangle. It had been his parents' last house, as unlike the houses they'd grown up in in Salford, where their parents had kept chickens in the yards and prayed in Yiddish to the Almighty, as was possible to imagine. All this in one generation—from a stable in a Mancunian shtetl to a baronial hall with a drive big enough to take a dozen Mercedes, a lake for rare fish and a view of Alderley Edge. A piece of purple-hazed, grassy England, holding Stone Age mysteries, theirs to look at and even feel proprietorial about, all thanks to car parts. Strulovitch liked his own house in Hampstead better—he preferred older money to new, even when the new was his own—but there were strong arguments for keeping Mottram St. Andrew. He had professional interests in the north, he had a daughter doing performance studies at the Golden Triangle Academy (latterly the North Cheshire Institute, renamed to remove all associations with poor-schools)—an arts-based independent college for the privileged of all ages, where Strulovitch, as a benefactor, was able to pull strings—and he believed the country air would be good for poor Kay. His mother, too, had wanted to go on living there, and would have been happy, in her own words, "to die in a shed in the garden," but Strulovitch had insisted on building her an extension big enough to house her carers. "Must I have so many people around me, Simon?" she asked. "You can't have too many," he told her. "You might slip in the bath, you might fall coming down the stairs. There's always an accident waiting to happen when you live on your own." Ironical that it was to Kay, a woman half her age and with a husband and a daughter in attendance, that the accident waiting to happen happened.

His mother slipped all right—but quietly, without a sound, slipped out of life under the kind supervision of a host of carers.

Strulovitch inadequately mourned her. He had loved her but his affections were becalmed. If you can't love your wife—daren't love your wife without howling for the loss of her—who can you love?

Your daughter.

Somewhere in the house, when she wasn't gallivanting, Beatrice lived. She was too young, in Strulovitch's view, to be sharing a place with other students of the performing arts who might be twice her age. Though in her own view she lived at home out of deference to her mother. She was not particularly good with her mother. She was afraid of her illness and impatient with the rituals of communication—who had time to wait for words that might or might not make sense to dribble out of the side of her mouth or appear illegibly on a chalkboard? But she was also ashamed of herself on these very counts and knew it was incumbent on her, at least, never to be too far away. Dreading what would happen to her if she went to college in London, dreading who she'd meet, who she'd fall in love with, and what they'd tell her, dreading her coming home one afternoon with a kafia round her throat, Strulovitch stoked her guilt. Yes—he commended her on her decision—it was a good idea to stay in the north and live at home. He knew her mother would be relieved, whether she'd be able to show it or not. In reality, the geography of Beatrice's education made no difference; they'd stuff her with the latest foie gras of anti-Jew psychosis and tell her that the sickness was her father's wherever she went. He wanted not to be too far away from her, though, in case . . . well, just in case. Which didn't mean he was tailing her. If she sometimes saw him flitting in or out of one of the art rooms, inspecting students' work, that was because he had suggestions to make and promises to honour. That was the price a daughter paid for having a father who ran the Strulovitch Foundation. Whichever institution she'd attended would have wanted something he had, the offices of a philanthropist, of no matter what religion, being always in demand.

"Don't use yourself up," his mother used to warn him. "There's only one of you."

It was only as he was getting out of the car—again conscious of something not quite right in Brendan's demeanour, not quite what one expected of a chauffeur—that he realised he had again not attended her grave.

The day had held too much excitement. And as his mother said, there was only one of him.

But there was always an excuse.

So what was Brendan's? He hadn't been behaving rudely exactly. He hadn't driven too fast, or cornered aggressively.

He hadn't been slow or resentful in opening the doors for his passengers. But he seemed ruffled. So who or what had ruffled him? The presence of Shylock, was it? The Christian-baiting? The Jew-talk?

Strulovitch wondered how his dogs would react. But they took no notice when he let himself and his guest in. They didn't even look up.

He suggested a drink and maybe something light to eat before bed. But he didn't want it to sound as though he couldn't bear to be left alone. Needy was he? He had just come, in a manner of speaking, from burying his mother. He had no wife he could talk to. He had no daughter he could trust. He had scores to settle—some social, some religious, some metaphysical—never mind what scores, just scores. Of course he was needy.

Shylock declined food, but found the idea of a drink agreeable. Strulovitch offered him grappa. He shook his head. Kümmel, perhaps. Strulovitch didn't have kümmel. Slivovitz, then? Strulovitch didn't have slivovitz. Shylock shrugged. Amaretto? Strulovitch thought he had amaretto somewhere. Shylock didn't want to put him to trouble. I'll have water, he said. Or cognac. Strulovitch had cognac. Shylock was in no hurry to retire. He didn't sleep much, hadn't slept much for a long time. And he seemed to be stimulated by Strulovitch's furniture—the leather and steel armchairs, the art deco rugs, the prints of resurrections on the walls, the uncannily lifelike clay sculpture of a half-naked couple wrapped around each other in a death embrace.

"Is it permissible to sit in this room?" he asked. "Or should I be standing to inspect its contents?"

"Sit, sit," Strulovitch said, ushering his guest into a chair. Had Shylock been in such a house before, he wondered. It must have been this thought that led him to say something stupid about the changes he must have seen.

"Yes," said Shylock. "I've seen a few."

Strulovitch opened his eyes wide. "Such as?" he still more inanely said.

"You don't have the time," Shylock told him.

"And you presumably don't remember."

"On the contrary I remember everything."

"So go on, humour me, what's the biggest change?" Shylock closed his eyes and pretended to take something—a straw, a raffle ticket—from an imaginary hat. "They used to spit on me, now they tell me Jewish jokes."

"Good jokes?"

"Not the way they tell them."

"But kindly meant, presumably."

"Tell me a joke that's kindly meant."

Strulovitch didn't try, but made a weighing motion with his hands. "Well, on balance I'd say joking, kindly or otherwise, has to beat spitting."

Shylock peered deep into his glass. When he concentrated, his eyes seemed to recede and close over as though they contained more of darkness than of light. Strulovitch knew he could appear stern himself, but the deep shadows cast by Shylock's eyes unnerved even him. Was this look another of his reprimands, he wondered. Have I trespassed in some way? Is it for me to decide for him whether joking beats spitting?

"What strikes me as more interesting," Shylock said peremptorily, as though to make it clear to Strulovitch that he was not keeping up conversationally, "is that they can't see a Jew without thinking they have to tell him a joke. Do they sing 'Suwannee' every time they meet a black man?"

Strulovitch wished he knew the answer to that. "They might under their breath. But I take a joke to one's face to be the equivalent of a little white flag. Look, we come in peace."

"And when they joke about my unbending, mercenary nature?" He was evidently unmoved by Strulovitch's pacifism. "When they finger banknotes in my face, when they jeer at my separatism, wondering that I consider myself favoured when everything about my existence declares the opposite, when they question my morality—though until we taught them they didn't know morality existed—when they dispute the principles by which I live, the things I believe, the food I put in my mouth, and when they expound their theories on where, given my faith, I should be living—are they still waving a little white flag?"

Strulovitch remembered boys at school making fun of his name—Strudelbum—and telling him to go back to where he came from. Where did they think that was? Ur of the Chaldees?

"So where are they sending you?" he asked.

"To hell, eventually. But in the meantime to nowhere in particular—that's their point. We had a chance at a Homeland and we blew it. Belonging was never what we were good at anyway. Being a stranger is what we do. It's the diaspora, they are at pains to assure me, that brings out the best in us. Which neatly sidesteps the question of what brings out the best in *them*. But they feel no embarrassment in proclaiming that the proper Jew is a wandering Jew. Citizens of everywhere and nowhere, dandified tramps subsisting wherever we can squeeze ourselves in, at the edges and in the crevices. Precarious but urbane, like flâneurs clinging to a rock face, expressing our marvellously creative marginality."

"My daughter thinks the same."

"I could speak to her . . ."

Strulovitch risked an ironic expression.

Shylock's face gave nothing away. His olive skin was polished to a mirrored bleakness, reflecting all that there was of sorrow. "Who's to say I won't make a better job of speaking to yours?" he said. "Since I'm here I might as well give you the benefit of my experience."

"*That*'s why you're here?"

"I'm here because I'm here. What other explanation could satisfy an unbeliever such as you?"

The men sit in silence for half an hour, neither looking at the other. Finally, Strulovitch does the unhostly thing and rubs his eyes.

"You can choose any bedroom you fancy," he says. "But the best are at the back of the house looking out over the Edge. If you stay up late or wake early you might see one of the wizards come tobogganing down."

"Ah, so it's a magic place," Shylock says, sniffing paganism.

Strulovitch remembers the sketch in which the Italian comedian Dario Fo attempts to eat himself. Shylock looks as though he means to eat Alderley Edge.

Strulovitch laughs with deep appreciation. Nothing beats my people's disdain for folklore.

He regrets he doesn't have more Jewish friends with whom he can exchange black thoughts and scoff at nature.

This pang of cultural loneliness might explain why he

suddenly asks what book Shylock was reading to his wife earlier in the day. One last convivial conversation about literature before sleep.

"You should be able to guess," Shylock says.

"It looked well worn. If it's the Bible, I'd be honoured if you'd read to her from one of mine. I have a Geneva Bible that's beautiful to hold and opens easily."

"Thank you. But we are giving the Bible a rest. We fear we have exhausted Jacob and his sheep. And besides, these days Leah prefers a novel. Last week we finished *Crime and Punishment* for the second time. I've promised her *Karamazov*. But for the moment she is disposed to laugh, and takes heart from hearing me read to her from *Portnoy's Complaint*. Some of the chapters are embarrassing but I feel it would be wrong to leave them out."

Needy or not, Strulovitch would have liked those to be the last words exchanged between them for the night. He felt he could sleep soundly on them. Sad, that he had no wife capable of taking heart from what he read to her. But sometimes it's possible to feel pleased for the hearts of other people.

Shylock, however, showed no signs of wanting to retire. Strulovitch was beginning to feel crowded by him. He was a guest one needed all one's energy for. Though his eyes leaked no light, and his mouth was resolutely unplayful, he still suggested a sort of irascible sociability, as though conversation, however desolate, were his medium and he dreaded its cessation. Or was it just sleep he dreaded? Did he ever turn in, Strulovitch wondered. Was this to be the price of having him here—that there would be no more sleep for him either? Only talk of daughters and identity, anger, betrayal, monkeys . . . ?

To keep himself awake, he asked if Shylock could remember the last joke the Gentiles had told him.

"Do you want it how I tell it or how they tell it?"

"How you tell it."

"Then I'll tell it how they tell it. '*Grr*eenberg goes to the doctor because he's not feeling vell . . . ' As a matter of interest have you ever met anyone who talks like that?"

"No . . . except maybe the occasional rabbi."

"It seems more likely that they're aping what frightens them."

"Let me tell you that no one's frightened of us any more."

"You must speak for yourself. I can still scare dogs." Strulovitch didn't say that his own dogs hadn't been scared. But then they were used to keeping company with an inordinate Jew.

"I don't doubt," he said, "that you, personally, still have the power to terrify. I meant 'us' collectively."

"I'm not sure that the distinction between 'I' and 'us' quite works. The individual Jew brings the collective Jew with him into any room. It's the collective Jew that Christians see. Person to person, I grant you, they can be very nice. I have received proposals of marriage from Christians sincerely wanting to make amends. I've had my portrait sympathetically painted. A German apologised to me in a cemetery once. But when I extended my hand he seemed afraid to take it. Why? Because at that moment it wasn't the individual Shylock's hands, it was the hand of the collective Jew. And collectively, we still connect to the uncanny."

Strulovitch felt the surge of dark forgotten powers. The uncanny . . . If only.

"Shall I go on with the joke?" Shylock said.

Strulovitch remembered his manners. "Yes, please. Grreenberg's at the doctor's . . ."

"'Grreenberg,' says the doctor, 'you're going to have to stop masturbating.' 'Stop masturbating!' exclaims Grreenberg, 'Vy is that?' 'In order,' says the doctor, 'that I can examine you.'"

Strulovitch laughed. It was one of his favourite jokes but he wouldn't have got it if he hadn't known it already. He had never heard it told so badly. Job could have told it better. Maybe that was Shylock's point. Telling it how *they* told it. He knew Shylock to be a man of savage humour. The fact of his never smiling was the irrefragable proof of that. Perhaps he was one of those who had to write his own material. And write it out of extremity—at the edge, or in the crevices. No wonder people couldn't always tell for sure when he was jesting and when he wasn't.

"I love that joke," Strulovitch told him, remembering the consternation it had caused Ophelia-Jane.

"You should have stopped me if you knew it."

"I wouldn't have stopped you for the world. But now you tell me something—why are there are so many stories about Jews masturbating? Onan, Leopold Bloom, your Alexander Portnoy, Grreenberg. Is that how Gentiles see us? Or is it how we see ourselves?"

He expected Shylock to take his time replying. But a scholar who had written a neglected paper on the subject could not have been more prompt with his reply. "Both," he said. "After so many years of being told what Gentiles see when they look at us it's hardly a surprise that we end up seeing something similar. That's how vilification works. The victim ingests the views of his tormentor. *If that's how I look, that's what I must be.*"

"Well, if they must see us as something depraved it

accords better with our own instinct for self-mockery that they see us as masturbators. Better that than misers."

"There's no difference. Jews hunched over their private parts, Jews hunched over their money. In the eyes of Gentiles it's one vast fevered panorama of degenerate self-interest. We spend as we hoard, exclusively, keeping our sperm and money out of general circulation. They claim their hatred of us has economic justification but if you ask me the genitalia are the root of it. They haven't been able to draw their imaginations from us sexually for centuries. You know they used to believe we bled like women, then they accused us of castrating Christian children. Even just thinking about us dirtied their minds. It's a mix of ignorance and dread that goes back to circumcision. If we would do that to ourselves, what might we not do to them?"

A gentle knock at the living-room door roused Strulovitch from the dark trance of thought into which these words had plunged him. It was his wife's night-time carer. Could Mr. Strulovitch spare a minute? Mrs. Strulovitch was asking for him.

"My wife wants me," he said, rising. He had intended the subject of his ailing wife to go largely unspoken between them. Sympathy was not what he was looking for. And Shylock, anyway, did not strike him as the man to give it. "I'll be back presently," he said, making everything sound as ordinary as possible.

But his heart was thumping. Could Kay have compounded all that was not ordinary about the day by actually calling for him by name?

The answer to that was no. The carer was worried about Kay, that was all. She had heard noises in the house and seemed more than usually distressed. But by the time

Strulovitch got to her she was asleep in her chair, her head lolling to one side, no word for Strulovitch on her nerveless lips. He straightened her up, kissed her brow, and went downstairs again. He wondered whether Shylock would still be there. Or whether he had ever been there at all.

"So where were we?" he asked, finding him as he'd left him, folded tight in his chair, all light excluded from his face.

Shylock shrugged.

Did that mean he was tiring? Strulovitch would have sat with him, swirling liquid in his glass, enjoying the dark quiet, but the longer he didn't speak the more he thought about Kay.

"And now?" he asked, after as prolonged a silence as he could bear.

"And now what do the Gentiles think? I'd be surprised if they're not thinking what they've always thought. Certainly their minds are no cleaner."

"No, I meant what now for you?"

"Me personally?"

Strulovitch decided to risk the other's wrath. He had invited Shylock into his stricken home. Now Shylock had to invite Strulovitch into his.

"Yes, you personally."

Shylock rubbed his face with his hands. Would it still be there when he took his hands away? His fingers, Strulovitch noted, were coated with a dark fur. Is he closer to the apes than I am, he wondered.

"For me *personally*," Shylock said, charging the word with all its long history of insolence and obloquy, "there is no now. I live when I lived. I have told you: where the story stopped, I stop. But sometimes, for the hellish pleasure of it, I roll the exit line of another dupe of fools around my tongue. I hanker, as you will easily imagine, for a resounding exit line."

Strulovitch made as though to rack his brain for the exit line in question. But it was late for tests.

"*I'll be revenged on the whole pack of you,*" Shylock said impatiently. How long did Strulovitch need? "I have always had a soft spot for Puritans," he explained. "Which I suppose is not surprising since they have a soft spot for us. We return each other's compliments. I like the idea that I, a heartless Jew, should be fortified in my unforgivingness by a Puritan."

"I'm surprised," Strulovitch said, displeased to have been found wanting, "that you take hellish pleasure in those words. They sound feeble to me, like an old man wagging his finger at small children."

"That's because you know they can't be acted upon. Malvolio, too, stops where the story stopped. He won't ever enjoy that revenge. But the intention echoes onwards through time. He has finally tasted blood. Until now he has only played at being a moralist, his Puritanism the stuff of pantomime. We are all the stuff of pantomime until we run up against reality. Now he knows whereof the little jesting world of men and women is really made."

For a man who reined in his agitation, Shylock had grown excited. Deep grooves appeared, like brackets—bracketing all that had not been and never would be said—about his sunken eyes.

Strulovitch looked at him warily. "You aren't, I hope, intending violence."

"That would depend . . ."

"On what?"

"Your definition of violence."

SEVEN

Plurabelle—who wanted to be loved for herself, that's to say for what she was rather than what she had, but who was as hard to distinguish from what she had as people generally are, and she more so than most because it was what she had that gave her the confidence and the leisure to be who she was—thus vexed and double-vexed, Plurabelle could not stop asking Barney to reaffirm his valuation of her. Once you have presented yourself as a prize wrapped up in an enigma it is difficult not to want to go on being guessed at and bid for. On her television show blindfolded contestants sipped dainty bits from a saucer, like cats, and hoped to prefer what she'd prepared. That way they'd win her company for the evening, and who could say what else? Back in the real-time world of the Golden Triangle, Barney had to second-guess which dress she liked herself in most that day, which earrings were the best accompaniment to what she had chosen to wear, which hotel in which country she wanted to be taken to on her birthday, whether she wanted her lobster cracked or in the shell, thermidor or Newburg, whether she wanted sex straightforward or perverse, with the lights on or off, with the windows open or closed.

"You just don't know me," she'd say when he mispicked. "I don't know what we're doing together."

On occasions she even cried over their incompatibility of whim.

His impulse was to go and do some work under the chassis of her Volkswagen Beetle but he knew he couldn't go on hitching his wagon to that lone star—she'd think it was the only trick he had.

He spoke to D'Anton who was, in a manner of speaking, responsible for the daily pickle in which he found himself. Without quite saying "You got me into this" he did say get me out of it. Not out of the relationship, which in other ways had so far proved as beneficial as he'd dared hope, but out of forever being tried for indiscrimination and forever being found guilty.

Although D'Anton would never have dreamed of coming between Plurabelle and Barney, he liked it when his friend, still bedwarmed, so to speak, still with the perfumes of Plurabelle on him, appealed to him for help. He didn't care to see himself as a go-between—such a role diminished his ongoing influence—more a sort of gentleman of the bedchamber, a confidant at the highest pitch of intimacy, a priest of the nuptial mysteries, no matter that Plurabelle and Barnaby were not yet man and wife.

"What you need to do," he said, "is man up to this aesthetically and critically."

"What does that mean, exactly?" Barney asked.

"It means daring to trust your own judgement. Stop doing what she wants you to do."

"I don't know what she wants me to do."

"Stop trying to figure it out. Follow your own impulses. Go out and buy her something decisively surprising that proves the confident refinement of your taste."

"I'm not sure I could afford that."

"I'm not talking expensive or meretricious. I mean an object of value in itself and in the fact that you have chosen it. Not something you guess she might like but something you do. Whatever she thinks of the gift, she will love you for being definite in your selection of it."

Barney put his hand to his cheek like a fallen cherub in the presence of the Creator. "I suppose I daren't risk a banger?"

"No you dare not. You don't want to undo your good work with cars."

"What then? Jewellery?"

"Too obviously expensive."

"I wasn't thinking sapphires."

"Then too obviously cheap."

"Perfume? Lingerie?"

Few words disgusted D'Anton more than "lingerie." "More obvious still," he said.

Out of ideas, Barney decided to second-guess D'Anton. "Are you thinking a work of art?"

"It's not for me to think anything, Barnaby. But art is good, yes."

"Do you have something she might like?"

"You are not entering into the spirit of this. This is about you, not me. Besides, Plury knows what I find and what I like. She would recognise my hand in it if you came to me."

"So what am I to do? I have no eye."

"You must have seen something beautiful that you like."

"The *Mona Lisa*."

"A step down from that."

"The Singing Butler."

"A step up."

Barney looked hurt. Being able to look hurt was a gift that had always served him well. Like the best lyric poets he knew how to convey his hurt into every heart.

"I simply mean," D'Anton said, remorsefully, "that I don't think Plury will go for that."

"You've just told me not to consider what she'd go for."

"Yes, but we don't want actively to offend her."

Barney threw up his hands. If, as D'Anton's expression implied, between the *Mona Lisa* and *The Singing Butler* a wide chasm of the beautiful yawned, he was damned if he knew how to cross it.

Unable to bear seeing his friend continuing at a loss, D'Anton reached out for him and put a protective hand, like an upturned cup, over his. Beneath D'Anton's fatherly fingers Barney's fingers quivered. D'Anton did not dare look at him. He suggested that they go together to Capes Dunn Fine Art Auction Galleries in Charles Street, Manchester. There was a sale coming up the following week. Never having been to a fine-art auction, Barney was worried he would not know what to do. "All that's required of you is to see something that takes your fancy in the catalogue," D'Anton assured him, "and I'll bid for you."

The very thought of the outing—just the two of them in pursuit of beautiful things—delighted D'Anton.

But Barney had a further concern. Money spent on Plurabelle was never, of course, wasted. "Give and ye shall receive" was one of the many Christian truisms about sensible investment his Christian mother had taught him, and to date he had surely taken from Plurabelle a sizeable interest on what he had put in. But there were limits to the store he could go on putting in from.

"We will worry about that," D'Anton said, with gentle understanding, "when the time comes."

One of the reasons D'Anton's friends loved him as they did was the comforting sense he gave them of an inexhaustible store of assistance, should such be needed.

The mistake Barnaby made, when the time did come, was to allow himself to be delayed by Plurabelle asking him to choose her a book to suit her mood from a Tolkien, a Murakami and a Jackie Collins. "I couldn't say no to her, could I?" he explained to D'Anton who was sitting waiting in a taxi, looking at his watch. D'Anton was so far irritated with his friend—believing he had forgotten an outing which in prospect meant so much to him—that he didn't even express curiosity as to which book Barnaby had chosen. And he continued to stare out of the taxi window as Barnaby, sparing no small literary or domestic detail, set about telling him. The Murakami, apparently. Because Barnaby knew Plury loved Japanese food. As though D'Anton gave a damn. The long and the short of it was that they arrived at the auction house just too late to stop an early study by Solomon Joseph Solomon for his painting *Love's First Lesson* from being sold to Simon Strulovitch. Barney had seen enough of this work in the sale catalogue to know that here was something he truly loved on his own behalf while feeling confident it would be loved every bit as well by Plurabelle, so like her was the naked Venus with her glowing cheeks and tiny nipples, and so like him was the naked Cupid in her lap, looking up at her with undisguised if slightly insolent devotion.

Particularly he liked the little bow and arrow.

"Can't we offer to outbid him?" he wondered.

"Too late, I'm afraid," D'Anton said. "What's sold is sold. Did nothing else take your fancy?"

Alas, nothing else did.

For the second time in a week D'Anton was lanced in the heart by the look of bewildered dejection on his friend's handsome face.

"Leave it with me," he said, with a sigh that would in turn have lanced Barnaby's heart had he possessed one.

EIGHT

Untrue what Strulovitch said about not exactly tailing his daughter.

It had been going on a long time. She was thirteen when it started. Thirteen in fact, twenty-three in appearance. Luscious. A Levantine princess. A pomegranate. She was luscious to herself, too. He had caught her looking at her reflection in the mirror once, pouting her lips and laughing at her own fullness, smoothing her thighs, pushing out her breasts, amused by the too-muchness but overwhelmed by it at the same time. As though it imposed a responsibility on her. Was this really her? Was this really *hers* to do with as she chose? He could understand it only too well. When he was thirteen and untouched he felt he had already gone to waste. A great prince in prison lies, he would say as he went alone to bed night after night. And he was no pomegranate. Of course she had to deploy herself. Of course she had to feel her beauty had a purpose beyond her own gaze and, yes—because she knew he tailed her, knew he followed her into her own bedroom even—beyond *his*.

He got it. He got it all. But he couldn't allow it. It was the waste he couldn't bear. The *other* kind of waste. The waste of his and Kay's ambitions for her. The waste of their love. The waste of that excitement he'd felt when he saw her for the very first time. The betrayal of the covenant. The waste of her, not as a pomegranate but a promise.

She was throwing that promise away. On boys who were beneath her. On crazes that demeaned her. On drinks and drugs she didn't need. On music that didn't merit a second of her attention. She had grown up in a house that was filled with Mozart and Schubert from morning to night. How could she not tell the difference? The first time he tailed her was to a party in a stinking house in Moss Side where a disc jockey scratched records with his dirty fingernails and shouted "Make some noise!" It was that injunction—*make some noise*—that brute invitation to the inchoate, that enraged him even more than the sight of her sitting cross-legged on the floor, smoking weed and stroking the matted hair of a half-conscious troglodyte lying with his head in her lap. "Make some noise," Strulovitch hissed into her ear as he dragged her down the stairs, "have I brought you up to value noise as an entity—just noise for the sake of it, Beatrice—while some chthonic arsehole fondles your breasts!"

She fought him on the stairs and fought him as he dragged her into the Mercedes while the chauffeur looked on, saying nothing. "That's what this is really about, isn't it," she said. "It's not the music, it's got nothing to do with music, it's the fondling. Well no one was fondling me as it so happens. I was fondling him. The only fondling of me that was going on was in your head."

He slapped her face. You don't accuse your father of having sexual fantasies about you. She got out of the car. He ran after her. A stranger shouted "Hey!" when he saw them

struggling. "Fuck you!" Strulovitch said, "I'm her father."
"Then try behaving like it," the stranger said. It was a line
Beatrice was to borrow. "If you want me to behave like your
daughter, try behaving like my father."

A couple of days later she walked into his study laughing
like a witch. "I've just remembered your description of the
boy fondling me," she said. "A chthonic arsehole. Congratula-
tions. You make me proud to be your daughter. No other girl
has a dad who could come up with a phrase like that."

Strulovitch felt a twinge of pride. It wasn't a bad phrase
for the spur of the moment. And it had the merit of being
deadly accurate. "I'm grateful for your appreciation, Beatrice,"
he said. "I'm sorry I hit you."

"You're sick," she said. "*Chthonic arsehole*. What you
really mean is a goy boy. You wouldn't have minded if he'd
been a Jew."

"Not true."

"True!"

"All right, I might have minded less. Not on religious
grounds, but because a Jew isn't interested in the idea of
making noise."

She laughed again. "Shows what you know," she said.

Was she right? Was chthonic arsehole just a euphemism
for a non-Jew?

He didn't think so. When he saw a Christian he didn't
see a creature of the prehistoric dark. That, surely, was more
what Christians saw when they saw him. Why, it was sometimes what he saw when he saw himself.

The fact remained that a Christian husband was not what
he wanted for his daughter, any more than his father had
wanted a Christian wife for him. Yet it was with him exactly
as it had been with his father. They both took non-Jews as

they found them, enjoyed cordial relations with them, respected them, loved them—his father's trustiest pal was a chalk-white Methodist from Todmorden; his partner, a man he cherished like a wife, an ultramontanist from Wells—and they both, father and son, reserved their highest admiration for Gentile geniuses—Mozart and Beethoven, Rembrandt and Goya (*Goya!*), Wordsworth and Shakespeare (whether he was a Shapiro or he wasn't). With what the Gentiles were in themselves Strulovitch had no quarrel. Only when it came to who his daughter would marry (and maybe sleep with) did he have reservations. Only when he thought of the covenant did a Christian become a troglodyte.

So in the name of that covenant, how many more times did he bundle her into the Mercedes?

He was lucky she never ran away with any of the freaks—he felt he needed another word—who fondled her breasts, even for one night. When he hated her he said that was because she knew which side her bread was buttered, when he loved her he said it was because beneath it all she was a young woman of profound good sense. Either way, he went on tailing her until she grew so accustomed to his presence in the shadows of a car park or at a table in the far corner of a bar wearing dark glasses and reading the *Financial Times* that she would turn and ask him for a ride home when she felt she'd been out long enough, or a loan when she ran out of cash.

One bank holiday Monday he followed her to the Notting Hill Carnival. She'd said she was going to stay with cousins in Hendon—he'd even put her on the train—but he got wind of her plans. He knew it wasn't going to be easy finding her in the crowds but went, despite his loathing of street parties, public nudity, jungle music—*jungle music*? yes, jungle music—drunkenness, and masquerades, fearing the worst. The worst being? A Rasta junked-up to his eyeballs, swathed in a kafia and making noise on a steel drum. In the event it was Beatrice who found *him*. His anxiety must have lit him like a beacon. Boldly—and ironically because she knew his fears—she introduced him to a white man in a suit, pretty much his age, who shook his hand and said, "An honour to meet you Mr. Strulovitch."

"Do you know how old my daughter is?" Strulovitch asked him.

"Twenty-four."

"Is that a guess?"

"It's what she told me."

"You don't ask people of twenty-four what their age is. You guessed, and you guessed wrong. She's thirteen."

"Thirteen and seven eighths," Beatrice corrected him.

"Out of the mouths of babes," Strulovitch said.

"Jesus!" the man cried, leaping from Beatrice's side as though he'd just learnt she had leprosy. Strulovitch was half-inclined to feel sorry for him. He nonetheless said, "If I discover you're still seeing her I'll cut your heart out."

For some reason this threat didn't upset Beatrice. "Well *he* was hardly what you'd call chthonic," she said, when Strulovitch got her home. "He's the deputy mayor of Kensington and Chelsea."

"Doesn't stop him being chthonic," Strulovitch said. "I can name you a dozen chthonic mayors, never mind deputy mayors."

But the only reason his threat to eviscerate the bastard hadn't upset her more was that she didn't love him. Once the loving kicked off in earnest he knew he'd have his work cut out.

And then it did. He recognised the signs. Loss of appetite, absent-mindedness, teeth marks in her neck. One night he followed her to Levenshulme—a suburb no daughter of his should have been seen dead in—kicked down the door of a council flat and began throttling the first person he encountered inside. He was someone's grandfather, too old to ravish Strulovitch's daughter, though he might easily have been acting as a lookout while some younger person did. It took five people—one of them the putative ravisher, too puny, in the event, to have ravished a mouse—to pull him off. You were lucky, Beatrice told him, that you didn't kill him or that no one called the police. "As far as you're concerned," he retorted, "I *am* the police."

It was at this time—otherwise Beatrice would surely have fled for ever—that Kay had her stroke. One of her doctors was a friend of Strulovitch's and assured him that while his running battle with his daughter could have contributed, other factors played a more important part in the aetiology of her sickness. She had always been a frail and nervous woman. The stress brought on by the long wait for Beatrice, and then her own anxiety for the girl's welfare, would also have contributed. Strulovitch knew it. You can want something too much.

But he was a superstitious man. If you do wrong, you suffer—that's morality. Superstition, which operates on a grander scale, has it that if you do wrong, someone else suffers. Someone you love. Would his wife have been with him still had he allowed Beatrice to throw her life away on whom she chose?

Which he doesn't doubt she is going to do anyway.

———

Feather-bedded, cocooned in silk, the apricot and indigo of the Chihuly chandelier reflected in his narrowed eyes, Shylock lay awake within the force field of magical influence emanating from Alderley Edge, thinking of Jessica. Wizards or no wizards, he could not unbury her or uncurse her. Nor could he abruptly unfather himself of concern for her. The story ended where the story ended, but while he grasped the finality of that for him, he could not stop himself imagining the misery waiting in store for his daughter.

This much he knew:

Those who hated him so much as to profit from his loss of her and laugh openly at his sorrow would never reconcile themselves to the fact that she was Jewish. Blood would out. She was not daughter to her father's manners, she said, but Lorenzo, the rascal who pilfered her, along with those who conspired in the misappropriation, could not stop commenting on her difference from the man she was ashamed to call father, her gentler (for which read more Gentile) disposition, her greater chance of making it to heaven, the fairness of her looks—ivory to his jet—and when all you can remark is difference then all you are aware of is similarity. That she came bucketed in his ducats only went to show how present he was in their estimation of her. How long before Lorenzo woke to find his limbs stretched out by Shylock's?

The naivety of daughters! To think that Lorenzo's love would make her Christian when nothing in his character or behaviour bore the notation of Christian as a Christian would describe Christianity. Was it Christian to avail himself, without pausing long enough to scratch his backside, of her father's gold and jewels? Was it Christian to make merry with her betrayal and watch her empty her pockets in a single mad night in Genoa? A subtle gradation of morality attaches to profligacy: to blow a fortune of one's own is reprehensible, to encourage another to squander hers is iniquitous. Or is that iniquity what Christians mean by virtue? Virtuous to divest another of his worldly goods so long as you deplore the means by which he came by them . . . ?

He remembered her as a child in Leah's arms and mourned her as he mourned her mother. What had he done to make her hate him? "Hatred" was not too strong a word. The monkey proved that. To buy a monkey with the ring Leah had given him was a profanation of them both. But whatever she had sold to buy it with, a monkey was a profanation of her ancestors and education, everything he and Leah had taught her since she was a child. Not for a wilderness of monkeys would I have sold that ring, he told Tubal, and as he said it he saw the wilderness, the vast expanse of feral nothingness, lawless, godless, governed only by greed, hyenas, and the blind impulse to reproduce.

Was that what Jessica hated, not him or the mother who'd prematurely left her, but the idea that the wilderness should be civilised—the wilderness in her heart and the wilderness that was the company she kept? Christianity, when all was said and done, counted as no more than an interregnum: the only true distinction was between Judaism and paganism, and when a Jew felt the old paganism itching in his blood he had no choice but to reject the interdictions he'd been brought up to listen to. Jessica wasn't interested in Christians. What she wanted was to be back in the wilderness with the monkeys.

Strulovitch found his guest in the garden when he woke. It was still early. And cold. He was wearing his overcoat, with a black scarf around his shoulders—to Strulovitch's eye not unlike a prayer shawl—and was sitting on his Glyndebourne stool talking to Leah. A few remaining droplets of dew sequinned the lawn, lighting him up from below like footlights.

"So, Leah, it would seem that I am presently to become a Christian," he'd been saying.

This was a familiar theme between them. He had waited for her, as always, to say something in return. But presumably she was too amused for words. "Some Christian you'll make!" he knew she was thinking.

He couldn't resist indulging her sense of humour. "You can just see me, Leah," he liked to go on, "taking my pew, gowned in white for when the sacred moment of baptism arrives, my head bowed, waiting in beatified gratitude for the sermonising to start. 'We have in our presence today, by the grace of Jesus Christ, a Jew notorious for . . .'"

He rose from his stool and did a stately dance for her, rubbing his fingers together—the Waltz of the Money-grubbers.

But there it had to come to an end. He sat down again. His conversion to Christianity was the ultima Thule of their graveyard pillow talk. They might approach it forever, nose it like sharks circling the smell of blood, but they would never be able to move in for the final kill. Before Shylock had been able to convert, or pretend to convert, the footlights dimmed.

Had he or hadn't he?

Well that was simple to answer. He hadn't.

Hadn't been given the opportunity.

But would he or wouldn't he?

Hearing Strulovitch's soft tread, he stood up quickly and extended a hand. He was impressed by his host's attire, a dressing gown that might have been painted by Matisse, and crested slippers. A gown and slippers of comparable sumptuousness had been left for him in the guest bathroom, but he was uncomfortable in other men's clothes. And he didn't want to look as though he intended to make himself at home. Strulovitch might fear he would never go.

"Shall I leave you?" Strulovitch asked him gently. He felt obscurely honoured—no, not obscurely, simply and deeply honoured—that Shylock felt the presence of his wife in Strulovitch's garden. It was one thing to accept Shylock's conviction that there was nowhere on the wheeling planet that Leah wasn't buried, but for her to be specifically buried *here* . . . !

Strulovitch lowered his head. He wasn't a religious man but he still believed that the beloved dead consecrate.

"We were enjoying a joke," Shylock said. "We try to keep it light."

Strulovitch privately hoped he was a better jokesmith with his wife. Poor Leah, otherwise, having to lie there, year after year, feigning amusement.

"May I ask the subject of the joke?" he said. "Not another one about Mr. Grreenberg being unvell, I take it?"

"No, nothing to do vid Grreenberg. We like to speculate on my becoming Christian. The idea entertains my Leah."

"I'd have thought it would horrify her."

"Would *have* horrified her had it come to pass, but time was on our side. It closed its fist before it could fulfil its purpose. We can smile that *something* was on our side."

"Do you feel you baulked the Christians of their prize?"

"That presupposes that they knew what their prize was."

"They sounded sure enough. *Get thee gone* . . ."

"*Get thee gone,* is no proof of anything. *Get thee gone* is simply what those in power like saying to Jews."

"But they didn't only want you gone from their presence, did they? They wanted you gone from yourself, stripped of your faith and your self-worth . . ."

"And my money, don't forget my money."

"So they did know what their prize was."

"Who can say? What if it wasn't time alone that closed its fingers before I could be Christianised? What if, having said what they'd said, they were now content themselves? Content to have saved one of their own and be seen to have swindled me out of my money. It was all about appearances, as show trials often are. And make no mistake, no matter how it began, this became a show trial in the end. How to Jew the Jew. And thereafter, what if they didn't much care whether I followed the conversion procedure or not? Though the order was malignantly meant, once having restored the status quo ante Iudaeus they had other things to think about, honour was satisfied, the merchant had won while briefly enjoying the masochistic ecstasy of losing, and ultimately it was my loss if I stubbornly went about Jewing it as before, hobbled as to cash, humiliated, orphaned either end, and without the intercession of Christian grace to save my soul. You can't suppose they really cared about the state of my soul."

Strulovitch thought about it. "They might have cared to the degree that they could boast of having changed its complexion."

"There you have it!—cared for how it reflected on them. But they'd had their victory. And their own souls were evidently in good shape. They'd spoken of pity and exacted a cruel revenge. Very Christian of them."

"But would they have believed such a conversion of you, anyway, given the contempt you'd always shown for Christianity?"

"Who can say? On the one hand Christians considered Jews too immured in obstinacy ever to convert, on the other they didn't see how we could resist the light of Jesus once we beheld it. They were right on the first count about me. I hope I'd have taken a knife to my own throat rather than kneel abjectly in front of a painted mannikin."

"So when you declared yourself 'content' to be converted you didn't mean it?"

"I was answering a question in the form it was presented to me. 'Art thou contented, Jew?' If that was not a sneer, what was it? I had no fight left in me, but my reply—'I am content'—at least returned the compliment."

"It was never your intention, then?"

"I only say 'I hope' I'd have taken a knife to my own throat. I can't pretend to know what I'd have done had they summoned the energy to do more than congratulate one another and actually drag me off to church. But 'content' I would never have been. Do I strike you as a contented man?"

Strulovitch was sorry Shylock had not chosen to wear the gown and slippers he'd left him. He would have liked him to feel at home. Stay a while. Try a little of that contentment he scorned. Explore the area. Admire the winter landscape. Exchange reminiscences. Or just go on talking about Jews, a subject of which Strulovitch tired in principle but not in fact. The heat with which Shylock discussed it shocked and fascinated him. I the Jew, they the Christians—no two ways about it, no weasel words. Was it better like that, he wondered. A naked antagonism. No pretending that fences could be mended. An unending, ill-mannered, insoluble contrariety. Did it mean that all parties at least knew where they stood? That at least you knew your enemy. And would go on knowing him until the end of time.

Until the conversion of the Jews.

Such extremity of thought and language. Such eternities

of mistrust and hostility. If Shylock does stick around he will need to learn to moderate himself in Beatrice's company, Strulovitch thinks—Strulovitch a man frightened for and of his daughter.

Shylock had gone on a short walk and was looking down at Strulovitch's fish. "Do you ever eat these?" he asked.

"They're strictly ornamental," Strulovitch said. The thought occurred to him that such a concept could be foreign to Shylock. If Strulovitch left him in the house, would he steal one for his lunch? Grab it from the pond with his hairy fingers and stuff it, wriggling, down his throat? I really don't know who this man is, he thought. He could hear his mother saying "You invited him into your home? Just like that?" His wife, when she had been his wife, the same. And Beatrice. "Who *is* he, Dad?"

Were men generally more incautious than women when it came to who you let into your house, or was it just him?

"Would you like coffee?" he asked at last

Shylock smiled. "Tea is probably better, thank you, given how you English make coffee."

"My coffee is good," Strulovitch said. "I import the beans myself."

Shylock put his hands together and then opened them. This was not the first time he had struck Strulovitch as making the sign of a man consenting quietly to arrest. "Shall I come in for it?"

"I could set a table out here."

"Too cold," Shylock replied, drawing his coat around him as he moved into the house.

The gesture was theatrical, the closing of a scene. Again Strulovitch thought, I do not know this man.

"I'm not sure how you breakfast," Strulovitch said once they were inside.

"The usual way. At a table, with cutlery."

"I'll rephrase. I'm not sure on *what* you breakfast."

"Toast will do me," Shylock told him.

"I should have asked you last night what you would like," Strulovitch said. "And whether you are . . ."

"Particular in what I eat? This side obsessiveness, yes I am. You are not, I gather."

"It is not that which goeth into the mouth defileth a man," Strulovitch said with pomp, "but that which cometh out of the mouth, this defileth a man."

"You consider Jesus the best authority on the subject of *kashrut*?"

"He lets me off the tedium of observance with a noble sentiment."

"You think it noble, I find it sophistical. Why cannot we be defiled by what goes out *and* what comes in?"

"Why do we have to talk of defilement at all?"

"I don't."

"Then if there's no defilement . . . ?"

"Why bother with the distinctions? Because it is always worth distinguishing. Life, to be valued, should not be random and undifferentiated. I no more want to stuff everything down my mouth regardless than I want to experience every sensation. When I fell in love with Leah, I knew I did not want to love another woman. I distinguished her from other women, as she distinguished me from other men. To keep a kosher kitchen is to practise morality in the same way that keeping a faithful marriage is. The habit of conscientiousness in itself ministers to goodness."

"You are sure you don't confuse morality with neurosis?"

"There is less neurosis in observing than there is in lapsing. You secular Jews are more punctilious in your non-observance of the law than the Jew of faith is in his performance of it. You have as many things to remember not to do. As many festivals to miss, as many mitzvahs to forget, as many obligations to turn aside from."

"That assumes I lapse meticulously. I am less deliberate than that. I simply don't notice."

"Somewhere along the line you made a choice to lapse. And that's where *your* neurosis comes in. That original choice of yours must have been highly principled, whatever you say, because you are, in so many other ways, cut out to be the full Jew. Diet aside, look what a fanatic separater you are. You separate ideas. You separate people. You have separated yourself. You separate your daughter—"

"I *try* to separate my daughter."

"You try uncommonly hard. You have a kosher mind. So why jib at a kosher stomach?"

"I jib at making it a reason for offending or inconveniencing others."

"Does my diet offend or inconvenience you?" Strulovitch laughed. "Me? No. Not yet it doesn't."

"I will be happy with toast so long as I am under your roof."

"I suspect you never said that to the Christians you refused to eat with."

"Do you think it would have made any difference? Do you think they would have liked me more?"

"They might have *dis*liked you less."

"Are you speaking now from your own experience of being liked? If so, then tell me: are you the more loved for what you give? For your bequests and benefactions? Or does a still greater repugnancy attach to you on account of your having the wherewithal to make them?"

"Repugnancy?"

I am not you, Strulovitch thought. I don't arouse such aversion. I am someone else living in another time.

But he almost regretted it were so.

"If the word offends you," Shylock said, "find another. But they won't ever forgive you in their hearts. You might as well whet your knife on the sole of your shoe."

"Is that your advice to me?"

Shylock said nothing.

"Nonetheless," Strulovitch continued, "you did on occasions eat with them."

"Yes, and I live to regret having done so. But it wasn't in order to win their affection that I went. It was to provoke them. I went to make their food taste like ratsbane in their gullets. There has to be some pleasure in life. It can't all be work and prayer."

Ah, Strulovitch thought, there's a provocation I do understand.

Silence between them.

Shylock eating dry toast.

Strulovitch wondering if it was true he had a kosher mind.

Beatrice . . .

Where was Beatrice?

Strulovitch wondered if she could have overheard this conversation. And if so, what would she be thinking—a modern girl who did what she wanted, kissed whom she wanted, ate what she wanted?

"Who is this guy, Dad? What's he doing here? Is he trying to convert you?"

And what would Shylock's reaction be when he met her? Would the sight of a living daughter, still at home, break his heart?

"So, your daughter . . ." Shylock mused into his coffee, his punctuation implying he had been keeping pace with Strulovitch's thoughts, "is she in residence?"

NINE

Among D'Anton's more lovable qualities, in Plurabelle's view—and he was a man made of lovable qualities—was his capacity to listen. Especially to listen to her. She had only to say she wanted a thing—for herself or for a friend—for D'Anton to seek ways to get it.

And so it was with a Jewess for the footballer Gratan Howsome. The minute she learned he had a thing for Jewish women, Plurabelle decreed that they should find him one. And Plurabelle had only to decree—especially in a matter that bore on Gratan's felicity—for D'Anton to act.

Even as they were speaking he remembered being struck by the appearance of a student he had encountered at the Golden Triangle Academy, an institution on which, in his most princely manner, he bestowed time, delivering occasional public musings on beauty and renunciation. Her looks weren't pleasing to him personally but, with his gift for altruistically entering into a foreign aesthetic, even a limited foreign aesthetic, he was able see how they could be pleasing to someone else—like Thai scorpion soaked in whisky or black bed linen. Something about her, perhaps even something about her family name, to which he wouldn't have paid much attention, lodged in his memory. He smiled at Plurabelle's good-hearted suggestion and tapped his nose. "Leave it with me," he said, more spiritedly than Plurabelle could remember him having said anything.

Plurabelle liked her from the beginning, immediately forgetting she'd been procured for the footballer. "You remind me of me when I was your age," she told the girl, in all likelihood remembering the time before she'd had work done on her face.

She loved the idea that the girl was studying with a view eventually to being a performance artist and expressed the hope that she would one day perform at one of her weekends. "We could put a stage up for you," she said.

Modestly, the girl explained that a performance artist didn't employ a stage. Hers was, or would be, a different sort of performance, subverting expectations of what performance space was, even violating what people normally thought of as their space. Art should go where it was not normally welcomed, she said.

Plurabelle listened to her in wonderment. So precocious. So lustrous and bejewelled, though the bejewelled part was an effect of her natural beauty only. "Well your art will always be welcome here," she said. "My house is yours, violate it as much as you like. I will invite some important people to be violated by you."

"I'm a long way from being ready for that, Plurabelle," the girl had replied with a becoming blush.

"Call me Plury," Plury said.

The girl thought the sky above her head would burst, it had so many stars in it.

It was Plurabelle's suggestion, one evening, that they

dress for dinner as boys. The girl was uncomfortable. She wasn't sure how she'd look. But she went along with it. Plurabelle had wardrobes of dressing-up clothes.

"Suits you," Plurabelle said scandalously, knotting a scarf around her neck and putting a cap on her head. "I feel we're brothers."

Gratan Howsome, who of course was at the table, was smitten at once.

Thereafter, they did this often. It always ended the same way, with Plurabelle smothering the beautiful girl with Levantine lips in rapturous kisses, laughing wildly, and calling her "My little Jewboy."

And with Gratan burning into her with his eyes.

This was how, unknown to Simon Strulovitch, his daughter Beatrice became an intimate of Anna Livia Plurabelle Cleopatra A Thing Of Beauty Is A Joy Forever Christine.

TEN

S he's in residence in a manner of speaking," Strulovitch said. "Certainly she *officially* resides here. But where she's living in her head or in her heart . . . Look, to be brief with you, I'd say we're heading for a showdown."

"Your doing," Shylock wanted to know, "or hers?"

"I'm not sure we're separate enough for me to be able to answer that. We seem to want to bring things to a head, and then step back again, at exactly the same time. It's what's kept her here so far . . . it's what's kept us together."

"Your simultaneity of rage?"

"I couldn't have put it better. But it's an equally simultaneous fear of that rage too. We both, I think, dread the final collision. Somewhere I believe she is sorry for me."

"Sorry for *you*?"

"Yes, since Kay took ill at least. Before that she thought I was out of my mind. Now she thinks I'm still out of my mind but doing my best for a father without aptitude or assistance."

Shylock appeared on the point of saying something, but before their conversation could proceed further, Beatrice herself appeared, a little the worse for wear, in an indigo

Stella McCartney robe which Strulovitch had bought her for her last birthday, and a towel around her head. A couple of strands of wet hair fell about her face giving her, to Strulovitch, for all the indolent, burnt butteriness of her skin and the laconic way she moved her limbs, a bewitching mermaid look. She could have come in straight from swimming with the ornamental fish. It pained him, how lovely to his eyes she was.

"Talk of the devil," he said.

"Thanks, Daddy."

He hesitated over the introduction, but it had to be done. "My daughter Beatrice, Shylock."

"Yeah, right," Strulovitch thought she said, that's if she said anything. She was a mumbler, otherwise uninquisitive in the not quite impolite style of a preoccupied teenage girl, asking Shylock if he was an old friend of Daddy's, pretending to listen to the answer, wondering if the men had plans for the day. Globally indifferent.

Did she know who she was talking to?

"We haven't discussed what we're going to do," Shylock said. "Your father might be busy. I'd be quite happy to sit here and read the papers or listen to some music if that wouldn't inconvenience you. Do you have any Bach, or George Formby?"

Beatrice looked at her father. She didn't know who George Formby was. Hers was the first generation, Strulovitch thought, that came into the world without memory.

Strulovitch helped her out. "'When I'm Cleaning Windows.'"

"That's not Bach," Beatrice guessed.

"No he's funnier than Bach."

"I am never amused," Beatrice said, "when I hear facetious music."

"My own Formby favourite," Shylock said, "is 'Happy Go Lucky Me.'"

Is he poking fun at himself, Strulovitch wondered. Or is he making fun of her? If so, to what end? Is he flirting with my daughter?

Beatrice seemed neither to notice nor to care. She loosened the towel around her head and shook her hair, sprinkling with the lightest spray Shylock's fine woollen trousers.

Unless that was her way of flirting back.

"What about Al Jolson?" Shylock asked.

Beatrice shook her head again. The Dark Ages, Strulovitch thought. For all her precocious brilliance, she lives bubbled in an electronic ignorance that makes the seventh century appear a carnival of enlightened knowledge. He was ashamed of her for having heard of so little that happened in the hours before she was born. But he was also worried that this suddenly light-spirited, not to say skittish Shylock might think of helping her out in the matter of Al Jolson's identity by singing "Mammy" complete with jazz hands. Beatrice knew nothing of what he knew at her age but she knew what was and was not culturally allowable and she knew a white man wasn't permitted to black up as a minstrel.

"The CDs are on that shelf," Beatrice said. "Just help yourself. They aren't mine. And you needn't worry about disturbing me. I'm off in a few minutes. I have to be at college for a twelve o'clock." She stuck her chin out at her father— see: contrary to what he supposed, she was taking her coursework seriously.

"What are you studying?" Shylock asked, lowering his voice as though to exclude Strulovitch. The question was almost a caress.

"Oh, it's a general arts course, pretty basic, but I want

to concentrate on performance art," Beatrice replied. Rather coyly, it struck Strulovitch, as though hearing what she described as "studying" was a novel experience for her.

Strulovitch felt a rush of shame. *Performance art!* Why didn't they just call it showing off? He wondered if Shylock had ever encountered the genre or knew it was just another word for shedding your inhibitions in public. Given what he thought of Carnival, he didn't see Shylock much caring for performance art. (But then you never knew: who would ever have picked him as a fan of George Formby?) Jessica had been trouble enough, but at least she hadn't told her father she was hoping to explore the empty parameters of audience–performer relations. "Not an occupation for a Jewish girl," he'd have told her, shutting the windows. That was pretty much Strulovitch's position too, even though most of the performance artists he'd heard of were Jewish girls.

Were the parameters they were testing those that existed between Jewish girls and their fathers?

Was the ecosexual exhibitionist Annie Sprinkle, born Ellen Steinberg, what came of teaching modesty?

Whatever Shylock understood of this, he inclined his head with Old World politeness. Beatrice might have been telling him she was studying to be a seamstress.

Then suddenly he asked her, "What does that entail?"

He's doing this to discomfit me, Strulovitch thought. He means to keep Beatrice here all morning, leading her on, catching her out, plucking at my nerves.

Beatrice smiled at him. "Being a performance artist?"

"Yes."

"I'll tell you when I have more time," she said, bewitchingly.

Strulovitch wondered again if she knew whom she was bewitching.

But something inviting in her smile made him apprehensive. Was she thinking about asking Shylock to accompany her to college. He saw her introducing him to her friends. "Hey guys, this is Shylock. Ring a bell? No, me neither. But he's cool." And maybe taking him along to one of her performance classes. He saw Shylock engaging in bitter dispute with Beatrice's teachers, not moderating himself as a modern Jew knew he had to, not knowing what a bear pit the place was. But that fear was quickly overtaken by a further—what if Shylock had designs of some sort on his daughter, not erotic, surely not erotic, but possessive-paternal, and who knew where possessive-paternal stopped and erotic began? Was he looking at her greedily? *A performance artist, eh?* Strulovitch knew from the inside how a man, without moving a muscle on his face, can comprehensively take in a woman. And why wouldn't he take in Beatrice who was luscious in the older style of young women, plumper and more contoured than was the fashion, not pared down like a half-gnawed carrot but full and rubicund, a Song of Solomon beauty. Like Leah, perhaps. Another Jessica. Yes, without doubt, Shylock saw and appreciated her. An appreciation that Beatrice noted— how could she not?—and appreciated in return. "And you let this man into your home," he heard his mother say. "Don't you have concerns enough with that girl?" All too impossibly Mephistophelean to imagine Shylock on an errand of this sort, Shylock here with the express purpose of replacing Jessica—no, surely not—but it is deranging to lose a daughter as he had lost his and who's to say what derangement won't bring about?

An eye for an eye, a daughter for a daughter.

Why should Strulovitch have a daughter and he not!

He felt the ignominy of his suspicions when Beatrice,

having dashed down a piece of cold toast, told Shylock it had been a pleasure to meet him, and Shylock, again inclining his head formally, said, without irony or knowingness, "Likewise—good luck with your studies."

Strulovitch was ashamed of himself. There's something not right somewhere, he thought, when a father can't see his daughter in the company of another man without envisioning foul play. Let's not beat about the bush: there's something not right with *me*. Beatrice didn't need to buy herself a lubricious monkey to suggest a world without moral bearings. The lubricious monkey was him.

Did Shylock see that? Did Shylock mean Strulovitch to see he saw it?

Before she left the room she asked Strulovitch if he'd checked his diary yet.

"I will," he said. "I promise."

"You promised last time."

"This time I really will. I'll leave a time under your door."

"Just text it."

They listened in silence to the girl banging about the house. Their eyes met in a way Strulovitch found intrusive. They shouldn't have been listening to her together. They were not bonded in his daughter.

The noise she made collecting her things and throwing books around—it sounded like throwing books around, though Strulovitch doubted she had any books—as a rule irritated Strulovitch. It seemed such an unnecessary insistence on her independence. But today he had no choice but to listen with the ears of Shylock. He thought how much he'd miss her if she went.

When she went.

The silence roared in his ears.

———

"She's a beautiful girl," Shylock said after they heard the front door slam. "Lovely."

"Beautiful, yes," Strulovitch said. He was still angry with his guest. Still felt intruded on. And Shylock seemed to know and enjoy it. "Lovely I'm not so sure about."

"I can only speak for her appearance. For the impression she gives."

"Yes. And what's not lovely about her is what's not lovely about all of them. She has natural discernment but it's not strong enough to overcome the culture she's been born into."

"You are in danger of sounding like an old man."

"Weren't you? Isn't a father by definition an old man? You locked your doors on yours."

"I had to. I'd lost one woman. I didn't want to lose a second."

"That's called being an old man."

"I knew the danger she was in."

"From shallow foppery and drumbeats? How great a danger was that, really? Don't we create the thing we fear by hyperbolising it? You kept a sober house, but a sober house is no place for a young girl."

"And are you telling me you let yours run wild?"

"I can't stop her."

"But you try."

"I try. I have a sacred obligation to try."

"That was all I was doing."

"And we both failed,"

"You haven't failed yet."

Strulovitch looked long into his guest's fierce, melancholy

eyes. His own were undistinguished, a pearly, uncertain grey, the colour of the North Sea on a blustery day. Shylock's were deep ponds of pitted umber, like old oil paint that had somehow—not by restoration, more by inadvertent rubbing—regained its sheen. They were dark with that Rembrandtian darkness that holds light. Ironic that when Strulovitch looked into them he felt as though he were in the crypt of a church. We are not the slightest bit alike, he thought, except in what we feel for our daughters. So what was it Gentiles saw that told them they were both Jews?

Shylock knew, from the intensity of Strulovitch's scrutiny, what he was thinking. "No we aren't remotely alike," he said. "Not in appearance nor in the manner we have lived our lives. You don't keep a kosher house, you don't attend synagogue and I'm prepared to wager you don't speak a word of Hebrew. So what does it mean to say we are both Jewish?"

"I'm more interested in what it means to *them*. What do they see that unites us?"

"Something older than themselves," he said.

"In you, maybe . . . I don't intend that unkindly."

"I know how you intend it. But in you too. It isn't wear and tear. It's an inability to be indifferent. You might think you don't believe but you're still listening to ancient injunction."

"That makes me no different from a Muslim or a Christian."

"Yes it does. Christians are so anxious to accommodate to the modern they have stopped listening. They sing carols and call it faith. Before long there will be none of them left, the long interregnum will have come to an end and we'll be back with just pagans and Jews."

"And Muslims."

"Yes, and Muslims, but they are out on their own, in an

argument with everybody but themselves. Look at you—you are riven. Islam does not encourage the schizophrenia you live by. When a Muslim listens to ancient injunction he attends with the whole of himself and finds a sort of peace in it."

"Peace? Iraq! Syria! Afghanistan!"

"Stop! You don't have to name every failed country in the Middle East. I'm talking about an inner conviction of peace, however we judge the political consequences. We Jews are more self-suspicious, always wondering if it's time to defect but knowing there's nothing we could finally bear to defect to."

"Not true of my daughter. She is the soul of defection."

Shylock understood this was his cue to invite intimacy. "So this is the showdown you said you were heading for . . ."

For answer, Strulovitch made more coffee. He had hoped to be complimented on it but Shylock was not free with compliments. "She wants me," Strulovitch finally confided, "to give her a date when she can bring her new boyfriend round for me to vet."

"To vet? You get to examine him like a dog?"

"I don't think that's on offer. She didn't in fact say 'vet,' she said 'meet.' I'm putting the best interpretation on it. If she wants me to meet him it means she's serious. I've been fearing this hour."

"You're lucky she values your opinion."

"Lucky! She's sixteen for Christ's sake! My opinion, as you call it, should be law."

"She's old enough to question law. It's not every daughter who cares what her father thinks."

"She doesn't. It's her mother she's feeling guilty about.

She believes that so long as she doesn't alienate me she is honouring her."

Shylock cleared his throat. "Why then are you so anxious?"

Strulovitch showed him all his ten fingers. If he were to count the reasons for his anxiety they would both be here till Judgement Day.

But he had to begin somewhere. "Here's the ridiculous thing," he said. "The last time she brought someone round I was expecting an uncombed boy in trainers and nose rings and the politics of . . . well, an uncombed boy in trainers and nose rings. He turned out to be a tutor whose politics were no better but at least he was clean."

"And 'not' . . . ?"

"Of course 'not,' Beatrice only does 'nots.' I say he was clean. I should have said he was too clean. When he called me Mr. Strulovitch he gargled the word. It was as though he were washing his mouth out. The joke is that while I'm plotting ways to put Beatrice off him, she gets rid of him herself . . ."

". . . and finds someone worse . . ."

"Far worse. Here I've been, steeling myself against the next over-principled, money-hating, ISIS-backing Judaeophobe with an MA in fine art she's going to bring back from college and she hits on someone who's probably never opened a book and certainly never heard of Noam Chomsky—a hyper-possessive uneducated uber-goy from round the corner. I've no idea how or where she met him. At a wrestling match, is my guess, or on the dodgems. But it's my doing. I was looking for danger in the wrong place. If I hadn't frightened her off Jewish boys by telling her she had to find one she might have met a nice quiet embroiderer of skullcaps."

"She was never going to satisfy you. What if your embroiderer of skullcaps had been a woman?"

"I wouldn't have minded. I don't hanker for grandchildren."

"You would have found something not quite right about her."

"Maybe. But there's something not quite right and then there's something in every way wrong."

"How serious is it?"

"Very, or she wouldn't be bringing him over. She wants my blessing. That's serious."

"So they've known each other a long time."

"She hasn't been alive a long time. But too long for comfort. She might be sixteen now, but how old was she when she met him? And how far has it gone?"

"You could ask her."

"She wouldn't tell me."

"I assume you've looked on her phone."

"And on her computer. But it isn't easy. She is guarded with more passwords than a bank vault. And I daren't leave any trace I've been there. Otherwise"—he made as though to cut his throat—"I'm a dead man."

"It could be that she isn't hiding anything. You might find you like him."

"It doesn't matter whether or not I like him. He's beyond the pale for all the obvious reasons. And then for several more."

"So you've already met him?"

"Met him, no. Know of him, yes. Everyone round here knows *of* him. He's a roué of repute and plays football for Stockport County."

"And that's bad?"

"From a football fan's point of view it's very bad. Stockport

County isn't even a League club. Though as a local personality he enjoys a modicum of fame. In the north anyway. He behaves badly on the field of the play, appears on television quizzes in the company of comedians, laughs like a ninny at their jokes, makes none of his own, and advertises underwear and trainers. Can you imagine having a man who advertises underwear for a son-in-law? Only on local buses, I grant you, but that somehow makes it worse. On top of everything else he has going against him he's provincial."

"You would prefer your daughter's suitor to be metropolitanly unsuitable?"

"Don't worry. He's that too. He makes it into the gossip columns and has had I don't know how many wives. I wouldn't be surprised if he's married to at least one of them still. Not all that long ago he was slapped with a seven-match suspension—itself suspended—for giving a Nazi salute after scoring a goal. Apparently it was his first in two seasons."

"His first Nazi salute?"

"His first goal."

Shylock took a moment to digest all he'd heard. Then he asked, "Have you decided what you are going to say to him?"

"I will ask him what a Nazi's doing with a Jewish girl?"

"I can tell you what he'll answer. He'll say he's saving her from the stain of having a Jewish father."

"Times have changed. He'll be both too stupid and too smart to say that. He has already publicly apologised for the salute which he puts down to a moment of excitement. He says he only intended to punch the air. He says he doesn't know where the Nazi bit came from. And he's promised he will never do it again. What if he sees Beatrice as a way of making amends?"

"He could be genuine."

"Genuinely what?"

Shylock looked out towards Alderley Edge, as though the word he needed could be out there. "Penitential?"

"It's not a term I associate with him, I have to say."

"You could be wrong."

"And how will I ever know that?"

"There are ways of finding out."

"What? By putting the question to him directly? *Are you penitent, Mr. Howsome?* He'll think that's a fancy way of asking him to take a penalty. Score and you get to sleep with my daughter."

"Which isn't all that wide of the mark. You could tell him if he really wants your blessing there'll be a price. He will have to make himself suitable."

"Suitable? What—divorce his other wives? Take elocution lessons?"

Shylock didn't bother to reply. There was mischief, Strulovitch thought, in his silence. A make-believe malevolence.

Strulovitch raised an eyebrow. "You're not saying he should convert?"

"Begin the process at least. Show willing."

Strulovitch laughed. "There are a few more obstacles in the way of his converting than there were in the way of yours."

"There was only one obstacle in the way of my converting—my invincible hostility to Christianity. Your future son-in-love has a soft spot for Jewish women, you say, which is likely to make him more malleable. And his not reading is also to your advantage. It helps to be theologically illiterate."

"This isn't only about what *he* might find acceptable."

"No indeed, there are the father-in-law's wishes to be

taken into consideration also. I don't minimise the difficulties. But they are not insuperable."

And with that he made a scissors motion with his furred fingers that caused Strulovitch to think first about Matisse, and then the red-legged scissor-man in *Struwwelpeter*, and finally the Jew of the fevered medieval imagination who kidnapped Christian children and castrated them.

"God fucking Almighty!" he said.

ELEVEN

When last encountered, D'Anton was giving vent to a sigh. What now needs to be told, before the depths of that sigh can be plumbed, is the true history of D'Anton's feelings, not about Barnaby but about Simon Strulovitch, and the true history of Strulovitch's feelings about him.

The two men grew up at more or less the same time in more or less the same part of the country (though D'Anton had been born to wealthy, missionary-minded parents in Guinea), and given their instinct for beautiful things and talent for acquiring them might have encountered each other sooner than they did, if not as schoolboys—for D'Anton very obviously went to a public school and Strulovitch very obviously did not—then in places where comfortably-off aesthetes congregated, at charity dinners and prize-givings, at openings of exhibitions and in the studios of artists, at private sales and in the drawing rooms of collectors. But neither was a fully committed northerner, Strulovitch spending a great deal of his time in London and D'Anton much of his in West Africa and the Far East, which was why they also missed each other at functions at the Golden Triangle Academy, to which Strulovitch loaned the odd painting and where D'Anton gave the odd lecture. Though it must be supposed, given this coincidence of academy and geography, that word of the one reached the other from to time, it was only when Strulovitch proposed making a gift of part of his art collection to the people of Cheshire in return for nothing more than some sympathetic easing of planning restrictions in relation to a once fine but now neglected Jacobean house just outside Knutsford, that the two men became overtly aware of each other. The house was at the time in the nominal care of Cheshire Heritage though in fact owned by the local authority which harboured plans of turning it into an ostrich farm and children's park. To Strulovitch, who wished to honour his parents, especially while his mother was still alive, with a Kunsthaus in their name—the Morris and Leah Strulovitch Gallery of British Jewish Art, he proposed calling it—the property in question seemed a godsend. It was the ideal size, enjoyed an ideal eminence, and it was in the right place, his mother having always loved shopping and taking afternoon tea in Knutsford. A Knutsford Kunsthaus!—how could he better that? To D'Anton, who was often called in to advise Cheshire Heritage in matters that pertained to the fine arts, Strulovitch's scheme had as little to recommend it as Strulovitch believed it had much. Indeed, where Strulovitch saw the hand of God, D'Anton saw the work of the Devil. His arguments were of the sort usually voiced by guardians of the local environment who are opposed to something for reasons they are unable to admit, namely that it violated bylaws, that it constituted a traffic hazard, that it would bring in more visitors than the Golden Triangle could cope with, that it posed a pollution problem both in regard to noise and appearance, that it dishonoured the distinctiveness of the house itself which was, let it not be forgotten, Jacobean and so enjoyed a history which Strulovitch's collection, by its very nature, could not match, and that, however it was viewed, it failed the first test of being culturally intrinsic to the area.

Arguing his case at a joint Cheshire Heritage and local council planning meeting, Strulovitch pointed out that it was precisely the "specific nature" of his collection that would preclude such numbers of visitors as might be deemed hazardous or troublesome. As for noise, he could assure councillors and trustees that the art he intended to display was silent in itself—the foster children of silence and slow-time—and would occasion silence in those who beheld it. And finally, with respect, he failed to see that a gallery of British Jewish art was any less intrinsic to North Cheshire than an ostrich park would have been. The painter Emmanuel Levy was born just up the road in Manchester, Bernard Meninsky had grown up a half-hour's drive from Knutsford in Liverpool, Jacob Kramer across the Pennines in Leeds, and at least three of the sculptures in his collection were done by artists whose grandparents had been born and lived in this very county. Correct him if he was wrong but he was fairly sure that that could not be said of the ostriches.

If the project was going to elicit so little in the way of interest and curiosity as to constitute no disturbance to the environment whatsoever, D'Anton, looking tragic, argued, then where was the advantage to the local community in supporting it? As for the fact that the odd obscure artist whose work would hang in the Morris and Leah Strulovitch Gallery of Jewish Art hailed from the area, that was an argument that could be adduced to support any venture. If he, for example, wanted to build a Museum of Sadism and Torture in North

Cheshire, would it advance his cause to show that a number of the perverts featured came from the Wilmslow or Alderley Edge area?

Strulovitch reminded council officers that the works on display would cost the local rate-payers nothing, that they were a gift from him to them, and that furthermore there was no similarity, from a cultural or educative point of view, between an art gallery and a chamber of horrors. D'Anton wondered from whose cultural point of view Mr. Strulovitch was speaking. He could, to be frank about it, imagine many who lived in the Golden Triangle finding more to entertain and instruct them in such a venue as he had humorously conjured out of the air than in that presented with so much heat, afore-thought and condescension by the applicant. What evidence indeed was there that there'd be any interest at all in a gallery of Jewish art, British or otherwise—most of which, as he understood the matter, was urban and avant-garde in spirit—in a rural area of outstanding natural beauty with its long history of quiet churchgoing? He wasn't arguing against the existence of such art—he was something of an avant-gardist himself—nor was he averse, in principle, to such a venture as Mr. Strulovitch proposed. He didn't doubt that in a more culturally apt place, by which Strulovitch took him to mean Golders Green or the Negev, it would be welcomed. But why, in the name of God, a Morris and Leah Strulovitch Gallery of Jewish art, *here*?

Strulovitch, who didn't like the way D'Anton enunciated his parents' names, saw his proposal turn putrid. It hung in the air of the council chamber like a malign presence. As D'Anton talked it even took a form, an incubus that would disturb the quiet of the Golden Triangle by day, and the sleep of its inhabitants by night. Strulovitch could feel its touch, smell it, taste it. He wished he could withdraw all memory of it, in order to spare his parents' very names the stench of alien malevolence with which they were now associated. But there was no reversing the ancient imputation of interloperie that D'Anton had, with such expertness, laid upon them. *Morris and Leah Strulovitch*—why, even he, the son, was ready to run from such an incantation of evil. *Morris and Leah Strulovitch*—stand on the highest point of Alderley Edge under a full moon and say the names three times and hell itself would open.

As happens when you make an enemy of someone you have never previously met, though you are neighbours, Strulovitch now began to run into D'Anton everywhere—in restaurants in the Golden Triangle, at charitable dinners, at parties thrown by wealthy art collectors, at a concert in the Bridgewater Hall in Manchester, even at a Society of Watercolourists' reception in London. Am I imagining him, Strulovitch wondered. Am I conjuring him up out of the hatred we bear each other? He was careful never to meet his eye and felt confident that D'Anton was no more eager to meet his.

What's happening to me, Strulovitch wondered. Was he turning into one of those Jews who saw insults to his Jewishness everywhere? God forbid. Such a person only insulted himself. Weren't there plenty of non-Jews he didn't like? I will not behave like this, he promised himself. I will not allow myself to feel slighted by the rustlings of a mouse.

And when the mouse was malignant? A malignant, moping, misanthropic mamzer of a mouse? To his rustlings, too, would Strulovitch cultivate a fine Anglo-Saxon indifference.

But one day as he was strolling through Knutsford after a long lunch with an old barrister friend who had chambers in the town, Strulovitch found himself at the edge of a small but ill-tempered demonstration outside the town hall, the object of which, he deduced from the literature being handed out, was a company that had a contract to recycle waste for the local council, but that also made parts for a pipeline that linked illegal settlements on the West Bank with Tel Aviv.

"So the purpose of this demonstration is what?" Strulovitch asked one of the protestors.

"To persuade the council to cancel the contract."

"For the pipeline in the West Bank?"

"For the rubbish and recycling services here."

"Here in Knutsford?"

"Yes."

"So what will happen to our rubbish?"

"There are others who can collect it. And anyway what's a little inconvenience . . . ?"

"No, exactly," Strulovitch agreed. But he wasn't sure how inconvenience to the people of Cheshire would impact detrimentally on a pipeline to and from the illegal settlements in the West Bank.

The protestor helped him out. "You make a noise where you can," he said.

"Hoping that it will reverberate . . . ?"

"Eventually, yes."

When a butterfly beats its wings in Knutsford, Strulovitch was thinking . . . then he spotted D'Anton moving quietly among the demonstrators. There was no time to make a decision one way or another, or remember what he'd promised himself. He simply acted out of impulse. "Hello there," he called out, and when D'Anton turned, Strulovitch waved at him.

D'Anton also had no time to think. Perhaps he too had vowed never to acknowledge Strulovitch—though he had no reason to think of himself as an aggrieved party—or, to the contrary, promised himself never to be offended by who or what Strulovitch was, but caught like this he could only nod an automatic greeting in return.

"A noisy gathering for our quiet county," Strulovitch said.

D'Anton turned his sad eyes away.

"Would you say," Strulovitch continued, "that this is a cause intrinsic to the area?" And when this time D'Anton turned his back, Strulovitch repeated the question in a voice that even to his own ear constituted a violent demonstration in itself. "Culturally, is all I'm asking. Culturally, would you say that this engages the interests of the local rate-payer, honours the area's long-standing history of gentle church-going, keeps the peace and respects the quiet—in a way that, say . . ."

But D'Anton was gone, lost among his fellow demonstra-tors.

Later, sitting alone in his garden, watching shadows dance like devils over Alderley Edge, and wishing he had a wife he could consult, or a daughter that wasn't out French-kissing troglodytes, Strulovitch wondered whether he was glad or sorry he hadn't emptied his stomach of all the bile it contained and called D'Anton what he believed him—no, what he knew him—to be.

Both, he decided.

Sorry, because the bile needed to go somewhere, and D'Anton deserved to be called the thing he was.

Glad, because the accusation he wanted to hurl at D'Anton's retreating back was of a sort that always returned to wound the thrower. How, sociopathologically, it had become a foul to cry foul, Strulovitch didn't know. But that was the state of things. No longer was it the hater who was unhinged;

the real madman was the person who believed himself to be hated. Better, Strulovitch thought, when our enemies wore their loathing on their sleeves, called us misbelievers, infidels, inexecrable dogs, whipped us, kicked us, dishonoured, disempowered, dispossessed us, but at least didn't deliver the final insult of accusing us of paranoia. See how the dog returns to the vomit of his self-pity, happy only when he thinks we wish him to perdition.

For which we wish him to perdition.

That, anyway, with no expectation that anything would occur to change it, was the state of Strulovitch's feeling towards D'Anton, in the period before Shylock showed up.

And D'Anton?

Well, he had no argument with Strulovitch, if he could remember who Strulovitch was. He certainly didn't hate him. He hated no man. Least of all did he hate on racial grounds—his French Guinean origins, the breadth of his travels, the number of languages he spoke, his love for Japanese and Chinese art, the natural affiliation he enjoyed with ceramicists, glass-blowers and miniaturists from all ages and all countries—attested to this. Strulovitch—and now circumstances had thrown the fellow into his path, yes, yes he could summon up an unwanted image of the man—had a persecution complex. One of those Jews who was far more conscious of his Jewishness than Gentiles were—indeed it would never have occurred to D'Anton that Strulovitch was a Jew had Strulovitch himself not forced the fact of it down his and everybody else's throat. But even then, his faith or whatever one was supposed to call it—his ethnicity, for Christ's sake!—played no part in D'Anton's distaste for him. He was a sore loser, that was all. Rich, tasteless, intrusive, belligerent, peevish, self-interested, self-pitying and self-destructive, imagining slights while slighting others, endlessly aggrieved, assuming the world owed him recompense for something or other—not qualities that pertained congenitally or irreversibly to a Jew, in D'Anton's view, until a Jew made them so.

But that being the case, though he would do anything for Barnaby, he knew it wasn't going to be easy to get Strulovitch to talk to him, let alone part with Solomon Joseph Solomon's study for *Love's First Lesson*.

Beneath it all, though, he was quietly confident. If he offered Strulovitch considerably more for the painting than he had paid, would the Jew be able to resist the allure of so quick a profit?

TWELVE

I'm not," the footballer said, "before you ask, what you think I am."

"A Nazi?"

"I'm not."

"So why did you bring it up?"

"Because I know it's what you're thinking."

"Why do you think it's what I'm thinking?"

"Because it's what everybody's thinking."

"And why is everybody thinking it?"

"Because I gave a Nazi salute."

"So easy to be misconstrued," Strulovitch said with a sigh but, before he could say more, Beatrice interposed her presence between the two men. "Correction," she said, tapping Howsome's wrist, as though with an imaginary fan, "because you gave a *parody* of a Nazi salute."

"Right," Howsome said. "Plus I didn't know it was a Nazi salute."

"Then how," Strulovitch patiently pursued, "could you have been parodying it?"

Again Beatrice saw this as something she was better

equipped to answer than her boyfriend. "Come on, Daddy," she said, "you know as well as anyone how ironic referencing works."

Howsome smiled at her in pride and nodded. This was what he'd fallen in love with the first time he heard her speak.

Strulovitch, too, was proud. He suppressed a pang for poor Kay, missing out on these flashes of smartness from a daughter who most of the time played dumb. So was it the smart Beatrice or the dumb Beatrice who had fallen for Howsome? He was surprised not to be more appalled by the footballer. He could half see what Beatrice saw in him. A sort of chthonic innocence, was it? He didn't look like a Nazi. But then one never really knew what a Nazi looked like until it was too late. He was touched by something in him, anyway. Maybe it was the sight of so much muscle constrained by an expensive suit made to look cheap by so much muscle. He sat on the edge of the sofa like a boy dressed up to meet his grandparents. His tie, with its big, perfectly triangular knot, had him uncomfortably by the throat. A tattooed green and scarlet dragon also had him by the throat. It was a wonder he could breathe. Though brought up to be a wearer of ties himself—"A tie shows respect," his father, who wouldn't ever wear a skullcap, used to say—Strulovitch forsook them when he became an art collector. He had thought about digging one up for this occasion but decided against, whatever its formality. There was no fine point of etiquette that said a father interviewing an accidental Nazi sympathiser who wanted to sleep with his daughter had to wear a tie. Should carry a pistol or brandish a horsewhip, but no mention of a tie. So he wore his customary black suit and a white shirt with long, soft, pointed collars buttoned at the neck. I hope he sees a connoisseur, he thought. A connoisseur of art, and men. I hope he sees how much I see and how little impressed I am by empty assurances. Or by tattoos, come to that.

For some reason or clutch of reasons he was not sure he wanted to investigate he had asked Shylock to make himself scarce while the interview was in train. Maybe stay in his room. Maybe not sing along to George Formby.

"Are you frightened I will put the wind up him?" Shylock wondered.

"Of course not."

But then what was he frightened of?

"Just call me if you need me," Shylock said, as much to help Strulovitch out of his embarrassment as anything else.

"Why would I need you?"

"Should he turn violent . . ."

"It's more likely to be Beatrice who turns violent."

"Ah, well then I'll be no use to you at all."

They laughed together—Strulovitch's laughter a bitter jeer, Shylock's a death rattle from the back of his throat—at what wasn't funny.

Unworthy daughters betrayed unworthy fathers. Where was the joke in that?

"What, Jessica? Why, Jessica, I say?"

He would never forget his last words to her. Do as I bid you. Shut all doors after you. Don't thrust your head into the street.

Was that really so much to ask?

He knew he should not have left his house. He could go on blaming her through all eternity, but he should have stayed home. There was some ill towards him brewing. He'd smelt it.

What news on the Rialto?

Why so jumpy? And if so jumpy, why go out?

I am right loath to go. Then don't.

Drawn to danger, like a cat, he went anyway, to eat a supper he didn't relish, in company he hated. There was, though, more than one kind of dining. Admit it, admit it to yourself, you went for the pure malicious fun of it, to dine on Christians. To feed, like a cannibal, your ancient grudge.

And while you were out . . .

And while he was out they fed on him.

Who, as a matter of dramatic interest, hated whom the more?

Not a wafer's thickness between them—

You called me dog . . .

I am as like to call thee so again . . .

But since I am a dog, beware my fangs . . .

They couldn't tear themselves apart from each other. A bond of mutual fascination. The magnetic force of indurated revulsion. Money the pretext. This one lent at interest; that one would do no such thing—although I neither lend nor borrow by taking nor by giving of excess, yet on this occasion—for someone else, a person dear to me—I will break my custom. Called having your cake and eating it, Shylock thought, remembering the fathomless impertinence of Antonio's "yet." As though he were doing Shylock a favour by asking. O father Abram, what these Christians are!

But if money was the battlefield on which they fought their ancient grudges, it was not the origin of their war.

Who, as a matter of historical interest, hated whom the more? A chicken-and-egg question. Attend that word "ancient." The villainy each saw in the other—the proud exclusiveness on this side, the proud pretence of loving kindness on that—pre-dated the rise of capitalism and usury. What movement of men and ideas, you might ask, didn't it pre-date? The divisive words of Paul the Apostle, maybe. Before Paul, peace. But then before Paul there were no Christians for Jews to hate or be hated by.

Well, if villainy was all the Gentiles saw, villainy would be what he'd show them more of.

And they? They would show him villainous mercy, dropping like poison rain, in return.

Does that mean he was ironic-referencing villainy?

And does that mean they were ironic-referencing mercy?

One thing he knew: they hadn't ironic-referenced stealing his daughter.

"I love Beatrice," Howsome said, tightening and then loosening his tie. Beneath his collar the green and scarlet dragon writhed.

"She's sixteen."

"Like that's some big deal," Beatrice said.

Howsome looked from one to the other, wanting to agree with both.

"*Sixteen!*" Strulovitch repeated.

"Play another tune, Daddy," Beatrice said, "you've been harping on about how old I am since I was born. *She's thirteen. She's fourteen. She's fifteen.* You'll still be saying it when I'm sixty."

"At sixty you'll have seen something of the world, and I won't be here."

"Me neither," Howsome said, which Beatrice's expression told him was ill-advised. You don't stress age difference when you're trying to prise a daughter from a parent.

It's time, Strulovitch thought, I spoke to my daughter's suitor in the old way—without the daughter present.

"Beatrice, you are making both of us uncomfortable," he told her. "Why don't you leave us for a little while. I promise I won't offer Mr. Howsome money to disappear from the country."

Which only went to show he'd thought of doing precisely that.

"There is no sum of money that would make me part with Beatrice, sir," Howsome said.

Beatrice rose and smiled at him. Good boy. Good answer. She could see her father thought so too. "I'll make tea then," she said, feeling confident. "And don't be horrible to him in other ways either, Daddy."

Such as what? Strulovitch thought.

"I want my daughter," he said, when Beatrice had left them, "to finish her education."

What he really meant was I want my daughter to *start* her education, but now was not the time to be discussing the merits of performance art.

"I want the same for her," Howsome said.

Strulovitch nodded. Good answer again. He could see what his daughter liked in the man. He was compliant. He made good use of the few words he possessed. He had a gentle smile, despite his bulk. And even his bulk—at least as he had disposed it among the soft fabrics of Strulovitch's sofa—was more protective than aggressive. What else she saw in him—whether or not he was sexually attractive—was a question that exceeded Strulovitch's fatherly brief. A man should not put his mind to what arouses his daughter, no matter that Strulovitch had put his mind to little else since Beatrice turned whatever age it was when he first knew her to be in danger.

Now sixteen, she was old enough—not legally, no, but

in society's eyes, and certainly in her own—to decide for herself. But he'd got her to this age without serious mishap, hadn't he? He'd navigated the dangers for her. Maybe she was secretly grateful to him for that. Maybe it wasn't only to avoid upsetting her poor vegetating mother that she didn't just up and go. Maybe she loved him too, and wanted his love in return. But since she had stayed, and was suddenly playing at being an old-fashioned daughter, wanting Daddy's blessing, he would go on playing the old-fashioned father.

"What else do you want for her?" he continued, looking hard into the footballer's swimming eyes.

Howsome was puzzled, on the lookout for trick questions. Daddy's devious, Beatrice had warned him. Be careful.

"In what sense?" he asked. "Do you mean like children?"

"Good God, no. Not yet. She's sixteen for Christ's sake. But you want her to be happy, I presume."

"Obviously."

It was a footballer's word. "Obviously." At the end of the day. At the end of the day, obviously, I want your daughter to be happy in the back of the net.

"And you want her to make her parents happy?"

That was less obvious, but Howsome acceded to it anyway. "Obviously," he said. He even nodded, Strulovitch thought, upstairs in the direction of poor Kay, as though he knew what had befallen her and where she was kept. And therefore as though he knew that this imposed a still greater obligation on him to look after Beatrice.

"You will understand then that the fact you've been married several times before doesn't make us entirely happy. In fact it makes us anxious."

He was glad Beatrice had left them. Who's this *us* suddenly, he could imagine her thinking.

"I made some silly errors," Howsome admitted. "I was young and had more money than sense. I am a different man now. In fact I'm a man now, full stop. I was a boy then."

Strulovitch nodded, not listening. He was preparing the only question that mattered. "You know, of course," he said, taking his time, "that ours is a Jewish family."

"I love Jews," Howsome said, bringing his body to the edge of the sofa. He loved Jews so much he was prepared to fall at their feet. "In fact . . ."

He stopped. He was about to say that the proof of his love of Jews was his having already married one, but decided in the nick of time not to. Jews appreciate being liked, but not collected, Beatrice had explained when he'd first tried wooing her with the line that she was not the first Jew he'd loved.

". . . in fact," he went on, "I've read many books on the subject."

Remembering the Nazi salute, Strulovitch tried not to picture the contents of Howsome's bookshelves. *The Protocols of the Elders of Zion? Der ewige Jude?* Bound copies of the *Guardian?*

"We make interesting reading," he allowed.

Howsome wanted to go further than that. "The Jews are wonderful people."

"Some of us," Strulovitch agreed.

Howsome had the look of one who had said all he had to say, had conclusively proved his suitability, and now awaited the go-ahead to carry Beatrice off to his bed.

But Strulovitch was not quite finished. "Since you know so much about us," he said, "you will know that we worry when our children fly the coop. I don't just mean leave home but, you know, leave the . . . clan."

A funny word "clan," but he couldn't say religion. Religion wasn't what he meant. It hadn't been in the name of religion that his father had buried him when he married out. What was it then? Faith? No, not that. And he couldn't say tribe. He'd heard Shylock fulminating against tribe. Culture? Too secular. If culture was all it was about, why the worry? So he let "clan" hang there, a poor substitute for a word he couldn't find.

Too late he remembered covenant.

"I so respect that," Howsome said. "And obviously I wouldn't expect Beatrice to stop being Jewish."

"That's good of you," Strulovitch said sarcastically. He marvelled at the magnanimity of his prospective son-in-law, a man who was happy to take Jewish women as he found them. "If nothing else, young man," Strulovitch thought about saying, "it sits smiling to my heart to know that the future of the Jewish people is secure in your benign consideration." But he held back. Why waste irony? Howsome was doing his best, considering the circles he'd been known to move in.

"If you eventually give your permission she can even keep her name," Howsome said.

"Beatrice?"

"No, her other name."

"Again that's good of you," Strulovitch said. "I think she'll be relieved to know that. But this isn't quite what I've been getting at."

The footballer apologised. "I'm sorry, I thought that was what you wanted to hear."

"It is. Indeed it is. But when I say I don't want my daughter to leave, I mean I don't want her to have a husband who isn't himself Jewish."

Howsome looked nonplussed. He opened the palms of his big hands piteously. I am who I am, his gesture said. I cannot be what I am not.

It was then that Strulovitch explained how he could be made what he was not.

THIRTEEN

D'Anton decided it was best all round, if he were to have any hope of getting the Solomon Joseph Solomon for his downcast friend, to write formally to the person who had it.

But the moment he took off his jacket, sat at his desk and, with his usual methodicalness, began to move books and papers around, he realised how difficult this task—no, this sacred obligation—was going to be. His stationery drawer refused to open. The ink dried in his pen. In his mind's eye he saw Strulovitch delightedly refusing his request, perhaps setting the paper it was written on alight, perhaps doing something even worse with it, whereupon his soul withered.

"It isn't proving as easy as I'd hoped it would," he said to Barnaby, conscious of a little lie in that he had hardly as yet tried moving mountains.

Barnaby threw him one of the most beseeching looks in his collection. "My heart is set on it, D'Anton," he said.

Ah, the potency of punctuation. Barnaby knew his friend was powerless to resist him when he finished a sentence *something something something comma, D'Anton.* The full stop taking an eternity to arrive, the name—*D'Anton*—lingering it seemed forever in his mouth.

And D'Anton knew that Barnaby knew it. But that made him no more proof against its influence. "I see that, Barnaby," he said, lingering over the other's name himself, "but could we not pay a further visit to the auction house and see what else they have? *Love's First Lesson* can't be the only artwork in the world you like."

"Well there's still *The Singing Butler*," Barnaby said pettishly. "And anyway it's not a matter of what I like, it's what Plury would like. The naked Venus is *so* her, D'Anton, I swear to you she could have posed for it . . . *Could* she have posed for it?"

"Only if she'd been born a hundred and fifty years ago." If Barnaby thought he detected an unaccustomed testiness in his friend he was right. For all the love he bore him—indeed, perhaps, because of it—D'Anton couldn't but think that Barnaby might have met him halfway on this, agreed to try at least to see if there was another picture that might catch his fancy, or show some sign of understanding the enormity of what he asked, no matter that it was D'Anton who'd originally proposed it. But he would not have dreamed of endeavouring to dissuade him further. His friend had set his heart on *Love's First Lesson*—again Barnaby repeated that very phrase: "My heart is set on it, D'Anton"—and what was close to Barnaby's heart was close to D'Anton's. His purse, his person, his extremest means lay all unlocked to his young friend's occasions.

So again, after pouring himself a large brandy, he sat down at his desk, extracted from his drawer a sheet of headed writing paper, handmade for him in an alleyway few visitors to Venice ever find, and, in the smallest of hands and with the finest of nibs, wrote:

Dear Simon Strulovitch,

Please grant me a moment of your time. Albeit I am not customarily a favour-seeker, I have a favour to ask of you.

I write to you on behalf of a friend—or rather, I am acting on behalf of a friend in the name of whose disappointment I make this appeal to you. We recently attended, he and I, an art auction in Manchester at which you were astute enough to buy an early study by Solomon J. Solomon for his painting Love's First Lesson. *It is an exquisite cartoon, lacking none of the grace of the finished painting. I commend your good fortune and your taste. I also commend your punctuality. We alas, who would have bid against you for the Solomon, were late. Our fault. But here's the favour I would beg of you. Might you consider parting with it? I make no mention of the price. Add what commission you please.*

It is, I repeat, not for me that you would be doing this, but for a young and impressionable friend who has his heart set on giving the painting as a token of his devotion to a woman who, I can assure you, will cherish the work every bit as much as we would wish her to.

When love calls, my dear Strulovitch, can any of us turn a deaf ear?

I await your response with keen anticipation.

Yours very respectfully,

—and signed it with a flourish designed to conceal nothing of the openness of the writer's own heart.

"So how did that go?" Shylock wondered.

Strulovitch was surprised Shylock had the nerve to ask. "I think we could both have anticipated how it would go."

"The footballer keeps his foreskin?"

"Correct. And I lose a daughter."

"You broached the matter in her presence?"

"No. But he was bound to go straight to her and tell her what I'd asked. 'Obviously,' he told me, 'I'll have to think about this.' Which meant 'Obviously, I'll need to speak to Beatrice,' who obviously was horrified."

"She told you so?"

"She didn't have to."

"And she's gone already?"

"Can't you hear her seething around the house? I've been divorced—I know the sound of resolute packing. Not the banging—that means they're not really going. Throwing stuff around means they're giving you a chance to stop them. It's the quiet folding of garments you have to fear. The measure of Beatrice's rage is that she hasn't banged a wardrobe door or said a word to me. But I know anyway what that word would have been had she said it."

"Savage?"

"Since that's the word that occurs to you, I wonder you didn't think of it earlier."

"Or you, since you're thinking of it now."

"I'm thinking what Beatrice might be thinking."

"You're thinking it because you fear it might be true."

"And isn't it?"

"There's nothing good or bad but thinking it makes so.

Our greatest weakness as Jews is forever to be thinking the worst of ourselves. What if we've fallen short, what if we are a light unto nobody, what if we're barbarians at heart. Our eternal refrain: what if we're not what we claim to be."

"Why shouldn't we ask ourselves that? Isn't periodically wondering if we're savages what keeps us civilised?"

"That depends on what you mean by periodically. Every five hundred years—fine. Every time a Jew asserts himself or acts in self-defence—that's something else."

"It's the self-defence part that's controversial."

"There is nothing controversial about protecting your daughter."

"I know all this."

"Then why are you having second thoughts?"

"Because I cannot be said to have protected her if she runs away."

"Then stop her. Explain your motives."

"I behave like a barbarian, Beatrice, because I love you?"

"You are still seeing with her eyes, when you should have the courage to see with your own. You have seen more of the world than she has. You have more understanding. Have you explained to her just what the rite of circumcision is? What it stands for? What it portends? How it's the very rejection of barbarism? Why it's a passage out of savagery into refinement?"

"That takes some explaining to a child."

"Everything serious takes some explaining to a child. Try sitting her down and reading to her."

"She doesn't go a bundle on Maimonides."

"It doesn't have to be Maimonides. Do you have any Roth on your shelves?"

"Joseph, Cecil, Henry, Philip? I have walls of Roth."

"Philip will do. Do you have the one where everyone is leading someone else's life?"

"That's all of them."

"A shame Leah isn't here. She'd know which I'm thinking of. It's the one where Roth lets the anti-circumcisionists have it with both barrels. Circumcision, he or someone like him argues, was conceived to refute the pastoral."

"Christ! And you think that would make it all right with my daughter? What in God's name does refuting the pastoral mean?"

"You ask me that! You who venture into your own garden as though it's snake-infested. Do you even own wellingtons? My friend, you are a walking refutation of the pastoral."

"And that's because I'm circumcised?"

"You were circumcised in order that you shouldn't, in the first days of your life, when you were still in a womb-swoon, mistake life for an idyll."

"Then it's worked. In fact I'd say it's worked too well."

"You're bound to think that. It's what you were circumcised to think. The heavy hand of human values, in our friend Roth's words, descended on you early. As it should."

"That's not going to convince anyone who sees precisely those values as inhuman."

"Those who are sentimental about being human will never be convinced."

"Worse and worse, Shylock."

"Look. The mohel's knife acts mercifully, to save the boy from the vagaries of nature. I don't just mean the monkeys. I mean ignorance, the absence of God, the refusal of allegiance to a people or an idea—especially the idea that life is an obligation as well as a gift. We are not born free of loyalties and oaths. The mohel's knife symbolises what we owe."

"Subdues us, in other words."

"Is that so terrible if the alternative is running lawless in the wilderness?"

Strulovitch was the wrong one to ask. What struck him as terrible one day, didn't strike him as all *that* terrible the next.

"We can't be saved from nature a little bit," Shylock went on. "It's all or nothing, it's human values or the monkeys."

Strulovitch's mind turned from abstractions of duty to the living daughter in whom, at the hour of her birth, he'd glimpsed the meaning of covenant. "Well that might fix it for the boys," he said, as though Shylock had both won and lost the argument, "but what help is there for the girls? There's no mohel's knife to subdue a daughter. Not in the civilised world, there isn't. In the civilised world, men who talk of subduing daughters are stoned to death."

"And that," said Shylock, in a tone of steely quiet, "is why daughters are a byword for disloyalty."

Were they a byword for disloyalty? I used to think *I* was an extremist, Strulovitch thought.

Shylock read his reservations. "You wouldn't anyway dispute," he said, much calmer now, "that it's because her footballer is a 'natural' man that Beatrice loves him. At least if you have described him to me correctly."

"He is not the question. *She* is. Does she love him? Who knows, but I'm pretty sure she'll give it a good try now. And my telling her that life isn't meant to be a womb-swoon won't deter her."

"She's a bright young woman."

"She's sixteen! That's too young to be giving up on life as an idyll."

"Then it's too young to be Jewish."

"Perhaps you should have thought of that before you glee-fully proposed this course of action."

"Did I propose a course of action?"

"In a dumbshow, yes."

"I mustn't have realised you were so impressionable."

"As to take you at your word?"

"I uttered no word."

"Call it what you will. But I must ask you what you meant by it."

"Mischief."

"Is that what you're here to cause me?"

"Cause you? No. The very opposite. But all isn't yet lost. By your own account, if you can hear her silence, she hasn't gone."

"And what do you propose I do to keep her?" He chanced a long look into Shylock's covert eyes. "Bar the doors?"

He let his words hang in the air, let the shutters to Shylock's windows swing open, let the sweet disgusting smell of goats and monkeys enter.

Two could play at mischief.

But he didn't bar his own door.

Fourteen

When Strulovitch has things to consider he considers them, if he can, in the presence of Kay.

If he could pretend they were still able to discuss what mattered to them, one of the things he would not have to consider was his part in her disintegration. Never mind that a doctor had told him he was not the cause, he knew he had made life intolerable to her, not just on account of Beatrice, but on account, quite simply of him—who he was, what he was like, what he believed one minute and then disbelieved the next, his inflamed Jewishness that blew hot and cold but was always in the way, like a deranged and disreputable lodger, disturbing their domestic quiet.

Yes, his father had welcomed him back into the fold when he married Kay, but she wasn't Jewish beneath her fingernails as he was even when he thought he wasn't being Jewish at all. She taught religious studies in a non-denominational school—respect for other people's beliefs, respect for yourself, respect for your body, respect for the environment. She happened to be what she was, others happened to be something else. End of story. She didn't start when she saw an

Arab in the street. She didn't start when she saw a Hassid in the street either. She wasn't beset by enemies outside the faith or fanatics within it. Strictly speaking she had no faith. Strulovitch—or Strulo as she called him—insisted that he too had no faith. And maybe he was telling the truth. What he had was stronger than any faith she had encountered. He had a madness, a frenzy. Had she been forced to teach what he had she'd have called it Judaeolunacy.

Judaeolunacy for A2 Year students.

"You couldn't be more wrong," he told her. "I'm indifferent."

But even his indifference, Kay thought, was a sort of delirium. He didn't go to synagogue because going to synagogue irked him, but not to go irked him just as much. "Look at them," he'd say if they happened to be driving past a synagogue on a Saturday morning. "Look at them in their fucking yarmulkes! What are they doing remembering to go every fucking week? Don't they ever just forget? Don't they have anything else to think about?"

"Leave them alone," Kay would tell him. "You don't want to go to shul, they do. It's not your business. What do you care?"

"I don't care."

"Then why are you swearing?"

"Because they're praying."

"So?"

"Being Jewish isn't just about praying."

"For you no. For me no. For them yes."

"It's not Jewish," he'd shout, "saying *for me no, for them yes.* That's Christian talk. We are a people who value x above y because x is true and y isn't. This is called ethics, Kay. It's what we're famed for. *For me no, so for them no!*"

"Strulo, why does it matter to you so much what's Jewish and what isn't?"

"It doesn't. I don't give a shit about Jews."

The next day he'd be throwing the *Guardian* in the bin, saying that Jews were on the brink of extermination and it was the *Guardian*'s fault.

Kay wondered why he had never gone to Israel and enlisted with the IDF.

"Israel? What's Israel got to do with anything?"

"I thought you were a Zionist."

"A Zionist, me! Are you mad?"

"So why are you burning the *Guardian*?"

"I'm not burning it, I'm binning it. Interesting, though, that you said 'burning.' I'd call that a Freudian slip. You're remembering the ovens. That's what reading the *Guardian* does to you."

"Why would reading the *Guardian* make me think of ovens?"

"Because the *Guardian* hates Israel and Israel is the only place that will save us when they start the ovens up again."

"So you are a Zionist!"

"Only when I read the *Guardian*."

And then Beatrice came along, Beatrice the child of their early middle age, their belated gift, in Strulovitch's words, from God. Like Isaac, miraculously born to a laughing, unbelieving Sarah. Isaac—laughter. Beatrice—joy.

"Oh, for Christ's sake, Strulo," Kay said. "It's not as though we're both a hundred. Can't we leave God out of this."

But she agreed to the child being called Beatrice.

It had been a precarious pregnancy and a difficult birth. Strulovitch saw that it took strength from his wife which she

never fully regained. It fell to him, he thought, to keep Beatrice on the straight and narrow, to ensure that the high
purpose he discerned in her delivery would be honoured.

Not a Jewish education—heaven forfend!—just a Jewish
consciousness, or at least a Jewish consciousness sufficient
to a Jewish wedding. And not so much a Jewish wedding as
a Jewish lineage. And even that was overstating it. Not a *not*
Jewish lineage—that was closer to what Strulovitch meant.

"I agree with you it would be nice if she found a boy we
could all approve of," Kay said. "But beyond that—"

"Beyond that! Beyond that, Kay, is everything that makes
us serious."

"You're a Judaeolunatic," she reminded him.

Beatrice, when she was old enough, cheered her mother
on. "Tell him, Mummy. The man's off his rocker."

"Don't call him 'the man,' darling, he's your father."

"Is he? Do you know what he said to me last night? He
said I was letting Hitler win."

"What were you doing?"

"Nothing. Snogging—not even that. Just pecking someone goodnight."

"Where?"

"Outside our front door."

"Who?"

"I don't know his name. Feng, I think. A Chinese boy."

Aha, Kay thought. Feng not Fishel. She wanted to know
if her husband really was telling their daughter that by going
out with a Chinese boy she was letting Hitler win. She would
divorce him if that were true.

Strulovitch knew to back off. "You should have seen what
she was doing . . ."

"I don't care what she was doing. Did you say she was letting Hitler win?"

Strulovitch knew to back off even further. "Not exactly *win*. More . . ."

"More what?"

"Kay, it was in the heat of the moment. You don't know what it's like out there. You don't know who she's mixing with."

"I'm prepared to bet Feng isn't a Nazi stormtrooper."

"Feng!" Strulovitch wasn't so sure. He had seen *Bridge on the River Kwai*. But he kept his counsel. Feng was better than Fritz.

Shortly afterwards he dragged Beatrice home by her hair. Shortly after that Kay was felled.

Strulovitch wondered if he should mourn her as one mourns the dead, but knew he had to go on loving her as one loves the living. The trouble was, he couldn't. Open the heart and it would break. But the forms of a domestic life—the greetings, the expressions of tenderness and concern, the passing on of news—those he thought he could manage. He fell into the habit of talking to her about what bothered him, quietly, without any excitement, much as Shylock talked to Leah, keeping all hint of Judaeolunacy out of his voice, censoring the news. When her face found repose she was still pretty, still recognisably the woman he had loved, the wife who called him Strulo, but ravaged by whatever had struck her down: disruption of the blood supply to her brain, a terrible tiredness, and him.

On this occasion, though, all that bothered him was bound to be disruptive of calm. He had a number of matters to consider but there wasn't one of them he dared disclose to her, for fear—just in case: for who knew?—she understood. So he sat with her for an hour, holding her hand, wiping her mouth, kissing her cheek, feeling very lonely but trying to imagine how much more lonely she must have been, locked inside wherever it was to which he and fate together had consigned her.

Which left him with a number of matters still to consider, and these he considered in his office, taking time off, occasionally, to look at Solomon Joseph Solomon's lovely study for *Love's First Lesson.*

The first and most pressing: whether to let Beatrice go unhindered for the time being, allow her her moment of outrage and then follow her—but follow her where?

The second: whether there was any compromise possible in the matter of circumcision; whether there was such a thing as demi-circumcision, a halfway house acceptable to Jew and Gentile alike.

The third: how brutish was circumcision—no half measures but the whole shebang—anyway? Were Roth and Shylock and the other Jewish sages right, was circumcision an act of the highest human responsibility, a badge not of backwardness but enlightenment?

The fourth: if Shylock was not here to cause him mischief—but had caused it all the same—why was he here?

Unable to decide what to do about Beatrice, since anything further from him would only make things worse, and wanting to clear his head of Shylock, he decided to start with circumcision. Shylock had said it all started with circumcision—"it" being the ancient grudge Jew and Gentile bore each other—but would it all *finish* with circumcision?

"I can't promise you," Strulovitch's first wife, Ophelia-

Jane, had told him early in their courtship, "that if we marry and have a son I will be able to consent to your mutilating him."

It wasn't so early in their courtship that Strulovitch couldn't ask her, in return, "Would you call me mutilated?"

"In appearance, do you mean?"

"I mean however you mean. 'Mutilated' is your word. But what other yardstick for mutilation is there?"

"There is the yardstick of psychology."

"You think I might be psychologically mutilated?"

"Well, scarred at least. I don't see how it could be otherwise."

"I have a few things to say to that. The first is that 'scarred' is not the same as 'mutilated.' Do I take it, therefore, that you withdraw the mutilation charge? The second is that 'how could it be otherwise' is not an argument in proof of what you say, it's just another way of saying it. You think I must be scarred because you abominate the ritual. Could it simply be that because you abominate the ritual you *wish* me to be scarred?"

She put both hands to her head and pushed her hair back, as though she needed more brain space to deal with his logic chopping.

"Let's leave it for now," she said.

But it was always present between them, like the fear of illness or an unresolved infidelity, and a week before they married she brought it up again.

"I really don't think I can go along with it," she said.

"The wedding?"

"The mutilation."

"Then let's agree to bring forth girl children only."

"And how do we do that?"

"We can't. But we can agree to bring forth neither."

"Is what I'm asking so much?"

Was it? Wasn't it? Strulovitch wasn't sure. Had he known how the birth of a child would affect him—how powerfully he would be struck by the concept of covenant, and even then in relation to a girl, where there was no question of ratifying it with circumcision—he might have decided that what Ophelia-Jane was asking was indeed too much. But he was young and ignorant of the sensations that can assail a father. He didn't fully know his own mind and suspected that if need be he would always be able to change hers. Besides which, his own father had talked of burying him, which made him not well disposed to the faith his father had talked of burying him in. To hell with the whole business. So no, she wasn't asking too much.

As it turned out, the god of both their non-faiths smiled on them and engineered their separation before they had time to have a child to mutilate.

But even in the absence of an actual boy child the penis, as a site of ritual disfigurement, had come between them.

"That psychological scarring we once discussed," she began.

"Whose?"

"Yours."

"What about it?"

"It's there every time you make one of your footling, thing-centred jokes."

"How could the trauma of mutilation turn me into a foot-ler? If I'm the trivial man you accuse me of being it must mean I wasn't mutilated enough."

"That's a naive understanding of cause and effect. You footle to disguise the pain. You cannot bear to accept that was what done to you was bestial in the extreme and so you try to joke it away—the proof of that being that your joking is always phallocentric."

He felt suddenly very weary. Compound words ending in "centric" had that effect on him. "You're right," he said. He couldn't tell her one more time that joking wasn't in his nature. Nor could he tell her he neither looked nor felt mutilated. That would sound like empty denial or brute insentience, and both only went to show just how badly mutilated he was.

A question, then, for Shylock:

How merry was your bond? When you set the forfeit at an equal pound of Antonio's fair flesh, to be cut off and taken from whatever part of his body it pleased you, what intended you by it? What intended you by it in the spirit of jest—that's to say how far in earnest were you, and how far playing the devil they expected you to be? And what intended you in the matter of anatomy? Did you mean salaciously, flirtatiously even, to designate Antonio's penis as the part it pleased you to take? Was *that* the pound of his fair flesh—weighing hyperbolically—you originally had your sights set on, before all jests went out of the window with your daughter?

They were sitting in Treviso, one of the Golden Triangle's best restaurants. Two Michelin stars. Italian regional—to make Shylock feel at home—with the longest wine list in the north of England. "I'm half hoping," Strulovitch had said when they first sat down, pausing only to ask the sommelier for her bloodiest Nebbiolo, "that Beatrice will walk in on her footballer's arm. Foolish I know. But you will appreciate my folly."

"So you haven't gone after her?"

"I don't want her to feel she's on the run. If I let her go

quietly there is a good chance she will not go far. I'm told he has a house close by. The natural thing is for her to go there, though I imagine it to be full of memorabilia of previous wives, maybe even full of previous wives themselves, and knowing Beatrice, she won't fancy that. She was disgusted to discover I still possessed photographs of my first wife. Not just disgusted with me but with her mother for allowing me to keep them. So I guess he's taken her to a hotel, and that it will be somewhere near. I've checked the fixture list and I see he has to turn up to play for Stockport County at the weekend, so he won't be going far. And as for Beatrice, she won't want to put too great a distance between her and her mother, no matter that she might not care how many miles she puts between her and me. Fast bind, fast find, didn't work for you. I will let my maxim be, long rope gives hope."

"Am I to take it from that that you will consent at last to the match?"

"No, I will not consent to the match. It is not a match. I haven't watched over her all these years for nothing. Besides, it has become a battle of wills and principle now. But I must weigh my options."

"And they include sparing him the cut?"

"Not necessarily. But the means of effecting it are not immediately to hand."

He waited to see if Shylock had any suggestions, but he had none.

Strulovitch poured him more wine.

It was in this convivial if inconclusive spirit, after Shylock paused to send back the linguine with spider crab, or at least the spider crab, declaring the linguine delicious, that the two men fell naturally to discussing Shylock's own original intentions, vis-à-vis Antonio's flesh. Had his aim been Antonio's privy parts, or Antonio's heart?

"What makes you so sure," Shylock wondered, "that I knew what I intended?"

"Are you saying you were making it up as you went along?"

"I didn't have to. It made me up. There is a weight of history when a Jew speaks. I watch the care with which you measure your words. There are impressions you are afraid to give, but you give them anyway. When you walk into a room, Moses walks in behind you."

"I have a degree from one of the oldest and finest English universities," Strulovitch reminded him. "When I walk into a room bishops and Lord Chancellors walk in before me."

"In your head, perhaps. But not in theirs. And you can no more escape what they see than what they anticipate. If a Jew strikes a bargain it is assumed it will be harsh. If a Jew makes a joke it is assumed it will be barbed. So why fight your history when your history is bound to win?"

"In order to confound it."

"Some other night you can regale me with your victories. In the meantime, since you have raised the matter, you must let me continue with mine. If this is how you see me, I in effect told Antonio, then I won't disappoint. He came to me loaded down with the weight of his implacable loathing, begging a favour without having the humility to beg it graciously—if anything, I was to understand (and be grateful), that the supplicant was me—in which circumstances how could I resist answering him in his own fashion, embodying his every fear, justifying every overheated rumour, every irrational superstition? If he spoke in metaphor and hearsay, I would speak in metaphor and hearsay in return. But note how little he actually hears of what I say to him. I am so to be disregarded as a man that he doesn't bother to distinguish what I say in earnest from what I say in jest, cannot tell whether I am obsequious or impertinent, doesn't even scruple to take umbrage at my salaciousness—for it is salacious to talk of taking flesh from whatever part of him pleases me, as though it is a sexual act and my fleshly pleasure is contingent on it. I am so to be disregarded, in fact—never mind *hath not a Jew eyes*: is not a Jew *there?*—that he barely weighs the consequences of what he agrees. In his arrogance as a merchant he believes he has nothing to fear from the transaction, and in his arrogance as a Gentile he negates the Jew he is doing business with. I do not exist, my words do not exist, my threats and my pleasures do not exist—only the loan exists, only what he wants and believes he can get, consequence-free. Why should you be surprised, in that case, that when he forfeits I rest implacably on my bond?"

Strulovitch makes to speak but Shylock puts up a hand to stop him. Even a waiter, about to ask if everything is to the gentlemen's satisfaction, steps back in fright.

"The question is rhetorical," Shylock continues. "I don't expect you to be surprised. No one should be. Antonio forfeits and what ensues must ensue—I must have my bond. Speak not against my bond. I am now become the thing he made me—my bond. I'll have no speaking. I will have my bond. To my bond you have reduced me, and to my bond, and nothing other than my bond, you must answer. Don't look for human pity. You never granted me the wherewithal to feel such an emotion before. How dare you expect it now? I am become the embodiment of your contempt. Prepare, then, to face the consequences not of who I am but of who you are.

It is as the bond and only the bond that I speak. The villainy you teach me I will execute."

Strulovitch was of a mind to say that however exhaustive Shylock's answer, it wasn't exactly an answer to the question he had asked; in fact to the two questions he had asked: had Antonio's privy parts been the original site of the compact and, if so, how had Shylock negotiated the actual and moral distance from those to Antonio's heart.

Shylock registered his companion's dissatisfaction. "You want an explanation for what cannot be explained," he said. "Did I know what I wanted in full earnest? Had I formed a definite scheme for what I would do in the event of Antonio defaulting that answered truly to some heartfelt wish—you must ask yourself what would I have wanted with Antonio's privy parts?—or was I threatening to exact, for the fun of it, or because I had no genetic choice but to exact, the very penalty that superstition expects a Jew to exact? Was I acting out my desires or theirs? When you can answer that about yourself you can come knocking on my door again. This, though, I can tell you—if there was salacious jest in the first proposed requital, there was none in the second. And that was my mistake. I ennobled Antonio by showing I had designs, even momentarily—and even if they weren't first and foremost *my* designs—upon his heart. The tragedy he had always sought out for himself I nearly gave him—though he was undeserving of so high an office. Attacking his privy parts would, after all, have kept him in his place—a man of high pretension and small merit. I lifted him out of farce."

Strulovitch thought best to leave it, for the time being, at that. People were watching. Though their table was discreetly positioned, Shylock's voice was loud and his mode of speaking, for the first time in their brief acquaintance, intemperate. Diners lost their temper at Ristorante Treviso, sometimes even walking out on their dinner companions. But it was rare to hear someone say "The villainy you teach me I will execute."

Besides, a meal was a meal. And they still had progress to make through the wine list.

The real reason Strulovitch chose not to pursue the subject, however, was that he had grown distracted, afraid he had been wrong, first of all not to prevent his daughter leaving the house, and then not to have gone after her. It seemed right at the time to let her go without a fight, in order to show that he was reasonable, and in the hope that he might thereby win her back more easily later. It didn't seem right any longer. Where was she now?

He still half expected her to turn up with Howsome, laughing brittly, looking beautiful, a little girl pretending to be a woman. It was while he was raking the darkest corners of the restaurant with his anxious stare that he saw D'Anton in the company of a number of younger men. He looked away. D'Anton was not a person he wanted to see at any time, least of all when he was sick with worry. So what was it that kept drawing his attention back? Partly it was the intensity with which D'Anton was scrutinising him. But also it was something not quite right in the composition of his party. Only as they rose to go—hurriedly, it seemed to Strulovitch, as though he might be the cause of it—did he realise what that something not quite right was. It was the presence of Gratan Howsome.

His first thought was to rise from the table brandishing his fists; his second was to stay right where he was. This was a good sign, wasn't it? Howsome here on his own? Howsome looking the very opposite to jubilant? Surely this could only mean that they had broken up already. That Beatrice had seen sense, given him his marching orders and returned home. He suppressed a third instinct which was to go over and laugh in the footballer's face before he could leave the restaurant. Why bother if she had left him already? He imagined her waiting up for him when he got back. *Sorry, Daddy.*

But she wasn't.

So where, in God's name—more to the point, where on God's earth—was she?

FIFTEEN

D'Anton had not at once sent off his letter to the Jew. Nothing was to be achieved by delaying, except the saving of his soul. It was not in his nature, as it had fortunately not been a necessity of his pocket, to go begging to any man, but to go begging to Strulovitch turned his stomach. Perhaps circumstances would change if he held back. Perhaps Barnaby would hit upon another gift for Plurabelle. Or, with a bit of luck, Strulovitch might suddenly put the Solomon Joseph Solomon back on the market. He called himself a collector, but it was said that he sold at times too, when the market was right, and D'Anton had no reason to doubt the veracity of such rumours. If he'd been told that Strulovitch had charts on his walls showing every smallest rise and fall in the value of art in every city in the world, he would not have been surprised.

D'Anton was not a dilatory man, but he didn't rush into things either. The advantage of having a melancholy nature was that it found a sort of pleasure in the slow passage of time, and since there was no true happiness to be rewarded with at the end of anything one did, there was no rush to do it.

And then Gratan came to him with a strange request— no, that wasn't fair, it had not yet assumed the shape of a request, it was more a plaint, an outraged perplexity, as though he felt he had been assaulted but had no bruise to show for it. "I'm in a bit of a pickle," he told him.

D'Anton often wished he'd been a marrying man and had brought up a family. I would have made a good father, he thought, though when he pictured himself playing in the garden with his children they were all boys. This wasn't sexual. Boys seemed sadder to him than girls, that was all. Boys nursed a secret hurt. He couldn't have put a name to it. He had never been able to put a name to his own. When he was a child he watched girls reading and painting and playing with their dolls—all right, with their soldiers too—and he saw in them a capacity for engrossment and self-forgetfulness that was beyond him. He was always alert to himself, not just easily wounded but attentive to those wounds, as though his only playthings were the slights he suffered.

Nothing very much changed as he grew older. Mortifications were still his playthings. But he felt them on behalf of other people now—other people of both sexes, but particularly men. The spectacle of their brave vulnerability, the woundedness which dared never speak its name, because men were meant to be strong not weak, consumed his emotional energies. If he could have made the world a better place for every man he saw in pain he would have done so. But you can spread your altruism only so far, so D'Anton made a double-friend of every friend he had, expending more concern on them than most ever thought they stood in need of. Never mind if they took advantage of him. Indeed the ones who took advantage of him the most were the ones he most helped. For they were surely—else they would not have made such exorbitant demands—the ones in greatest psychological want of his assistance.

Between Gratan and Barnaby in this regard—though obligation shaded into love for the one, while love shaded into obligation to the other—there was not much to choose. Barnaby came from the better family and had been given the better education, but he had no gifts beyond the boyish prettiness which, for D'Anton, was the outward form of his inward loveliness of spirit—a loveliness that needed all the help it could get in a world that didn't scruple to take advantage of innocence. Gratan had been initiated into cruelties that Barnaby could never have borne, had no education and was not by any stretch of the imagination pretty, but he had abundant physical skills and was able to earn an independent living with his body. On the surface he was not the sort of man who called out D'Anton's sympathies. But scratch a little deeper and the lonely, sorrowing boy could be discerned. Hence those little acts of folly like the Nazi salute which in reality was no such thing. D'Anton recognised a cry for help when he heard one. And when that cry for help was seconded first by one dear friend, and then another, he had no choice but to count Gratan as one of the deserving. He would, as he told Plurabelle—and as he had proved in the matter of finding him a Jew-girl to play with—do anything in the world for him. The phrase was automatic and denoted nothing in particular. But when Gratan drooped his normally manly head and announced he was in a bit of a pickle, D'Anton knew that the hour for another sacrifice—of his time, his energies, his influence, and maybe even his wallet—was at hand.

"Let's first of all rally your spirits," he told the footballer. "I'm eating out tonight with Barnaby and a couple of his old school friends who are up to watch some game or other . . ."

"Unlikely to be Stockport County against Colwyn Bay," Gratan said disconsolately. Even his career was ash in his mouth.

"No, I think it's rugby. Anyway, it's sure to be jolly."

The word "jolly" was so alien to D'Anton's vocabulary that even Gratan registered surprise. It was like hearing a man of God speak profanities.

"I'm not sure I'm in the mood for that," Gratan said.

"Oh come on. Why don't you join us for supper and you and I can discuss things in private afterwards?"

Gratan hesitated. Tonight of all nights Beatrice would be expecting him to be with her.

"If that's not convenient . . ." D'Anton said.

"No, no, I'll make it convenient."

But he wasn't sure how he was going to do that.

As it happened, D'Anton had to deal with a second pickle that evening, to which end he'd invited Barnaby—for this second pickle was his—to join him at the restaurant early.

"So tell me," D'Anton said.

Barnaby pointed to his left hand.

D'Anton shrugged.

"Don't you see anything missing?" Barnaby asked.

D'Anton counted his fingers. "Well they all seem to be there," he replied.

"Ring finger," Barnaby said.

"That's there, too."

"Yes, but ring isn't."

"Ah. Would that be the ring—?"

"Yes, that Plury bought me."

"And you've lost it?"

Barnaby pulled the face that always broke D'Anton's heart. The face of a little boy with no one to turn to. "Not exactly lost," he said.

"Given it to a whore then?"

"Of course not. I haven't even accidentally left it with a whore."

D'Anton could tell that Barnaby was looking for a little praise for this show of rectitude.

"Well I don't suppose it is any business of mine who you've given it to . . ."

"Why do you fear I've given it to someone?"

"Fear? Who said anything about *fear*?"

"Fear on Plury's behalf, I mean," Barnaby said, wondering if he'd presumed too far on D'Anton's jealousy.

D'Anton looked deep into Barnaby's indolent eyes. "Should I fear for Plury?"

"No you should not. I lost it. That's all there is to it."

"Then let's hope Plury believes you when you tell her that."

"Why shouldn't she?"

"Because it sounds like an excuse."

"I lost it."

"That's an excuse for carelessness."

"Christ, D'Anton, get off my case. You're as bad as she is."

A great wave of weariness with men and women and their tawdry ring culture overcame D'Anton. He had swapped rings himself when he was younger (always tentatively, it should be said, always because he thought it was what the other person wanted), and he understood the symbolism of both the giving and the losing, but the overblown poesy of men and women swearing eternal fidelity whenever they slipped a hoop of gold around one another's fingers, and then the commonplace accusations of betrayal whenever one of them slipped it off, as though the whole ritual had only ever been about trust and fidelity, a test that one or other party to it was bound to fail, a trap in other words, a snare as heartless as a springe, a wire loop attached to a twig to catch a rabbit—all this dismayed, depressed and disappointed him. Here was Plurabelle, an exceptional woman in every way, and yet Barney feared that the minute she discovered he had been careless of her love token—"He loves me, he loves me not"—she would turn into a fishwife.

"So why do you come to me with this, if you want me off your case?" D'Anton asked.

"I'm sorry, D'Anton, I shouldn't have said that. Forgive me."

D'Anton felt his friend was practising his apology to Plurabelle. He wasn't sure if that pleased him or it didn't. Uncomfortable, but flattered, he edged himself off the end of the imaginary bed. "So what would you have me do?" he asked gently.

"Couldn't you say you borrowed it?"

"I? Borrowed your ring? To do what with?"

"Oh, I don't know, to give to a whore?"

There was a moment of silence between them, relieved only by the appearance of the sommelier.

"I'm sorry," Barnaby said again.

D'Anton let his own silence linger a little longer. "I'll tell you what," he suggested at last, "I'll say I took it off you because I feared a stone was loose."

"It didn't have a stone. It was a plain gold band."

D'Anton remembered: a perfect, unbroken band to symbolise their perfect, unbroken love. Well, it had been his doing. Bringing people together was his speciality. Finding for others a happiness he could not find for himself.

"In that case I'll I say I took it off you to have it polished. I have my own polisher."

"Did it need polishing?"

"It doesn't matter."

"Will she be able to see the difference?"

"There won't be any difference because there won't be any ring."

Barnaby looked puzzled.

"You've lost it, remember."

"Ah, of course. So what happens then?"

"I'll say *I* lost it on the way to the polisher."

"That's a damn good idea. But better to say you lost it on the way back from the polisher."

"What difference?"

"I want Plury to know I had it polished."

"As you choose."

Barnaby took D'Anton's hands. "I'm forever in your debt."

D'Anton's eyes misted over. "Please don't say that," he said.

"All right. But can I at least promise that I'll never ask another favour from you again?"

"I'd rather you didn't say that either."

"I understand," Barnaby said, though he didn't.

But his spirits had cleared up so markedly that he hardly looked the same person who'd walked into the restaurant with his hair wild fifteen minutes before.

He settled back in his chair and smiled at his benefactor. "Now, how's that painting going?" he went on.

"Be patient," D'Anton said.

"Are you telling me you haven't persuaded the old skinflint to hand it over yet? What's the delay? Does he want more money?"

"First let me sort the ring."

Barnaby settled back even further in his chair. Yes, life had problems, but none that others couldn't solve for him.

"Here we go again," D'Anton thought when Gratan How-some eventually joined them, looking as much like a man in a pickle as Barnaby looked like a man who had come out of one.

Sixteen

To go back a bit:

In such a night as this, Beatrice thought, I shouldn't be sitting on my own looking at the moon.

Strulovitch had been right in this, if in nothing else: his daughter had not gone far. After leaving home with her boyfriend and her bags, she had gone straight to the Old Belfry to seek Plury's protection. Gratan's idea. They had met at Plury's, twisted eyebeams at Plury's, made philo-Semitic love at Plury's, and would now shelter at Plury's. Plury herself was away for a few days having corrective surgery to her corrective surgery, but in a phone call to Beatrice expressed her excitement and readiness to help, in a phone call to Gratan reproved his naughtiness but applauded his choice, and in a phone call to her house manager ordered the prettiest room to be made ready for the pair. Not the one she'd set aside for their personal use before, which had been pretty enough, but something more respectable and romantic. "Connubial" was the word she was looking for.

When Beatrice and Gratan arrived they found the pillows in what they were now to think of as their boudoir freshly

fluffed, bridal flowers in a vase, a bottle of Perrier-Jouët Belle
Époque on one bedside table and a box of Ladurée macarons on the other. They would also have found, had they gone
looking, D'Anton in demi-residence, rehanging paintings
in Plury's parlour—Plury loved to come home to D'Anton's
reconfigurations—though he was too preoccupied to see the
lovers arrive. Gratan was glad of that. He wanted to break
the news in stages to D'Anton, whom he looked on as a sort
of guardian, and from whom he expected sympathy but not
necessarily encouragement. It had been D'Anton who had
originally introduced Beatrice to their little world, and it was
possible he would not look kindly on Gratan's appropriation of
her. He could hear what D'Anton would say before he said it.
"I didn't bring the girl here for you to make off with, Gratan.
Not everything exists for your pleasure." A reprimand made
out of affection, but a reprimand nonetheless. "Just don't do
that again," D'Anton had warned after Gratan's Nazi salute.
He had pointed to Gratan's head. "Use that in future."

His manager at Stockport County had often said the
same.

Of course D'Anton might have guessed what was
afoot—he was a man lost in gloomy self-abstraction, but
there had been enough whispering in corridors and clumsy
disappearances for even him to notice. Failing that, Plury
might, in her vicarious erotic excitement, already have told
him. But if he still didn't know, Gratan figured it would be
best to keep him in ignorance for as long as possible, not to
say what he had done exactly, and in particular not to give
the person he had done it with a name. It would be more pru-
dent to talk in generalities—she, he, the father, circumcision,
stuff like that. D'Anton was a man of the world and would
be able to tell him whether, in an abstract way, circumcision

was something all Jewish fathers demanded of Gentiles who wanted to marry their daughters; whether they were within their legal and moral rights to do so; whether there were officers of the law who could enforce it; and whether it was likely to be painful.

Having carried Beatrice over the threshold, he had deposited her on the bed with less ceremony than she felt the occasion warranted, hurriedly explaining that he needed to nip downstairs a second.

"Where are you going?" Beatrice shouted after him, but he was already gone. "Just make sure you nip back up again," she added to herself.

D'Anton was up a library ladder when Gratan found him. "Does that look straight to you?" he called down without looking round.

Gratan was too caught up in his own troubles to know whether a picture was straight or not but he chose the easy option and said yes.

"So," D'Anton began when he was off the ladder. He could tell from Gratan's flushed appearance that he had something urgent to say. It was then that Gratan had poured out the edited contents of his heart, in response to which D'Anton had invited him to the restaurant . . .

To go forward a bit:

"I don't know," Gratan said to himself as he ran back up the stairs, "whether I'm coming or going." To Beatrice, who was standing at the window, as though awaiting his return by that route, he said, "Sorry, but I just have to slip out for a short while."

Beatrice stared at him in disbelief.

"First you have to nip down and now you have to slip out. Anybody would think you don't want to be with me."

She was not remotely sentimental. She hadn't supposed this was to be their honeymoon night. They had slept together many times already, and the evening wasn't otherwise to be sanctified by what had gone before. It was a night to get through, that was all. But for him to be nipping down and slipping out before she'd even had time to unpack her case was not how she, or indeed how any woman, would have expected things to go.

"Of course I want to be with you," Gratan said. He appeared hurt that she should doubt it.

"Gratan!"

"What?"

"We've only just got here!"

"I'm not going to be long."

"Where have you been?"

"I can't say."

"Where are you going?"

"I can't say."

"This isn't a good start, Gratan. Not after the day I've had."

He led her to the bed and embraced her in a manner that made it possible for him to keep an eye on the time. "It hasn't been easy for me either," he reminded her.

"No but you're bigger and more experienced than I am. And he isn't your father. Please don't go out tonight. Not tonight."

But Gratan had his appointment with D'Anton at Ristorante Treviso to keep. He needed D'Anton's advice—not later, not tomorrow, but now, in advance of his first night with Beatrice as runaways. It had dawned on him, in the course of the brief but fraught drive from Beatrice's house to Plury's, that however enraged and determined Beatrice was today, she might well feel differently about things—including him—in the morning. A father was still a father, no matter that he was a monster. And a Jewish father, from all he'd heard, even more so. He couldn't take anything for granted. What Beatrice said was not necessarily what Beatrice thought. He was pleased with himself for these insights into a woman's psychology. On Beatrice's behalf, as well as his own, it was important he talk to D'Anton. Otherwise he could easily make a false move. Say something he'd regret. Do something he shouldn't.

"Don't ask me to tell you where I've been or where I'm going," he pleaded. "Just trust me. When you know, you'll agree I was right to go there. It's for us."

"It sounds as though you're going to fetch a priest. Don't."

"I swear I'm not," Gratan said, putting his hand to his heart in a gesture that reminded Beatrice ever so slightly of his notorious Nazi salute.

"You haven't got another woman already?"

"Another woman! We've only been here an hour."

How long did it take, Beatrice wondered. "And you'll be back soon?"

"I promise," he promised, raising his arm to his chest again.

"You needn't do that," Beatrice said. "Just come back sober."

"As a lord."

"It's as drunk as a lord. A judge is what you mean. Never mind. Just assure me you are coming back. You haven't brought me here to leave me here?"

"Why would I do that?"

He kissed her with fierce passion. The first time he clapped eyes on her she'd been dressed as an urchin. Plury's doing. "My little Jewboy," Plury had called her. She looked a little like that again—more petulant than angry, more of a girl than a woman, more oriental than western, cross-bred, out of place, neither one thing nor another, a confusion to him. Was there nothing he wouldn't do for her?

"I won't be long," he said.

To go back a bit:
So Beatrice, on such a night, was left alone to reflect on what she'd done.

Was it any surprise she shed a tear?

She wiped her eye and wondered if Gratan had slipped out to kill her father. Would she have minded?

And what if, in the ensuing fight, her father were to kill Gratan? Would she have minded that?

Questions, questions . . .

She opened the champagne, though she didn't much like champagne, starting when it popped. Was that Gratan's gun going off? Or her father's? Her house was only a mile and a half away. On such nights, in the quiet of the Golden Triangle, sound travelled.

By the time I've finished this bottle, she thought, I will have forgotten who Gratan Howsome is. But I will not have forgotten my father.

My whole life, she thought, has been made a misery by him. She tried to remember a time when he hadn't pursued her, dragged her out of parties, punched her boyfriends, wiped the lipstick off her face with the back of his hand, pulled her down the street by her hair while clutching at his heart, as though to threaten her with cardiac arrest. *Look what you're doing to me. You're killing me.* Though it was he—wasn't it?—who was killing her.

Was it any surprise she laughed?

Once, she remembered, he threw her phone into a lake. The boy who'd rung her was talking as it drowned. That must have been two years ago. Was he still telling her how he couldn't wait to see her again, still guggling his appreciation of her breasts under water?

Once, her father jumped up and down on her laptop. Once, he kicked down the bathroom door and smashed his fist into her mirror. Once, he threatened to put out a contract on a boy she was seeing. She was just fourteen at the time. The boy a year older. Once he jumped on to the bonnet of an older boyfriend's car. Just keep driving, Beatrice had said, he's got no sense of balance, he'll fall off in the end. Once, he burst into a hotel room pretending he had a pistol in his pocket.

How could any other drama in her life compete with that? How could Gratan engross her to the degree her father had?

To show her how much he loved her—was that what it had all been about? To stop her falling in love with someone else?

Was it any surprise she shed a tear again?

The mad thing was—the maddest thing of all—it had worked. She couldn't fall in love with anyone else.

She tried to concentrate the tears upon her mother, but she could think only of her father.

Why hadn't he come after her?

He always came after her, so why not this time—the one time it mattered. If it mattered.

Had he given up on her? She had heard the story of how

his father, her grandfather, had buried him on the eve of his marriage to a Gentile. Had he now decided to bury her? *You marry a man with a penis like mine or I bury you!*

Was it any surprise she laughed?

Laugh over it or cry over it, such a commandment could mean only one thing: he loved her.

She put an unexpected question to herself with her fifth Ladurée macaron: were Gratan to agree to his demand would her father want the operation to be a success or would he prefer that Gratan bled to death?

To go forward a bit:

D'Anton was unable to believe his ears. "He said that?"

"Yes."

"You're sure?"

"He said it."

"In so many words?"

"I didn't count the words."

"He said, 'Get yourself circumcised and you can have my daughter'? He definitely said that?"

"He said, 'Get yourself circumcised and we can talk again. Until then there is no more to say.'"

"And you're sure he wasn't being figurative? He didn't say anything about circumcision of the heart?"

"What's circumcision of the heart?"

"Once upon a time, when this was a Christian country, a young man of your class would have gone to Sunday school and been taught about St. Paul. We can be better Christians, St. Paul argued, by understanding circumcision metaphorically, not following the letter of the law, but the spirit. We can be circumcised in the heart. Do you understand that?"

Gratan Howsome first nodded his head, then shook it. Whatever D'Anton was talking about, it didn't apply in this instance. "Why," he said, "would he want me to be a better Christian? I'm already too much of a Christian for him. He wants me to be a better Jew . . . Well, any Jew."

"That's what I mean. A Jew in the heart. Are you sure he wasn't asking you to be that?"

"There was no mention of circumcising my heart. I certainly wouldn't have agreed to that."

"So are you telling me you have agreed to something?"

"I said I would talk it over with Beatrice."

"*Beatrice!*"

Howsome slapped the side of his head. *The fool I am!* Two minutes with D'Anton and he'd blurt out anything. He wondered if he could invent another Beatrice, but saw that that would only make things worse.

"Yes, Beatrice."

"Plury's Beatrice?"

In for a penny, Howsome thought. "Well she's my Beatrice now. You have to understand, D'Anton, I'm in love with her."

"Since when?"

"Since I first saw her."

"Howsome, she's a child!"

"That's what her father said."

"Well don't you think he has a point. You're twice her age."

"So you think I should agree to let them castrate me?"

"I think you should agree to leave the girl alone."

"It's too late for that. She's run away with me. She's at Plury's now, waiting."

"Plury knows?"

"Yes. She rang to congratulate us. She left us a bottle of champagne."

"Well I'd give you almost anything, as you know, but I wouldn't give you champagne for this. Have you decided what you'll do if the father comes after you?"

"That's what I've come to you to ask. What should I do?"

"Give the girl back."

"I've told you, I can't. We love each other."

"And how does she feel about her father's demands? Does she want you to agree to them?"

"She thinks he's a fucking maniac. She hates him and his Jew money and his Jew foundation."

"Foundation! What foundation?"

"I don't know, D'Anton. The Whatsitcalled Foundation. The Fuckedif'Iknow Foundation. The Strulovitch Foundation, I suppose. Don't ask me."

D'Anton threw back the contents of his glass and let his eyes bulge.

"Did you say Strulovitch?"

"I think that's how you pronounce it. I don't think I'm obliged to know a man's name just because I've run off with his daughter."

D'Anton released his mind so that it might wander where it would. Beatrice Strulovitch . . . Beatrice Strulovitch . . . Had he known that? Had he known that was her name when he first recommended her to Plury, as an innocent diversion for Howsome, whose weakness for Jewesses so amused them both? Was he, in ways that were not clear to himself, a party to this mess? Had he connived at it, knowing or half knowing who Beatrice was?

Whatever he'd intended, he hadn't intended that Gratan would fall in love with the girl and either lose his foreskin or elope with her.

Unless he had . . . Unless, well unless breaking the

father's heart had always been what he intended, no matter who else suffered along the way.

He raked through the history of his rancid relations with the art collector, benefactor, upstart, sore loser, moneybags, bloodsucker and vampire, Simon Strulovitch. Was this—for him—its lowest moment or its highest?

Unable to decide whether Gratan Howsome's bombshell served his cause or impeded it, unable at this moment to re-member what that cause was, he ordered more brandy.

When Gratan finally returned he found Beatrice stripped naked, dead upon the floor.

He let out a cry so fearsome that Beatrice had no choice but to open her eyes and tell him she was acting out the space he'd left when he deserted her.

"How can you act a space?" he wanted to know.

"In such a night as this how could you have deserted me?" she asked.

But he was too transfixed by the sight of her breasts to answer.

The man has no feeling for art, Beatrice thought, yielding herself reluctantly to him.

SEVENTEEN

What chance that in two locations in the Golden Triangle, no more than a mile or so apart, two conversations about St. Paul's views on circumcision of the heart should have been taking place at the very same hour?

It was enough to make a visitor from another planet believe he'd dropped in on a Christian country.

Perhaps to describe what passed between D'Anton and his sentimental beneficiary Gratan Howsome as a "conversation" is an exaggeration. What passed between Strulovitch and Shylock ditto. Though it wasn't unevenness in the matter of comprehension that made this latter conversation not really a conversation at all. Rather it was that neither man spoke what he was thinking, though each knew the other was thinking it. A silent conversation, then. Or at least a conversation in which what was conversed was not what the conversation was actually about.

Not finding Beatrice waiting for him when he got back from the restaurant, Strulovitch fell into a despondency that even D'Anton might have envied. Whatever Howsome had been doing out on his own, it didn't signify what he'd hoped it signified. He slumped into a chair with a bottle of whisky and pointed Shylock to the drinks cabinet. "Get drunk with me, please," he said.

"I'm not able to get drunk," Shylock said. "I was never drunk then so I can never be drunk now. It's one of the disadvantages."

"Then just have the odd one and sit with me."

Shylock did as was requested of him.

They sat, looking at one another's extended feet, for upwards of an hour. Then Shylock asked if he could ask something.

"You've just asked it."

"Something else. The *bris* . . ."

"The *bris*!"

"The circumcision ritual."

"I know what a fucking *bris* is. I thought that word applied only to eight-day-old babies."

"And the footballer is what age again?"

Strulovitch laughed an ill-natured laugh. He would miss Shylock when he went. He needed a black-hearted friend. Jews had grown so careful now. *If you wrong us, shall we not revenge?* No, we shall not. We shall take it on the chin and be grateful. Unless we're in Judea and Samaria, where we're accused of being Nazis. Cowards or Nazis—which was it to be? The Rialto was not Samaria, but it too had bred a tougher Jew, Strulovitch thought. If he had, on pain of death, to be a Jew in Samaria, the Rialto or the Golden Triangle, he wouldn't have chosen the Golden Triangle.

Then he remembered that Shylock had not even met Gratan. "Are you psychic as well as everything else?" he asked.

"A little," Shylock said. "I enjoy a broad overview. But I

also listen to what you tell me. And I did manage to grab a look at him as he was leaving the restaurant. *Cavernicolo.*"

Strulovitch shook his head from side to side as though wanting to rid his brain of all memory of that savage exchange of glances. Why hadn't he gone over and collared him after all? "OK," he said. "So what about the *bris*?"

"Have you been having second thoughts?"

"If you're psychic you should know."

"I see you're blaming me. That's your prerogative. But you could always change the situation yourself by changing your mind. Let him off if your heart's no longer in it. Give Beatrice your blessing."

"She's sixteen!"

"As you keep telling me. But she's a very mature sixteen."

"That's the problem."

"How old do you think Jessica was?"

"It has never occurred to me to wonder."

"Precisely. Age isn't the issue."

"So what is?"

"Well answer me this: if you got the footballer to agree to your bloody terms—"

"Hold on a minute. *Bloody terms* coming from you—"

"No, you hang on a minute. I'm a guest in your house, so I ask you to forgive my rudeness. But you cannot presume to know how bloody or not I was prepared to be. You can guess, but you cannot know . . ."

"Do you know *yourself*?"

"Leave me out of this and let's go back to what I was saying. If you got the footballer to agree to your terms, however you describe them, would you be happy? Or do you expect him—*want* him—to reject them and leave your daughter alone?"

"Both. I want him to leave my daughter alone, and I want him to be circumcised, so long as . . ."

"So long as what? Why do you hesitate?"

"So long as I can be the one who wields the knife."

"I think you're fooling yourself. I don't think you could do it. You are not capable of that."

"Now it's my turn to ask how you can presume to know what I am capable of. You have only known me a matter of days."

"And how long do you suppose it takes? Mr. Strulovitch, I have known you forever."

"Do you know how insulting that is?"

"I don't mean it to be so. But let me ask you a question. How many *brises* have you been to?"

"You're psychic. You tell me."

"None. First, because you have no son. Second, because you scorn religious ceremony. But the real reason you haven't seen a *bris* is that you know you would faint. Many men do. Many fathers, uncles, brothers. It is an upsetting sight. A knife taken to an eight-day-old baby."

"Howsome is a mite older."

"Which would make it even more gory. And besides, what makes you think you want to see his penis, let alone take a slice of it? How many Gentile penises have you seen? How many have you held between your fingers?"

"I don't have to answer that."

"But you're confident you want to touch his?"

"I'll wear gloves . . ."

"Hold it, wound it, make it bleed, hear him scream? This is all bravado and you know it. You'd run a mile."

Strulovitch puts up a hand. "Just a minute," he says. "Just a minute."

Shylock puts up two hands as though he knows he might have gone too far.

"Can you tell me how," Strulovitch wants to know, "we have proceeded from metaphor to literalism? All this begins when I ask a Gentile who's been sleeping with my daughter to prove his good intentions. The next thing, under your tutelage, I'm slicing off his penis."

"Welcome to my world," says Shylock.

"So you, too, meant your pound of flesh metaphorically to begin with?"

Shylock makes his eyes droop in weary distaste. "Not that again."

"I'd stop asking that question if you'd answer it."

"Then ask it with more subtlety. Every transaction between Jew and Gentile is metaphorical. It's the only way we don't kill one another. But if you're asking me if I meant it jestingly then yes, partly."

"That's not quite the same thing."

"No, but there are degrees of earnest."

"Then let me ask you: did you hope that Antonio would fail to meet his bond so you could harm him?"

"At the very moment of the jest, maybe not."

"Then when?"

"As the tale unfolds, so does intention."

"And when was that intention firm?"

"I could say after Jessica was taken from me. After Leah's ring was stolen. After others thought they could renege on the bond for him. After they thought me manipulable. After I was backed into a corner. After I was left with no alternative . . ."

"So which?"

"All of them and none of them. I still don't know how firm my intention was. The story stopped . . . What didn't occur, didn't occur. Anything further belongs to speculation not philosophy or psychology. And not to theology either."

"But before it stopped . . . there was, there must have been, intention."

"*Intention,* well . . . What is intention? Whatever his intention, would Abraham have gone on to kill Isaac? I don't dwell in the Old Testament any more than you do, but I have, as you might imagine, a special interest in that story."

"The world has a special interest in that story."

"The world *did.* I doubt it has any more."

"That's as maybe. But the question has still to be asked. Would Abraham have gone on and killed his son?"

"Did Abraham ultimately have it in him to commit a murder? That too is an illegitimate line of enquiry."

"Illegitimate or unanswerable?"

"Both. It's the 'ultimately' we can't know about."

"So what is it legitimate to ask?"

"Whether anything in Abraham's character until that point would lead one to think of him as a child killer."

"The answer being no?"

"Exactly. No. And in mine neither. Was there anything in my personal history—mine specifically; mine as they knew of me, not mine as a member of a feared and hated race—to suggest I had a taste for blood? If there had been the slightest suspicion of such propensities the Gentiles would surely have kept their distance. But it was they who complained that I avoided them. Ask yourself this: would you agree a binding contract with a man who would cut your heart out if you reneged on it? Would you dare to steal from such a man? Take his jewels? Rob him of his daughter? Spit on him in the street? A man suspected of being free with his knife commands more respect than I did. More dread, too. Until I stood firm upon my bond they believed a few ducats' reparation would quiet my temper. In their contempt and confidence you can discern my innocence of violent reputation."

"They called you a cur and thought you wolfish."

"They thought Jews wolfish—not me in particular, *Jews*—but in reality they barely believed their own libels. In the eyes of Christians and Muslims we have never been warlike enough. We are emasculated men who bleed like women. That's what makes it so hard for them to forgive us when we do strike tellingly back. To lose to Jews is to lose to half-men."

"Wasn't there something of the warrior about Abraham?"

"Something, yes. But by the standards of the time he was a pussy cat."

"So if he had so little violence in him, how do you understand his readiness to kill Isaac?"

"By not calling it a readiness. A particular precipitating circumstance led him so far on the road to murder, is all one can say. But did he have murder in his heart, even then? We cannot know. He did not know himself. The story stops, and will remain stopped for all eternity."

"Abraham's precipitating circumstance was God. What was yours?"

"The same."

But Strulovitch couldn't leave the matter alone. A chance comes along, you take it. And Shylock was looking more relaxed than he'd seen him, sitting in the half-dark with his legs outstretched, listening to the silence whenever Strulovitch allowed it to be silent. A man easy to ambush.

"Not for the first time," Strulovitch resumed, "you elude

my questions with the story stopping. Yes, the story stopped, but you haven't. You are here. You have had time enough to reflect.'"

"Reflect! I do nothing but reflect. But reflection is not action. It is not even knowledge of action. I don't have the answer to your question. I don't know if I would have gone ahead and taken flesh from around his heart—or, even, since you have asked me this before, how the heart suddenly became the site of my revenge."

"Aha! You call it your revenge."

"I do, and willingly. I had much to avenge. My daughter, my wealth, my reputation . . .'"

"And a bloodthirst to slake?"

"Now you sound like them."

"Then show me where I'm wrong. Do you wish you'd not been stopped?"

"Stopped?" Shylock narrowed his gaze. Suddenly he did not look as relaxed as he had been. "I wish, for all the good it does me, that I had not been *thwarted*."

"From taking his heart?"

"From finding out whether or not I could have done it."

"So you wish you had?"

"That is not quite the same thing. Had I done so they would not have hesitated to take mine."

Strulovitch waved that consideration away. He wasn't interested in consequences; he knew all about what they did to Jews; what intrigued him was what a Jew might do to them. "Let me trespass on your good nature one more time," he pressed. "Would you have done it?"

"And one more time—I don't know. I have no more taste for blood than you do. Those men, I mentioned, who faint during a *bris*—well I am one of them. Twice I've fainted. It was that or cry louder than the baby. Like you, I'm made of the softest stuff and equally hate the sight and smell and even thought of blood. But understand—my own blood was up. My hatred for that superior, all-suffering, all-sorrowing, sanctimonious man boiled in my veins. There was, I believed, as he no doubt believed of me, no room in this world for both of us. We denied each other. He could not allow me to transact my way and I could not allow him to transact his. I stood for order, he for chaos. We both, of necessity, dealt in obligation. To be in business imposes obligation. And to be a husband, a father, a lover, imposes obligation too. I dealt in true obligation—I gave and I took. A quid pro quo that was agreed to on all sides and left nothing to doubt or misunderstanding. He dealt in false obligation. He could bear only to give. He would not profit financially or emotionally. So he must always be sacrificial, disappointed and alone. Which imposed a hidden but constant obligation on those he gave to. I could not function in a universe as raw and haphazard as his. And he could not function in a world as rational as mine. My legalistic rigidity, as he considered it, cancelled him out. His emotional coercion cancelled me. Which is why one of us has always to kill the other. So yes, it's possible—all right, more than possible—that in that fuming rage I would have found the wherewithal, the joy, the obligation—as though answering a commandment from a furious God—and as a long-owed return on those centuries of despising, as a requital of the slander, and as a perfectly ironic eventuation of all their baseless fears, yes, it's more than possible that I'd have found what was necessary—call it the heroic strength, call it the bliss, call it if you will the villainousness—to take what by any reasonable computation was owing to me . . . I felt myself to be, I won't pretend otherwise, the instrument of justice. By the measure I was used, would it be measured to them. And there's no violence a man is not capable of when he believes he is acting as God would have him act. And before you say anything, I am as aware as you of the blasphemy of claiming such entitlement. Let's include that, then, in what I might have been on the point of summoning up, the blasphemy of taking life, had it come to that, in God's name, except that it didn't come to that. So I am sorry, I cannot tell you what the act of murder feels like and whether, at the point of a knife, I would have gone ahead and done it. But I can tell you how it is to be brought to the threshold of murder and to wish, with every part of oneself that ministers to resolution, to cross over. Does that go any way to answering your question?"

But Strulovitch is asleep in his chair, worn out by too much anger and frustration, too much alcohol, and not impossibly too many questions.

Shylock, though, has another explanation.

This Strulovitch has a profound moral reluctance to stay awake, he thinks.

This Strulovitch asks but he doesn't want to know the answer.

Jews are sentimental about themselves, and this Strulovitch, though he can't decide if he's a Jew or not, is no different. A Jew, by his understanding, is not capable of what non-Jews are capable of. A Jew does not take life. I am a hero to him by virtue of what I permitted to be done to me, not by what I did or might have done. Good Jew—kicked. Bad Jew—kicks.

If you prick us do we not bleed, but if we prick back do we not shed blood?—he would rather not know.

These famous ethics of ours have landed us in a fine mess, Shylock would like to say to his wife. If we cannot accept that we might murder as other men murder, we are not enhanced, but diminished.

Do you agree with me Leah, my love?

But it's too late, and too cold to go outside. Always cold where she resides.

And anyway, he knows that Leah will point out the sophistry in the account of himself he has just offered Strulovitch. Antonio had been his to kill. "The law allows it, and the court awards it," the little lawyer with the squeaky voice had told him. That was the moment when history was his to make, and never mind "I cannot tell you what the act of murder feels like because it didn't come to that": it didn't come to that because he didn't let it. Give me my money and I'll go, he'd said instead.

Cowardice, was it? Or a pious adherence to Jewish law? The Almighty had fixed his canon against self-slaughter and self-slaughter it would assuredly have been had he shed a drop of Antonio's blood.

Either way—faint-heartedness or piety—does this mark the limit beyond which a Jew, with all his brave talk of vengeance, dare not go?

No wonder Strulovitch, otherwise so eager to keep him to the mark, has chosen to fall asleep.

Despite the lateness of the hour and the cold, he goes outside to face Leah's reproach after all. He had chosen to stay alive when there was nothing left for him to stay alive for. He could have killed his enemy and joined his wife. So why hadn't he?

EIGHTEEN

D arling! I've rushed back. I wouldn't even let them finish me."

Anna Livia Plurabelle Cleopatra A Thing Of Beauty Is A Joy Forever Wiser Than Solomon Christine skipped into the room carrying a posy of hand-tied forget-me-nots and roses. She had a bandage over one eye, like a pirate. The rest of her was lipblistered.

"You look like a bridesmaid," Beatrice cried, not knowing what else to say.

"Darling, I feel like a bridesmaid."

She searched the bed sheets with her one good eye.

"You can't be looking for blood?" Beatrice cried.

"Of course not. I'm looking for Gratan."

Then she nodded interrogatively in the direction of the bathroom.

"He's not here," Beatrice said.

"You haven't . . . ?"

"No, no we haven't . . ."

"So you are still . . . ?"

"Yes, we are still. But he hasn't been here much since we arrived."

"That was only yesterday, wasn't it?"

"Correct. He's done a lot of nipping down and slipping out in that time. He's just popped off again. I'm not sure why."

"Maybe he's making arrangements."

"What for?"

Plurabelle made as though to wink at her. "You know."

Beatrice scowled. "I can't promise you a wedding any time soon," she said.

The expression of disappointment that swept across Plurabelle's beleaguered face made Beatrice doubt the resolutions she had made the night before in Gratan's absence. He had come home, as he had promised, at a reasonable hour—supposing there was any reasonable hour for a man in his position to be out until—and, again as he had promised, as sober as a newt. But she had decided not to stay awake—and then, in a *coup de théâtre,* not to stay alive for him.

It did occur to her to wonder, as she lay there listening to the boards creaking outside the bedroom, that it could have been her father come to rescue her. In which case—but no, she decided against covering her nakedness. Let them all see what they had done to her. And how well she could perform it.

In the event it was Gratan.

That bloody father of hers. Never there when you wanted him.

She'd had a strange evening, lying there on pillows as fluffed as Plury's lips, sipping champagne like a thirsty bee, alternating glugs with macarons, and thinking about life's paradoxes.

However much of a fight she'd put up against her father's covenantal obsessions—a fight that seemed to her to have gone on all her short life—in some corner of her soul she respected them. Them, or her father's fanatic embrace of them? She wasn't sure that a bridal bower lent to her by Plury was conducive to the making of such fine distinctions. But she had read about hostages falling in love with their captors and their captors' ideologies, and she did wonder if that was what had happened to her—the captor being her father, not Gratan. Explain it she could not, and approve it she could not either, but now that the argument with her father had finally boiled over into flight, she saw him differently and thought he might be right. Not right in how he'd brought her up, exactly, but right in how he hadn't. She had girlfriends she could easily have envied for their freedom to come and go as they pleased. One, the daughter of atheists, had been sleeping with her boyfriend in the next room to her easy-thinking parents since she was thirteen. Another, the child of poets, was allowed to throw parties at her own home—parties her mother and father and even her grandparents attended—at which substances that Beatrice had never heard of were ingested through parts of the body she had never seen, and sexual practices she would not have thought practicable were openly encouraged.

So why didn't she envy them? Queer for her to hear herself say this but the reason she didn't envy them was that they lacked example. They swung free like gates come off their hinges, whereas she had had to learn resistance. Better your father be your adversary than your friend, she reasoned.

Don't waste yourself on chthonic arseholes, Beatrice, he'd told her. Wasn't she lucky having a father who thought like that? Less lucky, she thought, having a father who distinguished between Jewish chthonic arseholes and Gentile chthonic arseholes and measured the time she wasted on them differently. Wasn't waste waste?

She had never been happy with the Jew thing. "It's such a horrible little word," she remembered saying to her parents when she was just a little girl. "*Jew*. It sounds like a black beetle with spikes."

It was her mother who had smacked her then. Her father, she recalled, had laughed.

"So if we don't do Jewish things, and we don't have Jewish friends, and we don't eat Jewish food, and we don't celebrate Jewish festivals, why must I go out with Jewish boys?" she asked him later.

"For the sake of continuity," he told her.

"What do you want me to continue?"

"The thing you were born to be."

"Jewish?"

"Continuous."

"I just don't know what that means."

"Neither do I. But I do know you weren't born to toss yourself aside. You aren't random, Beatrice. You didn't begin with yourself so you can't end with yourself. Life is a serious business. You can't be shaken by every passing fancy."

You aren't a gate that's come off its hinges.

And now, to preserve that continuity—though he wouldn't be genuinely continuous even then—her Gentile chthonic arsehole boyfriend has to bleed. Maybe bleed to death. Explain to me how that works, Daddy . . .

He might love me but he's a butcher, Beatrice thought. His mind's an abattoir.

———

"So what's wrong?" Plurabelle wanted to know.

And Beatrice told her.

It was important to D'Anton, when it came to helping friends, to be even-handed. He now had two things to do for Barnaby. Get him the Solomon Joseph Solomon sketch and lie to Plury for him about his ring. So what two things could he do for Gratan? Extricate him from the mess with Beatrice was one, but Gratan appeared to have his heart set on the girl. Get Strulovitch to relent was a second, but he didn't immediately see how he was going to achieve that. Apart from Beatrice herself, he had nothing that Strulovitch wanted. And even if he found a way of prising her from Gratan and delivering her back to her father, what would that achieve for Gratan? Procuring a top-class surgeon to perform the operation—say the surgeon who attended to royal circumcisions, assuming they were still performed—was of course a third, but his gorge rose at the prospect of being in any way instrumental in this. I am not going to pimp for that Jew, he decided.

Then he remembered that several years before he had stood in the way of Strulovitch's opening a gallery of Anglo-Jewish art in memory of his parents. What if he were to say he would stand in the way of it no more? What if he were to go still further and offer to use his not inconsiderable influence to facilitate it?

I'll do that for you, Mr. Strulovitch, and all I want in return is—what? He did his sums again and came up with two things he wanted from Strulovitch. The Solomon Joseph Solomon and Gratan's release from the threat of dismemberment. What if Strulovitch would do a deal on one and not the other? What if it fell to him, D'Anton, to prioritise? Gratan's plight was clearly far more serious than Barnaby's, but if truth be told D'Anton preferred Barnaby to Gratan and felt more sympathetic to his suit. Gratan had got himself into this mess, blindly following that part of himself which, quite frankly, deserved to suffer retribution. Whereas Barnaby was just trying to please a lovely if whimsical lady. There, too, lay the other basis for his preference: he would rather be the indirect cause of Plury's felicity than Beatrice's, Beatrice Strulovitch being . . . well, a Strulovitch.

Solomon himself—the other Solomon—D'Anton thought, would have trouble sorting this one out. The irony was that Plurabelle's own television show, *The Kitchen Counsellor,* was the perfect place to adjudicate between these claims on D'Anton's givingness, but the Solomon Joseph Solomon was to be a surprise to her and a discussion of the rights and wrongs of circumcision would surely have a deleterious effect on ratings. Which left him back where he began, wanting to be even-handed but not knowing how.

He was being premature in his calculations, anyway, he reminded himself, in assuming that Strulovitch would play ball with him at all. He didn't doubt that his own loathing—no, he didn't loathe Strulovitch, did he? His natural aversion then, his discomfort, his reluctance to like—was reciprocated. What if Strulovitch would rather keep the Solomon Joseph Solomon *and* risk losing his daughter than accept D'Anton's condescension—as he would no doubt view it—in a matter that had once raised so much bitterness between them? Had there ever been a Jew yet—just a question—that was not inflexible and vengeful?

Thinking it over, D'Anton was pleased he had not yet sent Strulovitch the letter. Better not to show his hand yet. Better not to let Strulovitch know what he wanted. Did this not prove, once more, that time taken to plan a move was never time wasted? He went to look again at the letter, with a view to toning down any note of imploration, only to discover that it was no longer on his desk. There was only one explanation for this. His assistant, desirous as always to please a man so busily engaged in pleasing others, had hand-delivered it to the address on the envelope.

D'Anton bent over his desk as if in pain. He felt it was he who had been hand-delivered to Strulovitch. In his mind's eye he saw his mortal enemy, hunched as though over a money bag, fingering his words with diabolic satisfaction.

D'Anton shuddered. It wasn't just Gratan Howsome who had something to fear from the Jew's malevolence.

Nineteen

Timing, thought Strulovitch, is everything.

If he'd received D'Anton's letter before seeing him at Ristorante Treviso hugger-mugger with Gratan Howsome he might have looked kindly on the request. Well, "kindly" would have been to overstate it, but with an irony-drenched beneficence at least. How amusing that such a man should come cap in hand to him. And how amusing it would be to do such a man a kindness in return: sell him the Solomon Joseph Solomon for exactly what it had cost him, thereby depriving D'Anton of the pleasure of calling him a usurer and rogue. He liked the study for its pictorial flair and anatomical attention, but not as much as he'd have liked the sumptuous work it originally became. No one would have got *that* from him for any price. But the first attempt—yes, lovely as it was, he could bear to let it go, especially when the reward was so sweet. Here, D'Anton, my dear fellow, you must have known you had only to ask. I cannot tell you how delighted I am to learn you are a convert to Jew art at last.

Why, he might even have made him a gift of it.

But Strulovitch now knew him to be a friend and possibly

a co-conspirator of Howsome's. Difficult to see what the men could possibly have in common, but that wasn't his affair. Companions in nefariousness they clearly were. Who was to say D'Anton hadn't played a part in Howsome's making off with his daughter? They'd been together, looking shifty, on the evening of the day Beatrice had decamped, which strange occurrence suggested D'Anton might have given the lovers shelter that very night. Who was to say that they weren't there still, enjoying D'Anton's florid hospitality—Strulovitch guessed it would be florid; florid and abstemious all at once—drinking sake from fine Japanese porcelain and toasting Strulovitch's displeasure in Bellinis?

Strulovitch read D'Anton's words again. Had he missed the tone of them? What at first had looked like a begging letter now looked like a vicious leg-pull. He'd been planning the most deliciously ironic response, but what if the irony was all in D'Anton's court and he, Strulovitch, was its object?

That unnamed man, the "young and impressionable friend" who wanted the picture as a token of his devotion to a woman—there could be no doubt about his identity now. He was unmistakably Howsome.

Which meant that the woman to whom he was devoted—*devoted!*—was unmistakably Beatrice.

Which left only the title of the painting itself to consider. *Love's First Lesson!* The lubricious innuendo was unmissable. The young woman—Howsome's pupil in the erotic arts—would cherish the picture every bit as much as he, Strulovitch, would want her to, D'Anton had written. Meaning what? Either those words were rank sarcasm or they gestured at some lubricity locked away in Strulovitch's fatherly concern.

The joke's on me, Strulovitch realised.

He paced his drawing room, waving the letter in front of his face as though fanning himself with it.

Well we shall see about that, he said aloud.

Out in the garden Shylock was talking to his wife.

"I've been thinking," he was saying, "how our refined morality has left us incapable of enjoying that spontaneity of action other men enjoy."

"How so, my love?"

"Well take this man Strulovitch. What am I to him? I catch him staring at me sometimes when he thinks I'm not aware of him. A stare that seems to start from the deepest recesses of his mind and finishes I have no idea where. It disturbs me. Not even by you, my dearest, was I ever looked at with this intensity. I do not call it love. It isn't admiration either. It's an intensity of curiosity such as a parent might feel for a child, or a child for a parent, a sort of baffled pride as though anything I do, or have done, reflects genetically on him. I either bear him up or I let him down. He is not capable of indifference towards me. I am all lesson. I am all example. I need you to tell me I was never a trial of this sort to you, Leah. Or to Jessica."

It was always hard for him to mention Jessica by name. So much to hide, so much not to say, so much grief. Did Leah hear that? In her infinite tact did she detect how much this withholding of her name cost him? And was it costly for her as well?

"Anyway," he ruminated after a period of quiet, "it puts me in a false position to be an exemplar—not a role I'd ever have chosen for myself—the foundation of whose exemplariness has always to be kicked from under him. These Jews,

Leah, these Jews! They don't know whether to cry for me, disown me or explain me. Just as they don't know whether to explain or disown themselves. They wait for a sign that they are not as cringingly passive as they have been described, and when it comes they tear their hair in shame. 'We are a people on the verge of annihilation,' Strulovitch is fond of telling me, when he remembers. 'We cannot look to anyone to help us but ourselves.' Yet the moment a Jew raises a hand to do just that his courage fails him. Better we be killed than kill, I see him thinking. Look at him now, pacing his floor, plotting a revenge he won't in the end have the courage to carry out. The man lacks resolution, Leah. Tell me what I should do— spur him on or let him be?"

He waited for her to tell him what she thought. They spoke so often for so long when she was alive. They spoke and spoke. When she was no longer there to speak to him it was as though a cord connecting him to life was severed. He would go to the synagogue to speak to other men but their company could not replace hers. Theirs had not been a synagogue marriage. They spoke ideas, not faith. Leah had never been circumscribed by convention or tradition. She was like a fountain of clear, fresh thought. So when she went, his throat dried and his mind atrophied. He didn't want to see anything, because where was the value of sight if what he saw he could not share with her? He closed his ears to music. He stopped reading until he began to read to her again at her graveside. He saw no point in activity, and would sit for hours, thinking nothing, in a vacancy that was nearer to non-existence than sorrow. What had his life been to him before Leah? He couldn't remember. There was no before Leah. That his house became a hell for his daughter who couldn't rouse him or interest him in her life he accepted. Leah's death made him a bad father. Or, if he'd been a bad father before—a man who lived only for the love he bore his wife—the death of that too-loved wife made him a worse one. Poor, poor Jessica then, doubly deprived. No wonder. No excuse, but no wonder. And when he did rediscover some of his old energy it hadn't been out of any renewed concern for her well-being. He wished he could have lied to himself. And to her. *I lived again for you, Jessica, I remembered what I owed you.* But the truth of it was different. It had been the Gentiles who had pricked him back into animation. In their contempt he found the twisted stimulus to live again.

It is rage not love that propels a man to action.

When he looked up he saw Strulovitch occupying his own patch of garden, walking to and fro, a man without a wife to talk to, lost in reflection, moving his lips soundlessly.

He had no trouble reading what Strulovitch was saying. "I will do such things . . ."

He was sympathetic to the frustration. He too would once have done *such things.*

What they are, yet I know not . . .

But at least Strulovitch had what was still to come to look forward to. What things they were, yet he knew not. Whereas Shylock was busted. What he'd done he'd done, and what he had yet to do, he never would do now.

I miss the future, Shylock thought.

"So tell me," he again asked Leah. "Do I restrain him or whip him up into the vengeful rage he's been longing for all his life?"

The cold earth in which Leah was rolled around gave its deepest moan.

"Very well then," Shylock said. "In this, as in everything else, I will be guided by you."

———

"What do we do about it? What we do about it," Plurabelle said, "is this."

She made a sign with her thumb, meaning get them the hell out of here, on a train, a ship, a plane, anything. Just get them away.

D'Anton wasn't sure. "Do we want to rile a man as vile as this?" he wondered.

"The Jew?"

"The wealthy Jew, yes."

"The Hebrew?"

"E'en him. The moneybags, who else?"

They laughed. It was fun, even in worrying times, to play Jewepithets.

"Now I've lost my thread. Would you be so good as to repeat your question," Plurabelle begged.

"I asked how good an idea it was to rile the Jew."

"You mean the inexecrable dog—"

"Stop it, Plury!"

"Must I?"

"You must. I ask again: how good an idea is it to rile him?"

"Do you care about our friends?"

"I care about Gratan. Forgive me if the Jew's daughter means a little less to me."

"Well she means a great deal to me. I won't have her judged by that pig she calls a father."

"Pig refuser, surely."

"A pig can refuse a pig. But take my point. She is not him, any more than I was mine."

"Yours, I imagine, was another order of father," D'Anton said.

"Well he wasn't an Israelite, a werewolf, a castrator and a bloodsucker, if that's what you mean."

"I mean something along those lines, yes."

"But I love her despite her father the thick-lips—I assume he has thick lips, I haven't seen him."

"Thick and wet." He was careful not to look at her lips.

"As I suspected. Whereas hers are full and voluptuous."

"Like yours."

"Thank you. But stay focussed. Gratan loves her. And I demand that you love her."

"So why can't they stay here until the storm blows over."

"Because the storm might not blow over, and I don't want that hook-nose—I assume he has a hook nose: don't answer—banging on my doors. You know the press—they will love this. Besides, the lovers need some time on their own. Beatrice is looking a little flaky to me. She and Gratan have been fighting already. She could easily decide she's made a big mistake. And you know what Gratan's like. Two minutes of not getting all he wants and he'll be off looking for another wife."

"But how can they go away anyway? He's got a team to play for. He can't come running back every weekend."

"Isn't he suspended for that salute thing?"

"That was a year ago or more."

"Couldn't we get him suspended again? Get him to use the 'n' word? Or punch someone?"

"Only too easily But he wouldn't thank us for that. Another suspension could be the end of his career."

"Then let's get him compassionate leave. I know all the

managers. There isn't one of them that doesn't want to be on my show." She tossed her hair, knowing how silly she could be about herself—"Or in my bed. Trust me, I already have him in my pocket. What's his name?"

"I just don't know about this," D'Anton said. Things were getting complicated. He could no longer work out how any course of action impacted on any other. Where did this leave Barnaby's hopes? What would squirrelling the pair out of the country do to D'Anton's own plan of wrong-footing Strulovitch by promising to support his application for a gallery in return for the Solomon Joseph Solomon? Suddenly, everyone was looking the loser.

He wasn't sure either what removing the lovers from all society but their own would do to their feelings for one another. Plury was right: Gratan bored easily. And Beatrice, with no intrigue to distract her, and no father to fight, might discover that Gratan wasn't all that interesting a conversationalist. She might even tire of him erotico-aesthetically and decide that circumcision had much to recommend it after all. Leave aside the religious aspect, and D'Anton—a lover of beauty in all its forms—preferred the look of the foreskin gone to the look of foreskin intact. How it was that the Jews—a people with no instinct for beauty whatsoever—should have reached that conclusion all on their own, D'Anton couldn't understand. If anything he'd have expected them to go the other way— append a foreskin where nature had not intended one to be. Make ugly what had originally been lovely. He could only assume that somewhere in the course of their rejection of the ancient world they'd encountered a few pagan connoisseurs of male pulchritude. Whatever the explanation, it wouldn't surprise him if Beatrice before too long came around to his way of seeing. And then what?

One possibility was that Gratan would be persuaded by her pleas, Beatrice would be reconciled to her father, whereupon, all honour satisfied, a grand Jewish wedding would be held in Haddon Hall or Thornton Manor or even, given Strulovitch's labyrinthine contacts, Chatsworth.

For reasons he could not have put into words, such a prospect plunged D'Anton into the deepest gloom.

"I just don't know," he repeated.

At breakfast Shylock said, "I can't help noticing that you appear dishevelled and perturbed. I take it you have had no sleep and that your emotions are in disarray."

"You could just say I look like shit."

"I have seen you looking better. Can I be of assistance?"

"I am on a sea of indecision," Strulovitch said.

"Whether to return to port or steam ahead . . ."

"That's what a sea of indecision means."

"Which course would you prefer to take?"

"If I knew that I wouldn't be on a sea of indecision."

"Not necessarily. Your indecision might be to do with practicalities rather than preferences."

When are you leaving, Strulovitch wondered. Why did you come and when will you be going?

He didn't mean it. He remained awed by Shylock in his soul, and still sought his friendship as an idea, but in a day-to-day way, and especially given what was happening with Beatrice, he could find his linguistic exactingness, or was it his moral exactingness, or should he just call it his all-round Jewish exactingness, exacting . . .

"My indecision," he answered with a sigh, "is neither about preferences nor practicalities." He took a long time bringing out those words, as though their length were a severe trial

Howard Jacobson

to him. "It's about morality. My rights and entitlements as a Jewish father versus my daughter's rights and entitlements as—well, I don't know what as. Do I have a right to pursue Beatrice and drag her home? Does she have a right to go off where and with whom she chooses? Am I entitled to insist she has a Jewish husband, or at least the nearest to a Jewish husband I can manufacture for her? Would she be within her rights to get me certified? Are her new friends entitled to laugh at me? Would I be justified in paying their laughter back with interest, tenfold or a hundredfold, by fair means or foul? That too is a component of my indecision—what weapons to employ to make them suffer."

"The latter can't be called an issue of morality," Shylock said.

"You are being," Strulovitch answered, "peculiarly pedantic this morning. Have I offended you as well?"

"Not in the slightest. I just want to be certain we are talking about the same thing before I offer an intervention."

"If you are going to add to my indecision I ask you not to. My head aches."

"My intervention won't add to your indecision. On the contrary, I don't see how it can do anything but make you resolute."

"Resolute for what?"

"Recompense."

"On what grounds?"

Shylock hesitated only fractionally. "Violation. Gratan Howsome took advantage of your daughter when she was underage."

"My daughter is sixteen."

"She was fifteen when Howsome first slept with her. I believe that's against the law in your country."

Strulovitch suddenly found swallowing difficult. He spread his hands on the table as though to show there was nothing between his fingers. He seemed to want Shylock to do the same. "How do you know this?" he asked.

"I know what I know. It's late in the day for you to be questioning my modus operandi."

"It's not your modus operandi I question. It's your sources. You've just made a serious allegation. I have to know whether or not I can trust it. How do you come by your information?"

"That's not a question it profits you in any way to ask. Better you simply confirm what I have told you. Take a look on her computer. Check out her correspondence."

"You've been reading her emails?"

"I only suggest that you do. It might go against your morality but you have told me you have sneaked half a look already. Try sneaking a whole look."

"It goes against my morality."

"And what about your daughter being abroad with a man twice her age who slept with her when she was fifteen? How do you square that with your morality?"

Thou torturest me, Tubal.

What if Tubal lied?

Had Shylock ever considered that?

Your daughter spent in Genoa, as I heard, in one night four-score ducats . . .

You "heard," Tubal? You fucking *heard*!

On the strength of Tubal's "hearing"—mere hearsay— Shylock built a case against his daughter, and by extension every goy in Venice, that was bound to topple over into catastrophe. Even Othello took longer to be convinced.

Thou stick'st a dagger in me.

Was that Tubal's intention? To inflame his friend to the point of madness? It isn't necessary to find a motive. The inflaming of a friend is a motive in itself. The bigger question is why Shylock presented his chest with such alacrity to that dagger—with just so much alacrity as Antonio was to present his to Shylock's knife. When it came to a hunger to be gored, they were mirror images of each other—the merchant and the Jew.

As for whether Tubal spoke the truth—matters were too advanced for that ever to be tested.

But still Strulovitch, discomfited by Shylock's revelations, had to discomfit in return. A cruel vengefulness rose in his chest like bile.

"Did you ever consider that Tubal might have lied to you?"

Shylock was not slow to follow the logic of Strulovitch's challenge. "You think I might be guilty of reporting falsely to you? Haven't I said: go to her computer and corroborate what I tell you."

"Does that mean you wished you'd corroborated Tubal's reports?"

Shylock placed his elbows on the kitchen table and rested his chin on his fists. It looked painful, what he was doing, grinding his knuckles into his jaw. Or that might be what I want to think, Strulovitch thought. But he was not going to rush Shylock into speaking. His own silence was enough. Did you or didn't you?

"At the moment of his telling me, no," Shylock said, when at last it suited him to say something. His fists still supported his jaw, stopping him from speaking fluently. He seemed to want to find enunciation difficult. "Tubal told me what I dreaded, and what we dread we half want to come to pass.

But on reflection, yes. On reflection I sometimes ask if Tubal could have been party to the general mischief and if I lost my daughter by attending to him. I still hold myself potentially accountable for that. I exist in an equipoise of grief and guilt. But to what end should I have doubted him? My Jessica was gone. I didn't require a Tubal to tell me that. She had stolen what she alone knew where to find. So had I shaken Tubal to within an inch of his life what might I have rattled out of him that was more to my liking? That she'd gone through three-score ducats instead of four? Twoscore? Ten?"

"Such details matter. Was my daughter fifteen when Howsome slept with her or was she sixteen? Much hangs on the answer."

"Then go to her computer. I am just the messenger."

"Tubal would have said the same. But there are occasions when the messenger is no less odious than the message. Being 'just the messenger' doesn't make a man unimpeachable. What if Tubal was morally in connivance with the thing he was relaying?"

"And you would like me to have cut his heart out? Who's to say you aren't right. Perhaps I should have taken my knife to his chest instead of Antonio's. But messengers tell you how your repute stands, if nothing else. So they are always to be trusted in part. Jessica ran off. Where to and how much she spent when she was there is immaterial."

"And the monkey?"

"What about the monkey?"

"What if Tubal lied about that? What if he conjured the monkey out of his own Jewish terrors?"

"There was a monkey."

"What if he wished you harm?"

"Why would he do that?"

"Because Jews are kinds of devils, even to one another."

"There was a monkey."

An hour later Strulovitch was back at the breakfast table, his face flushed, his voice harsh. He looked as though he'd been drinking. But he'd only been at his daughter's computer.

"I'll kill him," he said.

Good, Shylock thought. Let's see if you have the courage. But what he said was, "First you have to find him."

Twenty

*O*y *gevalto,* we're on the Rialto," Beatrice said.
Gratan looked at her in bafflement. The air was
full of confused sounds—gondoliers singing, wait-
ers shouting, canals rising, church bells ringing, umbrellas
going up. "I didn't catch that," he said.

"*Oy gevalto,* we're on the Rialto."

He was none the wiser.

"It doesn't matter," Beatrice said.

She wasn't exactly disappointed. How many times had
she said that to herself in Gratan's company? But if she wasn't
exactly disappointed, what exactly had she been expecting?
Nothing—was that it? In which case what was she doing
here?

How many times had she asked herself *that* in Gratan's
company?

She'd been to Venice before, accompanying her father to
the Biennale, going from pavilion to pavilion listening to him
inveighing against installations, videos, whitened canvasses
or blackened rooms in which faceless women screamed in
agony or orgasm—all the stuff she liked. So she knew what

it was to be in Venice with an ill-tempered man, but she also knew what it was to be in Venice when the sun shone and the ill-tempered man was ill-tempered on aesthetic principle, rather than . . . Well, why *was* Gratan ill-tempered? Had she become a wife to him already? She sat under the dripping awning, watched water falling into water, and sighed deeply. Venice could do better than this, that was her point. And she'd spent enough time with Gratan to know that outside the environs of sex he couldn't do better than this. As for it being more fun to be with a Jewish man who got her jokes— she wasn't going to give her father the satisfaction of knowing she'd even entertained such a thought. But her expression would have given her away had he seen it.

"Anyone else won't know what you're talking about," he'd been warning her for years. "They won't get the cultural allusions. Just remember—your intelligence is five thousand years old, they were born yesterday. They can only think one thing at a time; you can think a dozen."

"I only want to fuck them," she'd answered back once.

He'd slapped her face.

So much for being truthful.

She'd wondered many times since why she hadn't called a policeman or taken him to the Court of Human Rights. You can't just hit your children because they use bad language.

Or had he hit her only because she wanted to fuck Christians?

Well, the lunatic had got his comeuppance now. The thing he'd most dreaded had come about. She was on the run, to all intents and purposes married (or would have been had he not been married already) to a Gentile who couldn't even think one thing at a time. And it had come about because he—her lunatic all-fearing father—made it come about.

If I could be sure this is where I want to be right now, and that I'm with a man I want to be with, I'd thank him, Beatrice thought. But she wasn't. Unhappiness didn't describe her state exactly. It was three days since Plury and D'Anton had bundled them on to a plane, and in that time Gratan had finally grasped that she didn't want him nipping off the minute they found themselves alone together. So she had his company, at least in the sense that *shomerim,* the Jewish sentinels of the dead, have the company of a corpse. And the rain was not without its consolations. It was almost fun—for her, at any rate—negotiating St. Mark's Square over duckboards and sitting in cafés catching rain in coffee cups. If this were any old break from the kind of man her father didn't want her to be with she'd have considered it only a moderate fiasco, and she'd had enough of those in her young life. But it wasn't any old break. They waited nervously for news. They kept their eyes open for police. Her father might have alerted Interpol. Gratan feared he might have breached his contract with Stockport County who, in his view, were looking for any excuse to terminate it. Already he was talking wildly about learning Italian (that was a joke: he had still to master the rudiments of English) and signing on for Venezia reserves. And there had been a disagreeable atmosphere at the airport where Plury and D'Anton had made it clear they were displeased—a change from Plury's initial excitement for them—and Gratan had told D'Anton he was not prepared, at his age, to be treated like a child, which D'Anton had answered by saying, "Then stop acting like one." So the risks had to be worth it—for both of them—didn't they? She had to conceal the fact that she'd been born five thousand years ago and he had to be the man she wanted to spend the next five thousand years with. He had to amuse and scintillate her. He had to take an interest in performance art and get her jokes. He had to make her knees shake when she looked at him. He had to make her feel proud of him when he opened his mouth. He had to look more of a mensch. And—?

And he didn't.

"*Oy vey*, why have I run away?" Beatrice wondered.

D'Anton rarely answers his own front door. It takes him too long to rearrange his face into something resembling civility. Nothing can be done in a hurry if you are a man of sorrows. Besides which, D'Anton doesn't welcome surprise. For this reason he has an assistant to answer the door for him, when necessary. In the Golden Triangle it is rare for people to call on one another without prior arrangement. It is unlikely that the person you want to see will be in, for one thing; and front doors are generally a long gravelly walk from where you will have parked the car. So it's easier all round to make phone calls and meet out. This is one reason why D'Anton has never installed an intercom system. It will almost never be used. The other reason he hasn't installed such a thing is that it's ugly. There is a plaited bell pull which, after much haggling, he'd been able to persuade the janitor of a monastery in Burma to sell him. But none of the infrequent visitors ever pull hard enough, and D'Anton is not going to put up a hideous notice telling them to do so.

Today, his assistant is off, nursing a sick relative in the country. They don't, in the Golden Triangle, call where they live the country, any more than they call it town. So when the mellifluous Burmese bell that never rings unexpectedly does so, D'Anton jumps with surprise and annoyance. He has to make the long trek down from his study in person, just as the monks had to come down from the mountain for afternoon prayers. It rings three more times before he has made it all the way. This person is impatient, D'Anton recognises. And rough-mannered. So not Barnaby or a Jehovah's Witness. Whoever it is that's pulling, pulls so hard that D'Anton fears the bell will be yanked from the wall. "Yes, yes," he shouts. "I am coming as fast as I can."

As fast he can, that is, in his Nepalese slippers with their Ali Baba points.

And when he unbolts and opens the door he finds Strulovitch.

The two men, who would rather not, in any circumstances, wish to be exchanging glances, direct their gazes over each other's shoulder. If D'Anton were a pirate with a parrot, Strulovitch would be addressing that. D'Anton himself is looking even further to the rear of his guest, as though at Strulovitch's grandparents in their headscarves and skullcaps, falling under the hooves of Cossacks' horses, muttering to their mouldy god while their hovels go up in flames . . . But enough of that, D'Anton tells himself.

Strulovitch, who is holding a sheet of headed paper which D'Anton at once recognises as his, is the first to speak.

"We can do it here or inside," he says.

"It?"

"Well if I tell you that, we are already doing it. You'd prefer it here then?"

"I am not frightened of you," D'Anton says.

Strulovitch smoothes the soft tips of his shirt collar. "I wouldn't expect you to be. We are both priestly men."

"A more priestly man would have made contact with me some other way before coming hammering at my door."

Strulovitch laughs. "Hammering? Is a bell pull not for

pulling? I could not have announced myself more peaceably. I twitched the rope as though plucking a loose thread from a tapestry."

"And so vandalising it . . . I see you have read my letter."

"What else would bring me here? You were hoping for a response. Well here I am."

"But you aren't carrying the picture."

"And you aren't handing me what I want in return for it."

"I can write you a cheque for it now."

"I don't want a cheque."

"So what do you want?"

"Not what, whom."

"I don't have your daughter, if she's what this is all about."

"You admit you know about my daughter. That saves us both time."

"I have met your daughter, yes. An unhappy girl."

"Is that for you to judge?"

"When she speaks to me of her unhappiness, I think it is."

"Why would she speak to you of her unhappiness? Who are you to her?"

"A friend of a friend. But you know that. You have seen us together."

"I saw you together on the night Beatrice ran away. Odd he should have been with you and not her that night. What is he to you, anyway?"

Strulovitch is pleased with himself for not answering his own question with the words "Rough trade?"

But D'Anton guesses what he's not saying. "I am not obliged to discuss the nature of my friendships with you," he says.

"And I am not obliged to let you have the picture you have asked for."

The last thing D'Anton wants is to have Strulovitch in his house, assessing him, looking over his treasures, picturing how he lives, but in his mind's eye he sees the unhappy Barnaby, already showing signs of petulant jealousy that D'Anton has spirited Gratan away to Venice with his floozie but has so far done nothing for him, not even in the matter of the lost ring that Plury is sure to be enquiring about any day now. In a tableau of the heart, D'Anton paints himself creeping up on Barnaby, lightly clapping his hands over his eyes, and leading him to a wall on which *Love's First Lesson* is hanging. *For you. For you to give to Plury, because I want you to be happy together. But of course the subtext of this gift is that it is from me to you.*

D'Anton loves being in receipt of gratitude, whatever its source. But gratitude from Barnaby is special.

"Come in then if you must," he tells Strulovitch.

There is no hall. They are already in a morning room every wall of which is hung from eye level to ceiling with miniature portraits. Watercolours on ivory, vellum and porcelain, oils on enamel or copper, snuffbox covers in filigree gold frames. I don't see any Kitaj or Kossoff, Strulovitch thinks, though his glance is of the briefest.

D'Anton doesn't offer Strulovitch a seat. "I am not able," he says, "to do business with you on the basis you suggest. I am not in a position to barter your daughter."

"Are you saying she is not here?"

"I wasn't saying that. But no she isn't. She never was here. I don't think she'd like it."

Strulovitch knows that D'Anton means to impugn his daughter's taste, but looking quickly around he knows he's right. "No," he says. "She wouldn't like it at all. But if she isn't here, where is she?"

"If I did know where she was why would I tell you?"

Strulovitch taps the letter which he still carries like a summons.

"You think I want the picture that badly?"

"Well someone does. Unless you were merely making merry with me."

"Yes, you are right—someone does."

"Gratan Howsome presumably. As a love token for my daughter. You can hardly expect me to hand it over lightly in those circumstances."

"If I tell you you are wrong, that it is for someone else entirely, will you name your price?"

Is this the moment, D'Anton wonders, to bring up my willingness to rethink my position on his gallery? He thinks it probably isn't.

"My price is still my daughter."

"Then it is too high. I cannot betray one friend to please another."

"You should not look on it as betraying a friend. You'd be assisting a father."

"A father can be as much a rogue as any man. Your daughter was made unhappy until she met Gratan. It would be wrong of me to intervene in this, even supposing I had the influence effectively to do so. And I would hardly be likely to encourage him to return to face your savage proposal."

"To 'return,' you say. So they have gone away."

"Your daughter is of an age morally to make her own decisions."

"Now she is," Strulovitch says.

"Meaning what?"

"Meaning that she wasn't when your friend began with her."

"I don't know what 'began with her' is supposed to mean."

"Then let me enlighten you. I have evidence that Gratan Howsome was sleeping with my daughter when she was fifteen. That this is a criminal offence I don't have to tell you. That others who knowingly connived in the offence could be prosecuted as accessories is something you might not have thought about, but I suggest you think about it now. One way or another, I want my daughter returned and your friend with her. How I proceed from there depends largely on your co-operation."

It is a matter of immense satisfaction to Strulovitch that D'Anton has to find himself a chair, though none looks suitable for sitting in.

"My guess," Plurabelle opined, "is that he's bluffing."

"It shouldn't be difficult to find out how old Beatrice was when Gratan . . ." D'Anton declined to finish. Some things, even when they concerned people he cared about, he preferred not to put his mind to.

"I don't mean bluffing about her age," Plury said impatiently. "I mean bluffing about what he's going to do."

"To Gratan?"

"To all of us."

"We can't be held responsible for what went on between them. How were we to know how old Beatrice was and what Gratan was getting up to with her?"

"I knew."

"You knew her age?"

"I never questioned her about her age. And probably wouldn't have done anything had I known. I had my first affair with a married man when I was twelve."

"Well then . . ."

"But I knew they were sleeping together. I gave them a room."

"That's not a crime."

"It is if I knew."

"You just said you didn't know."

"But what if I have to prove that? I don't want the police here, D'Anton. For any number of reasons. And neither, I would imagine, do you."

"Plury, I have nothing to hide."

"It was you, D'Anton, who brought her here. A Jewess to feed Gratan's appetite for Jewesses. You found the idea amusing. As did I."

"Amusing, but no more than that. I didn't imagine there was going to be a grand affair . . ."

"Just a squalid one—is that your point? I don't think that will help you. Especially when it's discovered that you found the girl at the academy where you lecture."

D'Anton winced at the word "lecture." "I have broken no academy rules. I didn't find her for my pleasure. I didn't 'find' her full stop. She was there. Hardly inconspicuous is she?"

"What's that got to do with the price of eggs? You end up in a court of law and no one cares what academy rules you did or didn't break, whose pleasure you procured the girl for, or how conspicuous she was."

"Procured!"

"Wake up, D'Anton! That's how it will look. Mud sticks. And the more salacious the accusation, the more people will want to believe it. You might think you are above this, but I don't think I am. What happens to my reputation, what happens to my show, what happens to the Belfry if I'm accused of running a bawdy house for paedophiles?"

"Oh, come on!"

"And what happens to your good name if you're accused of assisting me? They'll call us pimps, D'Anton. The country is in the mood for witch-hunts. The press tell them there's a pervert under every stone. They'll say we groomed underage girls here. Gratan will be finished. You'll be a hate figure on social media. And Barney will probably leave me."

"So what do you propose?"

"That we tell Gratan he must come back. He listens to you. Order him to return."

"And do what?"

"Man up."

"And what if what he has to man up to is three years in Strangeways? Why would anyone come back for that?"

"To help us, for one thing. To repay my kindness and whatever it is he owes you. Because he's the one who got us into this. And if he does return, then maybe the monster won't prosecute."

"You think he'll forgive and forget? He's not a forgiving and forgetting man, Plury."

Plury thought about it. She had been looking wild-eyed throughout this conversation, her eyes and lips more swollen than ever; now she resembled a figure from ancient tragedy and comedy combined, distraught and disfigured. She took D'Anton by his sleeve. "If Gratan gives him what he wants and agrees to his demands, he might."

"What are you saying?"

She made a distracted scissor movement with the index and middle fingers of both hands. Had she seen Shylock doing the same thing she couldn't have copied it any better. "Snip, snip!" she said.

Twenty-One

Gratan's response to D'Anton's text telling him to come home and face the music was immediate and terse. "No fucking chance," he wrote.

D'Anton texted back to say that was no way to talk to a man who'd always had his best interests at heart.

Gratan responded by saying that a friendship could only be tested so far.

D'Anton texted again to ask what Beatrice thought about returning.

Gratan responded in a similar vein to his earlier message. "Haven't fucking asked her."

D'Anton texted to ask why not.

"Sick to death of her," was Gratan's reply.

"Any particular reason?" D'Anton wondered.

"She keeps talking to me in some foreign language."

"What foreign language?"

"How would I know? It's foreign. Jew, I think."

"Then couldn't you at least see your way clear to sending her home?"

"No wucking fay," Gratan replied. "The sex is too good. It's the only time she shuts the fuck up."

D'Anton took that as a no, then, to any possibility that Gratan would countenance circumcision into the Jewish faith.

"Now what?" Plury wanted to know.

She was out with D'Anton and Barney at a bar in Manchester. They didn't want to be heard discussing any of this in the Golden Triangle. Where they were drinking nobody would understand the word "circumcision."

"We dare the Jew to do his worst," D'Anton said.

"I don't think that's going to work," Barnaby put in—an intervention that surprised him as well as his companions. Normally when there were councils of war he left Plury and D'Anton to do the talking. His role, at such times, was to make them feel better simply by virtue of his pleasing presence. But on this occasion his good name was at stake as well as theirs. If the Belfry was a brothel, what was he? The idea of Gratan getting away with something, no matter that he only dimly grasped the full extent of the offence, didn't please him much either. Gratan does something wrong and gets to stay in Venice for his pains, and he, Barnaby, does nothing wrong and has to put up with all this tetchiness and tension in Cheshire.

He was feeling badly let down by D'Anton in other ways too.

"So when's this ring I gave you coming back?" Plury had asked the moment they sat down to their drinks. "You swore to me you'd wear it till the hour of your death, and it's been off your finger for a week."

Barnaby had stared penetratingly at D'Anton. They'd re-hearsed this, hadn't they? D'Anton was meant to look at his own left hand where, after getting the ring polished by "his man," he'd worn it for safety, only to discover with magnifi-cently feigned horror that it had gone, goodness knows how, fallen off and rolled into a gutter or under the wheels of a bus, he could only suppose because his fingers were narrower than Barney's. "I would rather cut my left hand off than be responsible for this," he was to say, whereupon, amid prom-ises of restitution, profuse apologies, tears from Barnaby and the like, Plury would embrace them both and tell them that flesh-and-blood love such as they enjoyed, and she hoped al-ways would enjoy, far surpassed a trinket. But D'Anton, in his Gratan-centred distraction, forgot his lines, gazed into space, and with utterly uncharacteristic impatience snapped at Bar-ney for consuming his time and glared at Plury for making a fuss.

"I will deal with you," Plury said to Barney, "later."

(More than ever he needed that picture.)

D'Anton she glared at in return.

Are we in competition over this ring, she asked herself, and didn't much like the answer that came back.

Thus their exquisite world of mutuality and consider-ation, so often troubled but then redeemed by sadness, had begun to buckle under the pressure of short temper. Hence Barnaby—by any interpretation of events their only innocent victim—speaking what was on his mind.

"As I see it," he went on, "the Jew will not back down. I've never heard of a Jew who will. They believe they lose face if they relent. It's against their religion. My father who met many Jews told me the same thing. They have hearts of stone. Try standing on a beach and ordering the tide to go back—that's what it's like persuading a Jew to change his mind. So if Gratan himself won't return to face the music we have no choice but to find a proxy Gratan to satisfy the Jew's bloodlust."

Surprised by how much Barney knew about Jews and their beliefs, Plury was nonetheless perplexed by his reasoning. "A poxy Gratan I can understand, Barney," she said, "but what's a *proxy* Gratan when he's at home?"

I'm getting pretty tired of both these men, she thought. In fact she thought she was getting pretty tired of men altogether. Maybe she should have been the one who ran away with Beatrice.

"A substitute of some sort," Barney said.

"A substitute for what?" D'Anton asked.

"For Gratan. A substitute for Gratan in the eyes of the Jew."

"You'll have to explain that," Plury said. "Take it more slowly."

Barnaby didn't see how he could go any slower or be any clearer. "Someone who will stand in for Gratan. A scapegoat, is that the word? An understudy. Someone the Jew can do the equivalent to."

"Someone else he can circumcise, do you mean?" D'Anton wasn't sure whether it was he or Plury who asked that. Neither was Plury, so synchronised were they in consternation.

"Yes," said Barnaby. "That's what he wants isn't it."

"Darling," said Plury, "he isn't looking for any old person to circumcise for the fun of it. The point of circumcising Gratan is to get a Jewish husband for Beatrice."

"Or to scare him off altogether," D'Anton put in.

"I know that. I'm not the fool you take me for. But now, whatever Beatrice decides to do, it's a question of honour, isn't it? It isn't the flesh he wants—who'd want that, especially from Gratan?—it's the principle. He won't care how he gets it or who he gets it from. Jews aren't particular who pays what they believe they're owed. Give him what he wants and I'd like to bet we won't hear any more from him. And since we can't give him Gratan . . . we have to give him someone else."

A quiet descended on the party. Even the bar seemed to fall silent.

"But there's no point my offering, though I would do anything for you," Barnaby went on. "I faint at the very thought of blood."

"And since I am disqualified by gender . . ." Plury began.

"That leaves just me," D'Anton said.

You should sit in the dark more, D'Anton would tell the students who came to hear him think aloud. Not quite lectures, they were not quite classes either. He wanted more distance between him and his students than the word "class" implied. It isn't good for you, he would go on, to live in so over-illuminated a world. If I say you spend too many hours looking into screens I don't want you to mistake me for a moralist or a Luddite. My only concern is for your aesthetic welfare. Light is to be cherished, in the way great painters like Leonardo and Caravaggio cherished it, as an illumination of meaning, as a way of distinguishing between the mundane darkness of things and the glow that can come with understanding and discrimination. You lose a sense of beauty and volume if everything is light.

Did any of them listen?

Well one student, he remembered, did. "In your discussion of chiaroscuro you haven't mentioned Rembrandt," she put up her hand to say. "Wouldn't you agree that for Rembrandt, perhaps more than for any painter, light was a form of psychological insight?"

That student was Beatrice. He saw her clearly now, in shadowy retrospect, her golden bangles dancing about her wrists as though she'd raised an arm to shake a tambourine, her own innate darkness illuminated as though by the psycho logical insight—call it the operation of conscience—he was bringing to bear upon himself. Was that the moment when he lit upon her as a plaything for Gratan? Was she Susanna in Rembrandt's great painting, and he the more forward of the Elders? Such a scene answered to no prurience he recognised in himself, but he must have gone so far as to imagine how she might stimulate prurience in another man—otherwise why did he choose her? So didn't that make him a partner or co-conspirator—a pimp, Plury had called him—in titillation?

How many times was that in recent days that he'd sunk a line into his soul and drawn up the word "procurer"?

He sat in the dark—the dark he emitted as a man of sorrows, and the more mundane dark he controlled with the flick of a switch—and pondered.

He would have liked his eyelids to have been of thicker, more opaque tissue. He had read that only the prepuce and the labia minora were thinner-skinned than eyelids, but as light didn't come to him through those he found no consolation in the knowledge.

The light that did come to him, no matter what he did to shut it out, was violet, the colour of amethyst. This was the reason he rarely bought a paperweight or miniature that had amethyst in it: he found the stone too rich and the light it gave off too searing. Amethyst was the colour of his neurasthenia, the colour of what offended his taste, the colour of his antipathies. Strulovitch was one of those antipathies, though he'd have been hard-pressed to say whether, in this instance, the antipathy or the amethyst came first. Was Strulovitch amethystine in person? Was there something of the mineral's violet hardness in the sheen of his skin? Was it his voice that shattered with too much light D'Anton's attenuated nerves? He could more easily have explained why he hated Strulovitch morally. He hated the fact that Strulovitch bought and sold art, no matter that he bought and sold art himself. His own buying and selling had love at their centre; he traded because he loved the thing he traded in. Whereas Strulovitch, by his estimation, loved art incidentally, that's if he loved it at all, the ecstasy of it, for him, residing in the final balance sheet of beauty. This D'Anton knew, not from anything Strulovitch said, and not from anything he observed or heard about his practices as a connoisseur and buyer. He knew it because Strulovitch was not refined as he, D'Anton, was refined. To be alive didn't pain him as it pained D'Anton. He lacked excruciation. Beauty didn't run through him. If beauty perished from the world, would Strulovitch act any differently? D'Anton could not conceive existence other than as an exquisite torment of the feelings. If there were suddenly to be no beauty in the world he would feel it into being. But Strulovitch? No, Strulovitch wouldn't notice. He was too consumed by the materiality of things. And what was material was, to D'Anton, the colour of amethyst.

Beatrice too. A magenta spray of hair, her glance a gleam of mulberries, words like plums in syrup.

Was this what Gratan loved—the rich, pulsing presentness of the girl. Her insolent palpability?

Must have been.

So how did he know so well what Gratan loved?

D'Anton was a connoisseur of small things—miniature

portraits, teardrop paperweights, pricks of conscience. Though abstemious by temperament he was acquisitive, as only the vain can be acquisitive, of elegant self-torment. He punished himself mentally for having too much money; for being well educated; for having exquisite taste; for being multifariously gifted. People came to him for assistance and he didn't always give all they looked to him to give. Alternatively, he gave too much. In the amethyst dark of his fractious egotism he counted off his failings, of which one was perhaps the mirror image of all the others—too great a collusion in the afflictions of those he loved. Was Gratan's weakness for Jewesses an affliction? Well he'd fed it, however it was to be described. Fanned it. Stoked it. But what if he'd been fanning some comparable affliction in himself? Did he too, behind the purple veins of his eyelids, nurse a weakness for the colouration of Jews? Was Strulovitch not so much an antipathy as a corrupt esteem?

"Desire" was a word he wouldn't use. So far and no further. And "esteem" was far enough. But if there were some lurking, unholy, unacknowledged esteem, then he had done poor Gratan a great disservice, led him on to go where D'Anton himself wanted but did not have the courage to go. I owe the boy some recompense, he thought, with a shudder of that excruciation of which he believed Strulovitch to be incapable.

He had loved reading the lives of the Christian martyrs at school and tore out many illustrations to pin on his bedroom walls. One of his favourites was St. Lawrence who was roasted on a gridiron. D'Anton could, without difficulty, conjure up Tintoretto's famous painting of Lawrence's martyrdom, the light illuminating his suffering as cruel figures poked at him, prodding at his agony, from the darkness. There was a legend that St. Lawrence had ordered his tormentors, if they were going to cook him, at least to cook him properly. "Turn me over," he told them. "I'm well enough done on this side."

D'Anton had a taste for torment. Did that mean he also had a taste for his tormentors?

"Turn me over," he imagined begging Strulovitch.

"Are you really prepared to do this for us?" Plurabelle asked.

D'Anton closed his eyes. Sometimes there was no need for words.

"You are a saint," Plurabelle told him.

He shook his head, still without opening his eyes.

Sitting together in the little parlour that bore more the impress of his taste than hers—she had none, was his private view—they found a form of words they hoped would pacify the fiend who threatened the continuance of their idyll.

Plurabelle wondered whether these words should be witnessed by a Justice of the Peace. D'Anton thought not. A note on his paper would, he believed, suffice. Strulovitch, of all people, would surely know him as a man whose stern probity was beyond question.

"*I hereby pledge requital for your grievance,*" he wrote. "*Let my person stand as surety for Gratan's return within a fortnight.*" (Plury had wanted a week, D'Anton a month. A fortnight was their compromise.) "*If he is not back to face his punishment by then, take from me what you would take from him. I ask for no alleviation of his offence save this, and trust it will be the end of the matter.*"

And he signed it with that flourish of which Strulovitch had already seen an example.

He wished he could have included *Love First's Lesson* in the deal—*I ask for no alleviation but would appreciate your throwing in Mr. Solomon*—but it was important Plury remained in ignorance of any of that.

D'Anton sighed. How weary he had grown of these entanglements in the love affairs of others. How he wished he had never introduced anyone to anyone. How high the price of friendship had become.

"You really are a saint," Plury repeated when he showed her what he'd written. "Though no saint I was ever told about at school had your gift for language."

Some mole of probity in his nature—or maybe it was simply impatience—compelled him to shake off her praise. "If you knew more," he said, "you wouldn't say that of me."

Plury looked intrigued. "Tell me," she said.

He looked deep into her troubled eyes. "Can I count on your absolute confidence?" he asked.

"I swear," she said, "upon our friendship. I swear on the sacred melancholy that binds us."

"Not a word to another soul, your promise. Not even to Barney."

"Not a syllable even to him."

Whereupon he drew her to him, much as a lover might, and whispered words of wildness in her ear.

Anyone close to Plury would have marvelled at what she did then. She threw back her head and roared with laughter. It could have been enough to cure her of her sadness for ever.

"I can't wait," she said, between gasps of unaccustomed merriment, "to see the bloodsucker's face."

"The Jew's you mean?"

"The Hebrew's, yes,"

"You must be referring to the Israelite."

"The Christ-Killer, yes. The crooked-nose . . ."

"Plury, stop that!" D'Anton laughed.

There had not been so much mirth heard in Plury's Utopia for many a month.

Because she wanted to be certain the pledge would be received, because she knew herself to be no less culpable than D'Anton, because she wanted to see the devil with her own eyes, and because she was devising a little something extra of her own, Plurabelle delivered D'Anton's note in person, driving the short distance to Strulovitch's house—she was surprised to discover they were such near neighbours—in her housekeeper's Vauxhall. She couldn't have explained to herself her decision not to take the Porsche or even the Volkswagen Beetle, but she was miffed to discover a Mercedes in the drive.

She shuddered when Strulovitch himself opened the door to her. The hand with which he took what she handed him all but froze hers. This was a further surprise. She had come prepared to face the fires of hell. In her mind's eye Strulovitch was a man with the complexion of a devil and a scaly hand. What she hadn't expected was this icy blast. No wonder poor Beatrice had fled. I was right to have taken her in and warmed her through, she thought, and I am right to assist her now. God help us all.

But she was wrong about one thing. The person to whom she handed D'Anton's sainted offer was not Strulovitch.

It was Shylock.

Twenty-Two

Although he was used to her being away—at the academy in the day and the Devil knew where else at night—Strulovitch had begun to miss Beatrice. Yes, they fought the minute they found themselves together, but fighting was an expression of love, wasn't it? If truth be told, he couldn't remember a time when they hadn't fought, but since Kay's stroke the warfare which was another name for love had intensified. So he had to put a delicate question to himself: had she become a sort of wife to him?

He must have answered that affirmatively, because from the moment Beatrice decamped he had begun to spend more time with Kay. Loneliness, was it? Or guilt? He thought both. But then it was a habit of his mind to think both. Hence his being an on-again off-again Jew. Being a Jew was everything to him, except when it wasn't. Which is a debilitating characteristic of the Jewish mind; unless it is a strength. As far as Kay went, he felt every feeling it was possible to feel, while sometimes thinking he felt nothing. There was an advantage in feeling nothing; it enabled him to get on with his life and help Beatrice get on with hers. But if he'd failed with

Beatrice then he'd failed half the opportunities that feeling nothing for Kay had given him. It behoved him, therefore— since it looked as though he *had* failed with Beatrice—to return to Kay a proportion of what was owing to her.

After calling on D'Anton and delivering his ultimatum, he returned home and went immediately to sit with her. He acted as though she must have been waiting impatiently to hear what had transpired. He sighed deeply and breathed out. As though to say, Just give me a moment to catch my breath. "Well we'll have to wait and see what that yields," he declared at last.

Though there was concern about her chest, her windows were open in all weathers. If one of her carers closed them, she was able to convey to another that she wanted them open. After he'd delivered her his news, Strulovitch sat in silence and watched the curtains flutter as though they were the only things of living interest in the room. He held her hand absently and was surprised to feel the gentlest squeeze from her fingers. He turned his attention from the window to look at her. Had she understood him? Did she register his anxiety? Did she know Beatrice was missing?

"Are you all right, my dearest love?" he asked, and strangely it was his own words, not any movement she had made or any expression in her dead eyes, that caused his tears to flow. Was he weeping for himself?

He had shut his senses down, sealed his entire apparatus of memory and affection off from her, otherwise he would not have been able to function, and where was the point in both of them being as Kay was? Had he allowed himself to remember what he'd loved in her he'd have come into her room each morning, wrapped his arms around her legs, and sobbed until nightfall. You remember and you die; if you want to live, you forget.

But he had called her "my dearest love" and for a moment she was his dearest love again and he could even dare to persuade himself that he was hers.

And if he was—if somewhere locked away in there a memory of what she'd felt for him stirred as faintly as her sun-yellow curtains—was it to be welcomed? Was it of the slightest earthly use to her for such a buried remembrance to be disturbed? Or would she too have wept for the sadness of it had she been able?

He held her hand more firmly. He had no right to take such a risk with her feelings but he took it nonetheless. "You look pretty today, beloved," he said, and kissed her brow.

No response now from her fingers. If she had felt what he'd felt she'd dealt with it, shut herself down again because that was the only way any of it could be borne.

"Yes," he said. "We'll wait and see what my visit yields."

He continued to sit with his head down, letting the cold air graze his cheeks. He owed the woman whose dead hand he held in his some recompense. She'd given him a few years of happiness. She'd given him a daughter. She'd helped seal the rift between him and his father and in that and many other ways she'd improved his relations with his mother too. More people to whom he owed recompense. Over a year had gone by now since his mother died and what had he done to honour her memory? He'd allowed the plan to open a gallery in his parents' names to lapse. He'd put up little or no fight against D'Anton. He was a defeatist—an on-again off-again everything, son, father, husband, defender of the faith. In tearing at himself, his soul hardened against D'Anton.

Was there more soul-hardness to feel against D'Anton than he already felt? A soul can always harden more.

D'Anton: the Jew-hater who had stolen his daughter, interfered in the expression of his love for his parents, and bore responsibility—by implication, by association, by retrospective malice, by the simple fact of his sort existing—for the wreckage that was his wife.

"If I could kill him I would kill him," he told her.

He thought he saw alarm in her eyes. He imagined that she shook her head. *Don't, Strulo!*

If only.

"Then if you don't think I should, I won't," he said.

The idea that D'Anton owed his life to Kay only made Strulovitch more murderous towards him in his heart.

The note, when Shylock handed it over, disgusted him. How did D'Anton manage to beg and yet not beg? By what power was he able to turn a grovel into an insult?

"If I could destroy him I'd destroy him," he told Shylock. "But at least this way I will spill blood."

Shylock shook his head. "I'd proceed carefully," was his advice. "What D'Anton proposes neither brings back your daughter nor requites the footballer the wrongs he has done her."

"What about the wrongs they have done me?"

Shylock looked away. It was as though he wanted to spare Strulovitch the fires burning in his eyes. "I fear you are putting yourself at the forefront of this," he said. "It strikes me that you are allowing it to get too personal."

"Too personal? What's *too* personal?"

"Killing D'Anton is too personal."

"Too personal for D'Anton maybe. Not for me."

"But your argument is with the footballer."

"That clown? For him I feel only a minor contempt."

"Despite his violation of your daughter?"

"I know Beatrice. She is more than capable of leading a man on. And if he were to argue in a court of law that she struck him as ten years older than she was he'd as likely as not be believed."

"I commend your forbearance. But why then your insistence on his return? If you can allow what happened a year ago, when it was illegal, why can't you allow it now when the law has nothing to say against it?"

"She is still a child."

"In fact, though hardly in appearance. Or in assurance come to that."

"And he is still a Gentile. Didn't you say of Jessica that you would rather any of the stock of Barabbas had been her husband than a Christian?"

"You take me out of context. Those Christian husbands were falling over one another to shed their wives, so they could rescue Antonio from my clutches. A father wants his daughter to marry a man who values her above his friends. It was more the loyalty they swore to one another than the icons they prayed to in church that rendered them undesirable. And anyway . . ."

"Anyway what?"

"Though I can no more reasonably regret than I can look forward, I do from time to time wonder whether I'd have been better advised to let her marry a Christian than lose her altogether."

"That's for you to ponder. As things stand with me, I neither have a daughter nor approve her choice of husband."

"That could change if you signalled that you had changed."

"If I welcomed them back with open arms, you say?"

"You needn't throw wide your arms. A handshake would do as well."

"And what would that handshake denote? That he's forgiven? That I love him? That he may keep his foreskin?"

"It may have to be you who forgoes the foreskin."

"You will deny me my merry jest?"

"I don't deny you anything. The man presently cohabiting with your daughter denies you. Your daughter denies you. The opinion of the world denies you."

"You forget D'Anton's offer."

"But how would circumcising D'Anton serve your purpose?"

"It would serve my jest."

"Only in a spirit that would negate the jest."

"Look into your own heart and you will know mine. I too have a black humour. My first wife told me that. My second wife has found a way of telling me something similar."

"There is neither purpose nor profit in circumcising D'Anton."

"It might not come to that. The threat of it might result in his returning me Gratan."

"And if he doesn't?"

"Then I will have my satisfaction."

"This is exactly what they expect you to do."

"Then I will give them what they expect and be gleeful in the doing of it. Their expectation won't take from my gratification."

"I repeat, you are allowing this to grow too personal."

"Must I be denied my satisfaction?"

"If satisfaction is all it is. Yes."

"Then I will change the word. Must I be denied my bond?"

Well that didn't work out too badly, Shylock thought.

"If it were done when 'tis done then 'twere well it were done at my place," Plurabelle had told Shylock.

She had rehearsed several times in front of the mirror before leaving home, knowing Strulovitch to be a fiery Shakespearean and hoping by this means to soften him into agreement and maybe even admiration. By the time she came to deliver the words she had realised it wasn't Strulovitch who had opened the door to her, but she wasn't going to waste them. Who exactly it was she was talking to she didn't know, but his austere and belligerent demeanour declared him to be a person authorised to deal with whatever arose, a man privy to Strulovitch's affairs, a lawyer, perhaps, given his dress, retained to advise on the very business that brought her here.

"Hasn't too much already been done at your place?" Shylock had answered.

Yes, a lawyer fully conversant with the matter on which she'd called. Plurabelle had been in better spirits over the last hours than she had been for days, but a cold chill seized her now. If Strulovitch had employed and briefed a lawyer then the legal process to implicate her in scandal and turn her Utopian dream into a nightmare had begun in earnest.

Plurabelle had not spent a fortune plumping up her lips for nothing. She threw Shylock her most ravenous Venus flytrap smile. A beast in the courtroom he might be, but let him beware a flesh-eating beauty like her.

So much for Plury on the outside. Inside all was tumult.

Two ambitions fought within her breast. A) To keep all

this as confidential as possible. B) To seek as much publicity as the disputants themselves would allow her. Though a deeply private person, Plurabelle was also a deeply public one. I have never lost by being indiscreet, she thought. I have always been applauded for my candour and sympathised with for my pain. On the side of confidentiality was the truism least said, soonest mended. On the side of publicity was the shaming of Strulovitch. How that was to be effected she wasn't as yet entirely sure, but she was confident he would show up badly in any public confrontation and in the process discredit his own testimony. Who could blame Beatrice, or those who encouraged her, if she fled from such a father and sought affection in the arms of a man not ideal in every respect, it was true, but at least a man who loved her. Whether the other piece of information to which she was privy would discredit Strulovitch still further or simply make him look a fool she couldn't say, but she anticipated either outcome with eagerness.

And D'Anton? Which side of the confidentiality/ publicity debate was he on? She hadn't canvassed his opinion. He didn't know himself, she believed. Had she asked he would have said the quieter they kept this the better, but once she presented him with the fait accompli of Strulovitch abased, she didn't doubt he would be pleased with her. Sometimes you know a person's interest better than he knows his own.

Meantime, unmoved by her labial allure, this grave, legal figure stood between her and the effectuation of her plan.

"I hope I am not misunderstood," she said. "My offer to make amends is not to be taken as any sort of admission of guilt. I befriended the girl. She was obviously unhappy at home. I had no idea that she had formed an unsuitable relationship under my roof. I would never have allowed it had I known. My close companion and advisor D'Anton feels the same, hence his brave acceptance of your client's demands."

"I'm an acquaintance of Mr. Strulovitch," Shylock said. "I do not represent him or work for him."

"Might I speak to him in person in that case."

"He isn't here. You can speak to me. He thinks of me as his conscience."

Plurabelle knew not to say "Conscience! Are you telling me that man has a conscience?" Instead, she said, "Then you will gather that what he asks for is extreme. Nothing less than bodily and emotional injury to my dear friend D'Anton. It would appear to be a public humiliation he seeks, which is why, in order to satisfy that strange craving, I'm prepared—should it come to this—to host the event in my gardens."

"The event?"

"It is Mr. Strulovitch himself, I gather, who would rather the course of action he proposes to take did not go unnoticed. Were he prepared to debate the rights and wrongs of what he asks with the person of whom he asks it, I'd be prepared to film that debate for my television show—"

"You have a television show?"

Plurabelle was dismayed. She didn't think anyone was unaware of her television show. If this man did not know of it, it only showed how remote and eminent he was. "*The Kitchen Counsellor,*" she said.

"It's a cookery programme?"

"Yes, but not only that—"

Shylock put up a hand to stop her telling him what else it was. "Mr. Strulovitch, to my certain knowledge, doesn't think of himself as being party to a debate, doesn't recognise an answering grievance to his own, and is therefore unlikely to be tempted to discuss the matter on a television programme of the sort you describe. I'm surprised you think your friend would be a willing party to it either. Circumcision is not a culinary happening."

A thought occurred to Plurabelle. Bicker. Her old interactive Webchat site was now defunct but she felt confident it could be reactivated, via one or other of the social media with which she enjoyed professional relations. Might this, she wondered, giving Shylock a brief rundown, appeal to Mr. Strulovitch more?

"What I can with some confidence say would not appeal to Mr. Strulovitch," Shylock assured her, "is the suggestion that the redress he seeks amounts to bickering."

"I see that," Plurabelle said quickly. "I don't mean to minimise this. Quite the opposite. Hence my offer to make an occasion of it."

"Are you planning a jamboree?"

"Should it come to it, should Gratan not return with Beatrice, as we all of course fervently hope he will, then yes, I will do as much or as little as Mr. Strulovitch sees fit. I only want it to be pleasant for everyone. If Mr. Strulovitch has an objection to my home and would rather not enter it—"

"Why would he rather not enter it?"

Plurabelle looked momentarily nonplussed. "Oh you know . . ."

"Because it has been the scene of debauchery?"

"You libel me," Plurabelle said.

"Then you have nothing to fear."

"I *have* nothing to fear."

"You are going to great lengths to bring this matter to a conclusion in that case. I'd say your celerity speaks guilt. But go on with what you were saying. If Mr. Strulovitch would rather not enter your house . . ."

"I will arrange for a marquee to be put up in the garden."

"What makes you think he draws a distinction between your house and your garden?"

"I don't know what he draws. I wish only to be accommodating."

"Will there be canapés?"

"If canapés are what he would like."

"I am still trying to understand why you would go to this trouble to publicise what you yourself have called the humiliation of your friend."

"Because," she said, "I want to show how deeply sorry I am."

"Your spirits," Shylock said, looking away from her, "shine through you."

Plurabelle, who knew a compliment when she heard one, ruffled her lips. This lawyer friend of Strulovitch's had a stern charm, she thought, though she doubted that anyone but her would see it. Not charm of the D'Anton or Barney sort—he was another species of man entirely, icily distant and repellent if the truth be told, insulting and contemptuous even—but then she had had her fill of approachably attractive men, princely suitors who lined up to second-guess her desires and otherwise be pleasing to her. With this man it would be she who would have to do the guessing. Not that she was thinking of him erotically. He was too old for her. But looking on him as a father—and she had never been much impressed with the father nature had given her—yes, she could imagine being an unlessoned girl again, trying for his love.

"Do you have children of your own?" she asked him.

TWENTY-THREE

Strulovitch had a dream. Jessica and Beatrice, both aged about nine, frolicking in a plastic paddling pool in his garden, splashing water on each other, the sun illuminating their young bodies, not yet sirens, but tadpole girls looking to win the attention of no one, not even their fathers stretched out in deckchairs drinking icy beers. Was there ever such a time of innocence? Yes, in Strulovitch's dream there was.

Kay was watering the garden with a hose that writhed, on account of the tap being turned full on, like a snake. Leah, standing by her, laughed her long Venetian's laugh. Strulovitch, not innocent himself, desired them both. Two Jewish wives, two Jewish daughters—no wonder his mother and father playing gin rummy in the shade were pleased with him.

Shylock was asleep. This was Strulovitch's dream, so Strulovitch could do with Shylock what he chose, and what he chose was to render him unconscious. So was Shylock dreaming too? Two Jewish daughters, two Jewish wives?

Tears flooded ancient Strulovitch's dream. Molten tears, the colour of gold.

For whom?

It's hard to tell in dreams.

"What news from the Rialto?" D'Anton asks his PA.

The answer never varies. "None."

The colour rises in D'Anton's cheeks.

Strulovitch asks the same of his. And receives the same answer.

There has been no colour in Strulovitch's cheeks for several days.

Left to his own devices, Shylock wandered the house, looking at Strulovitch's paintings. He had grown up in a beautiful city but had felt himself excluded from its splendours. Much of the art was housed in churches—indeed much of the art *was* the churches—and those were not for him to admire. If something he saw out of the corner of his eye struck him as lovely he kept it to himself. He didn't even mention it to Leah. He wasn't going to be caught appearing to covet what was not his.

Even here, unwatched in Strulovitch's house, he felt self-conscious about looking. It compromised his fierce mistrust to be an appreciator. If he were to love what men had made he would next have to love what men were.

So it was with reluctance that he picked out this and that on Strulovitch's walls. A small Mark Gertler nude, roseate and pert, a Christian body offered to a Jew's curiosity, but kept just beyond his grasp. Some Bomberg charcoal sketches of war-damaged English churches. A couple of early Lucian Freuds which must still have been worth a pretty penny, cruel-eyed and unforgiving, but showing no Jewish sensibility to Shylock's sense, the painter, if anything, hobnobbing

Freudianly with the English. If these were Jewish painters they were at pains to please Gentile critics.

More to his taste was a trio of densely worked portraits by Frank Auerbach which rendered, in a way that made him marvel, what it is to be inside the knotted matrix of a head, or at least, he thought grimly, clenching his teeth, what it is to be inside mine.

He couldn't decide what to make of Strulovitch's collection—not just the individual works but the fact of Strulovitch's wanting to own them. By religion as well as forced habit he was a word man. Sensual representation worried him. God had spoken the world into existence—"Let it be"—he had not painted it. Had God been a painter the world would have been other than it is. Better or worse? Well, less disputatious and declamatory, which might not have suited Shylock. Would he have known himself in a painted world? He thought in words, argued in words, stood his ground in words. On the other hand he had loved Leah from the moment he set eyes on her, loved the fleshliness of her, loved the atmosphere of her, loved her sleeping no less than waking, loved the silent being of her. When she died their relationship dwindled into talk—*dwindled* not because the talk was trivial but because talk now became all there was, an unending conversation he could not survive without, but still he misses her beyond bearing, so what he's lost cannot be her words but the look and smell and feel of her. It is a sacrilege to her to call himself a man of words only.

And it is a sacrilege to him, too, a sacrilege promoted assiduously by the Gentiles. The Jews were a people without sensuous appreciation, they insisted. What they saw they saw second-hand, through the eyes of others. Their natural medium was the law and the law enshrined itself in words. So by words were they made intransigent and cruel. And blind. That was the libel. And Jews—remarkably for an obstinate people (another libel)—acquiesced in it. Yes, you are right, they had told the Gentiles, we are bound by the cold formality of the word and leave all that's lovely in life to you. We think, and leave you to see. We judge, and leave you to enjoy. Lies, all of it. The word that created the world also created its physical delights. Let there be sea, let there be sky, let there be light, let there be beauty.

The God of the Jews, too, had not made enough of his sensuous side, not wanting to be confused with pagan idols.

Strulovitch, at least in his collecting, had refused the example of the over-particular Jewish God and refuted the libels of the Gentiles.

Shylock wandered between the paintings again, taking his time, noticing a group of portraits by Emmanuel Levy he had missed before, all of anxious and watchful-looking women, painted in a soft and melancholy manner, sensuous without being voluptuous, expressing a sort of love, he thought, whatever the painter's actual relations to them. And two more, equally fond but if anything more fraught, by Bernard Meninsky. Many of the paintings in Strulovitch's collection, he began to notice, expressed this keen, compassionate apprehension of the strain of being a woman. Jewish women were they? Burdened with loving Jewish men? He didn't know, but under their influence he began to relax his initial hostility, liking everything he saw more, this time round, for Leah's fleshly sake. It was as though he were using faculties he hadn't known he possessed. If he'd bought Jessica paintings for her room—what then? Could he have kept her by beautifying her surroundings?

Yet why, in that case, hadn't it worked for Strulovitch?

Here was beauty everywhere you looked, but where was Beatrice?

He thought he knew the answer: Strulovitch refused the libel with one part of his mind but accepted it with another. He hung what was forgetfully sensual on his walls and still went on being a man of words, arguing with everyone around him. The art he bought, he bought in order to gain entrance to a world which in his heart he didn't think by right was his. But he was wrong. He should look at what he owned more, Shylock thought. More often, more intensely, and with more pride. He should drink it in. Revel in it. It was his as much as it was theirs. He hadn't become one of them by buying art, he had become himself.

Never mind what God had said about graven images. There was another reading of that injunction. It was God, the great separater, keeping ordinance and beauty, religion and art, apart from each other. It was Jewish to obey the law. And it was Jewish to love colour, vitality and gentleness, as he had loved Leah, as he would still love Leah if only he could see her. Or as Jessica, in her desperation, had loved not him.

What wasn't Jewish was to love both at the same time.

"What news," meanwhile, "from the Rialto?" Strulovitch was asking, and not getting the answer he wanted.

After an afternoon of sightseeing in the Campo di Ghetto Nuovo, Beatrice and Gratan walked arm in arm through the rain in the direction of St. Mark's Square.

"You've had your treat, now I'm having mine," Beatrice laughed.

Gratan didn't see how an afternoon of sightseeing in the Ghetto could be called a treat for him.

Beatrice sighed and tried not to miss her father.

Once she'd kissed a boy with sunken cheekbones called Feng. A Chinese boy whose family owned three Chinese supermarkets and two Chinese restaurants in Manchester. She'd tried to captivate him with amusing observations not one of which he found funny.

"Laugh, Feng," she said, but he seemed not to know how.

It was while she was messing with his mouth, trying to turn the corners of it into a smile and force his lips apart, that she ended up kissing him. At which moment her father came out of the house and accused her of letting Hitler win.

Feng laughed.

So instead of missing her father she decided to miss Feng.

She wondered if there was anyone she didn't miss, anyone who wouldn't have been more fun to be with in Venice than Gratan.

"Nobody knows me in this town," he kept complaining. "I haven't signed a single autograph."

"Think of that as a good thing," she told him. "It means you can concentrate on me."

They took a seat at Florian's and listened to the orchestra play. She loved it here. When she'd sat here in the past with her father he'd told her it reminded him of a Viennese café, only outdoors—the best place for being Jewish that had ever been invented. Then Hitler came along and screwed it. "That's why," he'd begun . . . She didn't bother listening to the rest. That was why he couldn't let her kiss Feng. But she had felt at one with him here, he pretending to be a Viennese Jew, she pretending to be a good daughter.

It was no place to be with Gratan. "I don't like this sort of music," he said. "It's too sweet. It makes me miserable."

"It's meant to make you miserable. Sweetly miserable."

"It makes me angry miserable."

"That's because you're thinking of something else."

"Too right I am. I'm thinking of your father castrating me."

"Just try listening."

"I don't like the violins. They sound like sawing."

She didn't ask him what music he did like. She knew. Johnny Cash. Bruce Springsteen. Chain-gang music.

She despaired of him.

And he of her. Would she want to take him to hear music like this when they were married? Jews, or at least people with Jewish names, sawing and fiddling.

He grew even angrier when he saw the bill. "We've only had coffee," he said.

"And we've listened to Viennese music, and watched the world go by, and been in Venice. Compared to the sums people pay to see you miss penalties and give Nazi salutes I'd say it's cheap."

"I've stopped giving Nazi salutes," he said.

That night, in the casino, she played roulette, putting her chips again and again on *les voisins du zéro,* with whom she felt an affinity, and losing eight hundred euros of his money.

"I wouldn't have minded," he said, "had they been your father's."

"Well in a manner of speaking they were," she said. "You still haven't paid for me." He wasn't amused.

The following morning, to make it up to him, she bought him a stuffed monkey with her own money. A Venetian Carnival monkey wearing a black pointed mask.

He still wasn't amused.

Shylock wanted to talk to Strulovitch about painting, commend his taste, urge him to stop describing the works he collected as Jewish art since all art was in origin Jewish art, was it not?—let the others make the distinction if they must: call what they did post-Pauline art—but first there was another matter he needed to broach. His exchange with Plurabelle.

He hadn't hurried to tell Strulovitch about this. He needed to choose his moment. And besides: everyone else was thinking how events would best serve their interests; did he not have the right to wonder what would best serve his?

But he couldn't keep Plurabelle's offer to himself for ever.

He went searching for Strulovitch and found him sitting in a deep chair, sunk in black reflection. There was barely an inch of wall that didn't have a painting on it, but Strulovitch looked at not a one.

"If you want to milk this they will let you," Shylock said abruptly.

"*This*?"

"You know what *this* is."

"Who's they?"

"The Madame, the keeper of the bawdy house, or however she styles herself. And, I gather, by implication, D'Anton himself."

"You *gather*?"

"I have spoken to her. It was she who hand-delivered the note. I believe I was to understand it as an act of considerable condescension."

"Why didn't you tell me?"

"I judged you had enough on your plate deciding how to respond to the note itself. In my view, practical arrangements could come later."

Shylock folded himself deliberately into an armchair next to Strulovitch's. Both chairs had views of Alderley Edge on which a light snow was falling. Living here was like living in a snow globe, Shylock thought. Art or no art, he suddenly wanted to be gone. He missed the heat and the commotion of the Rialto. The brutality, too. This was no place for Jews. He had said as much to Leah. They live with their nerve-ends exposed in this country, he'd told her. You can maim with a look, in this place. You can kill with a word. Our friend Strulovitch has lost the robustness native to our people. He could be the spinster sister of a country clergyman, he is so sensitive to slights. And as a consequence of that, he cannot judge what's worth going to war for. So he goes to war, mentally, over everything. He had heard Leah laughing at him. "As though you're an example of moderation," she said. And she was right. Jews went to war over everything wherever they washed up. The bellicosity just showed up more obviously here, where the contours of the landscape were gentle, where footfalls in the snow were silent, and where the provocations were more subtle.

Strulovitch sat with his hands over his eyes. He no more wanted to look at Shylock than he wanted to look at the snow. The inside of his hand contained all that he could bear to look at of the physical world.

Shylock wondered whether he was going to be thrown out, snow or no snow. Get thee gone!

In the absence of such an order, he sat quietly, listening to the thump of Strulovitch's bad thoughts.

"So what's she like, this Madame?" Strulovitch asked at last. But he couldn't be bothered to wait for an answer. "And what do you mean when you say I can milk it if I choose?"

"If you want a spectacle they will give you a spectacle. You have not let me into your thoughts about the practicalities of getting the flesh you want, so I am not up to date with your intentions. How it will be done. Where it will be done. Who will do it. Who will weigh it."

"Its weight is of no interest to me."

"Symbolically weigh it."

"Symbols are of no interest to me either. What I ask for is literal to the point of tedium."

Shylock wasn't going to argue with that. "How it will be corroborated, then. Do you want an affidavit from a doctor? Or will you be wanting to inspect the offending tissue with your own eyes? I never paused to consider such questions myself. I let the moment take me. I'd advise against that. It is better to be a master of events. In this case you have the opportunity to be the master of ceremonies. They seem to think you might favour a party. Or at least the woman does. She will throw it, she said, in her grounds."

"Did she say whether there'd be dancing?"

"Whatever you desire. Fireworks, if you wish them. I believe she is in the catering business, so the food should be good. She is also offering a slot on her television programme if that appeals."

"Stop, stop, stop. Are you saying they want to film the operation?"

"I think more the debate."

"What debate? A debate implies there is something further to be decided. There isn't."

"If I understood what the woman was telling me—"

"I don't for a moment doubt that you understood her. Tell me something you don't understand."

"*If* I understood her, the question of whether D'Anton should be circumcised in place of Gratan would be put to a public vote."

"And if the public says yes?"

"We didn't get that far."

"And if it says no?"

"We didn't get that far either. I took the liberty of turning down television. I felt I was empowered to make that decision for you since you seem to think it was I who got you into this."

"But you said OK to the party?"

"I said I would relay the offer."

"When it suited you to do so?"

"None of this suits me. I am not here on some whimsical personal errand. Allow me to remind you that it was you who found me in a cemetery and invited me back to your home. For which . . ."

"*I found you*? I think you misremember. I had business of the heart in that cemetery. I needed to be there. You have still to tell me what brought you."

Shylock who never removed his fedora did so now and ran his hand through his hair. He had the look of a man who might just walk out into the snow of his own accord, whatever his host wanted. Walk out and not be seen again. Enough, his expression said. Enough of this.

He will never be my friend, Strulovitch thought. But then I will never be his.

He owed it to his guest, however, to remember his manners. "Forgive me," he said. "I am grateful for your counsel."

"Counsel is not what I'd call it."

"I am grateful for whatever you call it. Your attention. Your time."

"Then in my judgement," Shylock answered, "you should accept the invitation, not to please them, but to please yourself. There is much mirth for you here—"

"Mirth!"

"Mirth, if you seize the opportunity to look upon it in the right spirit. Think of it as one for the Jews. View it sardonically as a giant outdoor *bris*."

On Alderley Edge, the snow had begun to fall more heavily. Pretty, if you were in the mood. "Won't it be a bit cold for that?" Strulovitch asked. "For D'Anton, I mean."

"There will be a marquee. I'd be surprised if it isn't heated."

"Are you saying, since you've appointed yourself my event-planner, that they're prepared for the procedure to be witnessed by the guests?"

"That depends on your definition of 'procedure.' If you mean the public settling of an argument—the denouement, so to speak, the just distribution of honours and deserts, the mortification of the guilty and the exoneration of the innocent, or vice versa: vice versa being the more usual way of it in my experience—yes. If you mean the removal of D'Anton's foreskin, I doubt very much that D'Anton would consent to undergoing that before an audience. They are talking of a clinic."

"The snivelling coward," Strulovitch said, which was tantamount to an acceptance of Plurabelle's munificence in all other regards.

ACT FIVE

It is one of those better-to-be-dead-than-alive mornings you get in the north of England in winter, though the absence of light is more markedly felt in the Golden Triangle of Wilmslow, Mottram St. Andrew and Alderley Edge on account of the sadness that prevails there in all weathers.

Sadness is among the tools which those who would live nobly employ to distance themselves from the farcicality of existence engulfing everyone else. The unfairness, the banality, the repetition of cruelty. That some are delivered to far grander sorrows than these is proved by their sadness.

As it happens, it is also one of those mornings when a person neither sad nor hopeful might feel that the sun could yet show itself. Not this day, and not even the next, but in the weeks or months to come.

Plurabelle wished they'd waited. Her gardens would not look their best until spring arrived. But she was at the mercy of Strulovitch's impatience. And D'Anton's, come to that. And for herself, too, she knew that the sooner this was settled the better.

"Up," she said to Barnaby who believed that Sundays were

for lying in bed. Indeed, as a man who'd only ever had to look presentable for a living, Barnaby believed that most mornings were for lying in bed, and since his curly head looked so pretty on her pillow Plurabelle was usually content to indulge him. But today was different. "There is something in particular I'm going to want from you," she told him. "Can you guess what it is?"

Barnaby felt tested to within an inch of his life. He doubted he had an answer to any question left in him, or that he could find within himself a single further proof of his devotion. D'Anton had still not succeeded in getting him the Solomon J. Solomon sketch that would show Plury how much and how unconventionally he valued her, but at least he'd found Barnaby a ring much like the one Barnaby had lost. So it couldn't be *that* that she wanted from him. And they'd made love sweetly the night before, so it couldn't be *that* either.

"A clue wouldn't go amiss," Barnaby said, knowing that theirs was a multiple-choice relationship and that, as always, she would give him three.

"It's about today," Plury helped him. "A very important day, as you know."

Barnaby sat up on one elbow and turned his profile to her. That usually helped him out of trouble. "You either want me to welcome guests at the gate," he guessed, "go around with the raffle tickets, or dress D'Anton's wounds and I'm not going to do that."

Plury shook her head. "You can make yourself scarce for the day," she told him, "or you can make yourself scarce for the day, or you can make yourself scarce for the day."

Barnaby, being boyish, wondered if there was a fourth option.

"You can make yourself scarce for the day," Plury said, kissing him.

"Is this because you fear I will faint at the sight of blood?"

"No, it is because I fear my women friends will faint at the sight of you."

"I know," said Barnaby, "that that isn't the real reason you want me out of the way."

"And you are right. The real reason I want you out of the way is that your very presence is suggestive of sexual pleasure. You are so young and so beautiful and so indolent that no one will believe we devote ourselves to anything here but indulgence of the flesh. That is not the impression I want to give, today of all days. I was sad before I met you and it will better serve our cause—yours, mine and D'Anton's—for me to look sad again."

"Very well," said Barnaby, pleased she hadn't mentioned Gratan, "I will drive to Chester Zoo."

Plurabelle could tell he was hurt. But this was a day for sacrifices.

Strulovitch and Shylock had also risen early.

Strulovitch tried on a number of suits, all of them black, and spent much of the morning at the mirror. How do you dress for such an occasion?

At last he sought Shylock's advice.

"Taking one thing with another," he asked, "which of these three ties strikes you as the most appropriate?"

He was reminded of his marriage mornings. The same intestinal tumult. The same wondering if he was looking forward to the day's events or dreading them.

"As a rule you don't wear a tie," Shylock said.

"No, but I think today calls for one."

"Then any but the red," Shylock said.

"I am assuming," Strulovitch mused aloud, "that you will not be making any changes to your wardrobe yourself."

Nothing moved on Shylock's face. "There is, though," he replied, "the question of the hat."

"I was guessing you would wear it."

"The point is not what you were guessing but whether I *ought* to wear it."

"You are more threatening in it."

"Meaning I shouldn't wear it?"

"No, meaning you should."

Shylock looked at himself in the mirror. He too was nervous and reminded of an earlier time.

The final plans, hammered out by persons better suited than the principals to putting their minds to such things, were these:

The two men would be driven by Strulovitch's chauffeur Brendan to the Old Belfry where there would be a small champagne reception at which, if Gratan and Beatrice had not returned to face the music—Plurabelle had booked a string quartet just in case—Strulovitch and D'Anton would have a final conversation, confirm terms in front of witnesses chosen for their discretion, and then be transported in a limousine belonging to neither party to a private walk-in circumcision clinic in Stockport for surgery—a preliminary check of D'Anton's physical and psychological fitness for such an operation, minor as it was, having taken place at the clinic several days before. Strulovitch would see D'Anton across the threshold (and hang about a while outside to be certain he didn't make a run for it) and then return to the party. In due course—the procedure itself, barring complications, not being lengthy—news of its verified completion would be relayed to the Old Belfry, Strulovitch would sign papers to the effect that no further action would be taken against Gratan, no further restraints placed on Beatrice, and no further word spoken against the good names of Plurabelle and D'Anton. The latter would remain in the clinic for as long as necessary, receiving the best care that Stockport had to offer, and Strulovitch would take his leave satisfied. How much champagne he drank would of course be up to him. Ditto the making of a speech.

"As best man you might want to say a few words yourself," Strulovitch said to Shylock.

"I am not your best man."

"I am joking," Strulovitch said.

"Your joke is not welcome."

"It was kindly meant."

"I thought we had agreed that no joke is kindly meant."

Fifteen minutes of tense silence between them in the course of which first one, and then another, repaired to a bathroom to inspect his appearance in a mirror.

It was Strulovitch who spoke first. "I am wondering," he said, "if we ought to make sure that all is well at the clinic."

"Why shouldn't it be?"

"Ideological misgivings."

"It's a circumcision clinic."

"You can never rule out second thoughts."

"Second thoughts on the part of whom?"

"The surgeon."

"He does this operation all the time. It's a routine procedure for him. It's how he makes his living. If I were you I'd be more concerned about D'Anton turning up."

"D'Anton! Of D'Anton I have not the slightest doubt. I have sounded his nature to its dregs—not much of an achievement I grant you, given how little of his nature is anything else. But I know him, I have him, he is mine. He will need, more than anything, to demonstrate his bravery and in the process show us to be inhuman wretches. He might even be hoping we will kill him. I am only sorry we can't oblige."

"*We?*"

Strulovitch stopped what he was doing and looked across at Shylock who was not looking across at him. "Don't tell me it's *your* constancy I should be worrying about."

"Do I owe you constancy? I am not aware I owe anyone anything. I certainly don't owe this D'Anton harm."

"No, you don't owe me or D'Anton a thing. But our actions have consequences."

"You will have to explain that."

"There are consequences to setting an example."

"I set an example! *I?*"

Shylock would have liked at that moment to be in Strulovitch's garden, expressing incredulity to his wife. "My host seems to see me," he would tell her, "as a role model. Would you believe that?"

"I shouldn't let this go to your head, my dear," he knew Leah would reply, "but you were always a hero to me too."

"Then you are both fools."

D'Anton, though eager until the last moment to know if there'd been news from the Rialto, was perhaps the least anxious of the actors. Let the axe fall. What would be, would be. The readiness is all.

Considering his initial reluctance to Plurabelle's plans, he was in remarkably good spirits. But then she had worked on him and got him to understand how much hung on his co-operation. He too, she hoped she didn't need to remind him, could only gain from this in the end.

But she was impressed nonetheless by how calm he seemed on the day. "I am armed by the knowledge of our rectitude," he said, taking her hand and putting it to his cheek.

"And I by the quietness of your spirit," she said.

They both laughed.

When Strulovitch and Shylock arrived a small party was gathered in a snowy white tent, warmed by banks of the most efficient patio heaters money could buy.

It fell to Shylock, who was not wearing his hat, to effect the introductions.

"It seems odd," Plurabelle said, shaking Strulovitch's hand, "that we have not met until now."

"Since we don't move in the same circles, except those my daughter runs around me, and you around her, I don't find that odd at all," Strulovitch replied. What did, however, strike him as odd was the look of hurt surprise—like a person drowning where there is no water—which the thousand cuts of surgery had lent Plurabelle's every feature. May the knife do as ill with D'Anton, he wished.

He is as horrible as I imagined, Plurabelle thought, feeling a renewed surge of pity for Beatrice. No wonder her own father had hated Jews. For the first time she understood the tests he'd devised for her prospective lovers. They were calculated to protect her from the depredations of such monsters. Of the two examples here, she much preferred Shylock, a preference she emphasised by taking him by the arm and walking him into the marquee, scattering him like gold dust among her friends.

"Who are these people?" Strulovitch enquired, following her.

"They are well-wishers of D'Anton and friends of mine," she told him. "You were invited to bring an equal number of supporters."

"I have no need of supporters."

"I promise you they are not here to sway opinion, one way or another."

"There is no opinion to be swayed. I and your co-conspirator in the abduction of my daughter are agreed as to what will happen should Gratan not return Beatrice by noon, and I see we are only a few minutes away from that. It doesn't look as though they are coming."

At noon exactly, D'Anton emerged from the house and, with eyes becomingly lowered, his back bent slightly as though feigning weariness, he walked to meet Strulovitch. Strulovitch noted that under his coat and jacket he wore a shirt as snowy as the earth, the top three buttons of it open like a crooner's. Has he forgotten what we're here for, Strulovitch wondered. Does he think I have designs on his heart?

Neither man made an attempt to shake the hand of the other.

"The matter is settled then," Strulovitch said, looking at his watch. "You will submit to my wishes in place of your crony, Gratan—"

"He is not my crony."

"As you wish. You will submit in his place, and once the thing is done—"

"The slate between us will be clean. You will have no further call on any of us, including your daughter."

"My daughter will remain my daughter, I will not consent to thinking of her as 'one of you,' but yes, whatever she wants

I will consent to so long as I have written assurance that you have left the clinic other than as you entered it."

"That exceeds our agreement, I think. Will it not give you room from now until evermore to complain that I am still, in some respect or other, the man I was before?"

"How you remain, 'in some respect or other,' is none of my affair. The state of your mind, your character, your affections and temperament, your prejudices, are yours to do with as you please. They are such as the Devil himself could not change and I don't flatter myself that I could. You know what I ask. It is a strictly circumscribed demand."

"That I return, God willing, fit to be your son-in-law . . ."

"That you will never be."

"Nor will I ever want to be. I mean in your 'strictly circumscribed' sense only. Fit in your God's eyes to be a Jewish husband were I ever to desire to be one. Ha!"

Strulovitch wondered what it was about that phrase "your God's eyes" that made him want to put out D'Anton's. He had been hoping, even after the clocks struck, that Beatrice would turn up, with or without Gratan. Now he prayed she wouldn't.

He nodded his assent.

"Then do your worst," D'Anton said.

He looked around, hoping to see Barnaby. It was only a shame that it wasn't his but Gratan's debt he was paying. There was poetry in his heart for Barney. "Give me your hand, Barnaby," he could have said. "Bid your wife judge whether Barnaby had not once a love . . ." D'Anton was a man for a dying fall. "Bid your wife judge whether Gratan had not once a love" had a very different ring to it.

He was about to ask Plurabelle to commend him to Barnaby's favour, but Plurabelle had business of her own to attend to. "May I make a final plea," she said, addressing Strulovitch, "before this business is concluded. I understand a father's pain. My father died dreading what might befall his daughter. I won't say he did too much to protect me, but his precautions didn't exactly smooth my way. Sometimes a father must chance his child to the world—"

"I have chanced my child to the world," Strulovitch said, "and the world has undone her. I have struck a bargain which won't bring her back, but a bargain is a bargain. This gentleman is by repute—certainly by his own repute—a man of honour. By that honour he owes me the little I have left to ask."

"It is not a little to him," Plurabelle said.

Strulovitch coughed, looking to Shylock for corroboration of the infelicity, before remembering that Shylock wasn't a corroborating man. Without his hat he looked a more genial figure. Unamused but lenitive. The headmaster of a progressive, but not too progressive, secondary school.

"This is an operation," Plurabelle continued, "that can go terribly wrong. You mean it as a humiliation, and a humiliation it most certainly is. Do you also mean it as a fatal injury? You think I exaggerate but I have details here"—she brought from her pocket a computer printout bearing, Strulovitch noticed, the Wikipedia logo—"of accidents and, yes, fatalities that must surely make you think again. I am your daughter's friend. I believed myself to be her protector. As such I plead with you, by your own faith and hers, to spare a man who would not intentionally have hurt a hair on her head."

She seemed to be speaking by rote, not even looking into the eyes of the person she was trying to persuade.

"It's too late for any of this," Strulovitch said. "We have

struck our deal. Let's get it over with. So that we can be done with one another for all time. The car, I believe, is waiting."

He made a courtly motion with his hand to D'Anton. After you.

The men made to go but were again halted.

"Tarry a moment. A word before you leave."

Strulovitch turned in surprise. The speaker this time was Shylock who, until that moment, had been holding himself theatrically aloof, a man worthy of notice for his lack of interest in the day's events or any of the parties to them. Shylock bored. Shylock somewhere else. But that was then. Now, as though snapped into action by some external agency, he was another man. Shylock urgent. Shylock here. Conciliatory in tone, gently spoken, hatless, avuncular, but insistent on being heard.

"What's this?" Strulovitch said.

"A moment of your time," Shylock said. "No more."

"It's all been said."

"Not all."

"Have I forgotten something?" Strulovitch asked. "Or have you?"

"Forgotten something? I, no." Shylock paused as though the matter of their being different men with different memories merited careful thought. "But you, yes, you have forgotten something."

The banal sky felt thundery all of a sudden. Shylock could do that; he could affect the atmospheric pressure, perturb the weather with whatever was perturbing him. Strulovitch looked up, saw the future and the past. The weariness of the prophets descended on him.

"I have no time for this triteness," he said. "I am not in

need of a lesson. The matter is agreed." Here he inclined his head to D'Anton who was resigned to his fate, whatever the meaning of Shylock's intervention.

But Shylock hadn't finished yet. "You accept the terms?" he asked, looking into D'Anton's face for the first time.

D'Anton's eyelids dropped like heavy curtains. "Fully," he said.

"You allow them to be just?"

"Just? Does justice enter into this?"

"If you think it does not, then you cannot accept the terms."

"I accept the terms because I have to."

"By what reasoning?"

"I have no option."

"You could refuse."

"If I refuse, those I love will suffer consequences."

"And you? Will you suffer consequences?"

"I don't count what happens to myself."

"You are a willing sacrifice?"

"I am."

"Therefore by this action both sides will achieve the thing they seek. I call that just."

D'Anton nodded his head.

"So I ask again: You allow these terms to be just?"

"Cruel, but just."

"But just?" It is like extracting teeth, Shylock thought.

"Yes," D'Anton conceded. "Just." He smiled faintly at his own joke. "Just just."

Shylock, unamused, nodded and turned his face back to Strulovitch's. "Then," he said, "must the Jew be merciful . . ."

Strulovitch knew exactly what he had to say in return. You don't always have a choice.

"On what compulsion must I?" he asked.

Whereupon Shylock said what he too had to say. "The quality of mercy is not strained, it droppeth as the gentle rain from heaven . . ."

Strulovitch owned an etching by an unknown nineteenth-century artist that showed Ulysses lashed to the mast of his ship to protect him from the treacherous mellifluence of the sirens. The sirens themselves were a touch too Rubensesque for Strulovitch's taste but he liked the way their songs were drawn as musical notations that flew towards Ulysses like birds, assailing all his senses. Struggling against his bonds, his eyes popping out of his head, Ulysses clearly regretted his decision to be restrained. But what about the sailors whose ears were stopped with wax? Did a single flying melody get through to them as they laboured at their oars? Or was there just a wall of yammering and the mermaids miming?

Having no wax to din out Shylock, Strulovitch deafened himself, instead, by act of will, stringing a procession of black thoughts, like funeral bunting if such a thing existed, from ear to ear. Everything he could recall that had ever made him angry, every slight, every exclusion, every bad thing done to him and every bad thing he had done. It was more than a match, in its malignancy, for Shylock's honeyed peroration.

This, had he listened—but had he listened he would only have heard what he knew he was going to hear—was what Shylock said:

"The quality of mercy is not strained . . . You ask on what compulsion you should be merciful, you who have received no mercy yourself from him I ask you to show mercy to—you ask why you should requite what you have not received—and I say to you: Be an exemplary of mercy; give not in expectation of receiving mercy back—for mercy is not a transaction—but give it for what it constitutes in itself. Show pity for pity's sake and not the profit of your soul. Eyes without pity will become blind, but it is not only in order that you may see that you should practise it. Pity is not compromised by profit or deserts, it does not minister to self-love, it is not a substitute for forgiveness, but builds its modest house wherever there is need of it. And what need is there of it here, you ask, where justice alone cries out for what is owing to it. The need is this: God asks it. What pertains to him, must pertain to you, otherwise you cannot claim that you are acting justly in His name. And will God love the sinner more than the sinned against? No, he will love you equally. No man can love as God loves, and it is profane of any man to try. But you can act in the spirit of God's love, show charity, give though it is gall and wormwood to you to give, spare the undeserving, love those that do not love you—for where is the virtue merely in returning love?—give to those who would take from you and, where they have taken, do not recompense them in kind, for the greater the offence the greater the merit in refusing to be offended. Who shows *rachmones* does not diminish justice. Who shows *rachmones* acknowledges the just but exacting law under which we were created. And so worships God."

Though he wouldn't attend, Strulovitch waited. Manners too are a species of that compassion Jews call *rachmones*.

"You are finished?" he asked at last.

Shylock signalled to those who had applauded him that such an ovation was unnecessary. "Yes I am finished," he said.

"Then I and my co-signatory will proceed to the clinic as agreed," Strulovitch said.

Shylock bowed to him. He seemed to expect nothing else.

But Strulovitch wanted a quiet word before leaving. "Was it for this, then, that you came?" he asked in his lowest voice. What business remained between them was theirs alone.

"I'd prefer to think," Shylock replied in kind, "that this was why you found me."

Strulovitch swam in the unexpected blue of Shylock's eyes. When had they changed colour?

"Who did the finding and who the being found is not a matter that will easily be settled between us."

"No."

"I too admired your performance."

"You weren't listening."

"I got the gist of it."

Shylock lowered his head. His hair was thinner than Strulovitch had noticed before, but then he had not seen him without his hat. A sentimentalist when it came to men— especially to fathers—he was half-inclined to kiss Shylock where the hair was thinnest.

Shylock read his mind. "I am not in search of a son," he said.

"And I have had my fill of fathers," Strulovitch said. "I hope I can admire your theatricality for itself. But you couldn't really have believed that it would sway me."

Shylock laughed. A shy catch of the breath. When had he started to laugh? "Not for a moment," he said. "Affecting your resolution was the last thing on my mind. Not everything is about you."

When Strulovitch swept out of Plurabelle's drive with D'Anton at his shoulder, Plurabelle did not even see them go. She had eyes only for Shylock. God, I love this man, she thought. I fucking love him.

She was glad Barney was not here. It had been inspired of her to get rid of him though she hadn't really known why she'd done it at the time. Now she could only hope he'd lost his way and would never come back. Let him stay in Chester Zoo.

She approached the new man in her life and laid a hand on his arm, surprised by how hard it felt. "That was awe-inspiring," she said.

Shylock's eyes had reverted to their gunmetal grey. "But it didn't work," he said. "Mercy has not been shown."

"Oh, that needn't matter."

"Needn't it?"

"How do we ever measure what works anyway," she said, looking up at him with her swollen lips. "I can only tell you that it worked for me."

"I'm pleased to hear that. To whom are you showing mercy?"

"I will show it you if you wish me to."

"I am not in need of it."

"What are you in need of ?"

He paused, as though expecting something else. "And?" he said.

She was disconcerted. "I don't understand."

"I am waiting for what follows. Don't you usually have a riddle for those you think want something from you?"

She shook her hair as though wishing to rid her head of what he'd just said. "I have no riddle for you," she said. "With you, I feel at last that I can be direct. I know there is nothing you want. But is there anything I can give you?"

He wondered if she was about to offer to make him famous. I am too old for this, he thought. "Peace and quiet," he said. "Peace and quiet are all I am in need of."

She took that to be further encouragement. Peace and quiet she could give him. "You are not what I thought you were," she persisted.

"And what did you think I was?"

"I don't know, but I would never have imagined . . ." Whatever it was she would never have imagined she couldn't for the moment find the words for it.

Shylock helped her out. "That a Jew could be so Christian?"

She felt that he almost spat the words at her.

"No, no, that wasn't what I intended to say. What I mean is that you looked so forbidding when you opened the door to me at Simon Strulovitch's I didn't dream you could be capable of such humanity."

"That's just another way of saying the same thing. You saw a Jew and expected nothing of him but cruelty."

"I didn't see *a Jew*. I don't go around *seeing Jews*."

"All right—you saw cruelty and gave it a Jewish face."

"I'm only saying you are not what you seem. I am not a Christian. I haven't been to church since I was a little girl. But I know what Christian sentiments are. Is it so wrong to be surprised by the eloquent expression of sentiments one normally hears from the pulpit by a man who scowls?"

"You mean a Jew who scowls."

"I mean what I say I mean."

"Then I will answer you in that spirit. Yes, it is wrong to be surprised. It is wrong not to know where you got your sweet Christian sentiments from. It is morally and historically wrong not to know that Jesus was a Jewish thinker and that when you quote him against us you are talking vicious nonsense. Charity is a Jewish concept. So is mercy. You took them from us, that is all. You appropriated them. They were given freely, but still you had to steal them."

"I?"

"It shocks you to exemplify? It must. It shocked me. I was made to crawl for what I exemplified. So yes, *you*. You say my humanity surprises you. What was it you expected? And whose humanity is it that you think you see in me now? Your own! How dare you think you can teach me what I already know, or set me the example I long ago set you? It is a breathtaking insolence, an immemorial act of theft from which nothing but sorrow has ever flowed. There is blood on your insolence."

Plurabelle looked as though she were about to cry. She put a hand on her chest. "I feel you've laid a curse on me," she said.

"Well now you know the sensation from the other end," Shylock said.

And this time Plurabelle could have sworn he *did* spit on her.

"That's what you call telling them," Leah said.

Shylock pulled his coat around him. "It was not without a long premeditation," he admitted.

"It was none the worse for that," she said.

"A long premeditation invites anticlimax," he said. "One can think *too* long. What I said was musty. It could have been better."

"It was good enough."

"Is that all?"

"Good enough is good enough. You don't, I hope, think you are going to change history."

"I can hope."

"You'd be unwise to do so."

"You wish then that I'd stayed silent?"

"I haven't said that. Though I wish you'd shown a little of your *rachmones* to that poor girl."

"Ach, I wouldn't worry for her. She fucking loves me."

"Then maybe I should worry for you."

"I think you're safe. She's the wrong persuasion."

He didn't go immediately, but stood in the snow enjoying her proximity.

Some days were harder than others. Today he would have liked to feel her arms around him. There was quiet between them, as though each were waiting for some word from the other. At last it was she who spoke.

"Caring about the right or wrong persuasion has not done us any good," she said.

"It's not only our doing," he reminded her.

"No, it's not. But it's us I'm talking about. You and me and Jessica."

"Oh, Jessica will be fine."

But he read from the long echoing silence that ensued, that she knew, after all, that Jessica was not and never would be fine.

So had Leah all this time been concealing what she knew from him, just as he had all this time been concealing what he knew from her? Did she know what he'd have given the world for her never to find out, that their daughter had betrayed them, betrayed the love they'd borne each other, betrayed her upbringing and betrayed her own honour, for someone, for something—describe it how one would—of no worth?

It had been worse, then, for Leah than for him. Down there, in the cold of her interment, Leah lay day after day, without the consolation of confession or conversation, with her arms wound tight around their disgrace.

He thought his heart would break.

By the time Strulovitch returned to the Old Belfry to await public word of D'Anton's operation Shylock was gone and of the friends of Plurabelle still dancing attendance on her none appeared to be of a mind to talk to him.

The little afternoon light there'd been was fading quickly. That suited Strulovitch. There was nothing he wanted to see. He dusted snow from a filigree bench far from the marquee and sat indifferent to the damp. He'd dropped D'Anton off at the clinic without looking at him or speaking to him. D'Anton had clearly wanted quiet himself after his altercation with Shylock. He shook a little, Strulovitch thought— though that might have been in fear of what awaited him. He recovered his spirits enough to say, "So this is it, then, over the top we go," as he left the limousine, but Strulovitch had met that with silence. Why the victim should have been in a lighter mood than the executioner Strulovitch didn't bother to enquire. Bluster, presumably. As it was bluster on his own part to say he hoped his adversary would die screaming under the knife. In fact he no longer cared what happened either way. Let D'Anton live, let D'Anton die—the outcome was immaterial to him. What would it change? It wouldn't bring Beatrice back. It wouldn't bring his wife back. It wouldn't cook Gratan's goose. And D'Anton would still be D'Anton when he was discharged. In all probability, and with some justice, more the Jew-hater than before.

He wondered if Shylock were feeling much what he felt right now. Knowing his words had all been for nothing. It wasn't just that there was no victory to be had; it was that there was no victory worth having. Victory and defeat were alike absurd.

On it stretched, backwards and forwards, the line of risible time—all the way from the conversion of the Christians to the conversion of the Jews. And would the world be a better place if the one hadn't happened and the other suddenly did? Beatrice with or without Gratan—what difference? The gallery he had failed to open in his parents' name—so what? His ruined wife—did it matter to her what sort of world she lived in? Action had stopped arbitrarily for Shylock, but time hadn't. Time had embalmed him. Would he have been better off had time ended for him when action did? Would he have effected anything less or anything more? The greatest illusion of all—that time would labour and bring forth beneficent change.

He didn't know how long he sat there, but the chill had barely begun to spread through him when Plurabelle called out that she had news. Her voice had an unaccustomed crack in it, like a choirboy's on the point of breaking. She looked shrunken and feverish. Knowing nothing of what had transpired between her and Shylock, Strulovitch took this to be the natural consequence of her fears for D'Anton. Good. If nothing else he had sown disquiet. And for a moment he hoped again his adversary had died screaming under the knife. But there was something not quite right about Plurabelle's agitation. She had news, she said tragically. If the news was that D'Anton had died screaming under the knife, why was she taking so long to deliver it? Why the music-hall posturing— the badly executed stagger, the laboured breathing, the pale hand to the brow?

She's hamming this, Strulovitch thought. She doesn't want it to end. He could understand her looking forward to all being well again in her brittle little world, and Strulovitch with his threats and menaces being gone from it. But that didn't explain the histrionics.

A small number of people were gathered in the marquee, hugging the heaters. "I have here a letter from the surgeon, dated, you might be surprised to learn, five days ago," Plurabelle finally announced. Her voice was suddenly strong and vindictive and, as she read, her sorrowing eyes of moments before became points of unabated fire.

> *To whom it may concern,*
>
> *I have today had the pleasure of examining this delightful patient (name supplied) with a view to judging his fitness to undergo circumcision by the "Forceps Guided Method" and am pleased to report that examination proved such a method, or indeed any method, supererogatory as the patient is already circumcised. The operation, as far as I can deduce and he recall, was performed when he was an infant, such procedures being common among families living in hot countries.*
>
> *Needless to say one cannot circumcise a person twice.*
>
> *Yours very sincerely,*
> *Pandhari Malik*

Was there laughter? Was there applause?

For the second time that afternoon, Strulovitch stopped his ears. If there is such a thing as hysterical deafness there is such a thing as rational deafness too. Why listen to what neither educates nor honours you? Why be demeaned by the unfolding of absurd predictability?

He didn't have the patience—with events or with himself—to track back over the subterfuge that had made a fool of him. No one had acted with principle. He had lost, that was all that differentiated him from D'Anton. Winning—the prize a bloodied D'Anton—would not have made him the better man.

Surprised only by how little he was surprised, he slipped away before Plurabelle could confront him with his defeat. Let her exult without him. He had no further business at the Old Belfry and nothing to complain of. He was glad of it. To the modern mind there is a dignity in being tricked. It confirms the preposterousness of existence.

I am content, he thought. Obsolete, but content.

He did not immediately return home. He asked Brendan, whom he found in earnest conversation with other chauffeurs, to drive him round. Anywhere. On ungritted lanes, preferably. A whited landscape. High hedgerows and the quiet crunch of tyres on snow. Stay away until nightfall. And not long to wait for that. Here, night fell in the middle of the afternoon.

Before getting out and opening the door for Strulovitch, Brendan turned around and handed him a letter. "It's my notice," he said.

"I've been expecting it," Strulovitch said. "I hope I haven't been a trial to work for."

"Sometimes one needs a change, sir," Brendan said. "That is all."

"You must do what your conscience determines, Brendan," Strulovitch told him.

It gave him no pleasure to reflect that in the absence of fiends and devils to blame, Brendan's conscience would be his scourge.

When he did finally get back he went straight to his desk where he scribbled a note to D'Anton. "To the victor the spoils," he wrote. "As a mark of my good grace I will arrange for the Solomon Joseph Solomon to be delivered to your home. I trust the pleasure it gives the person for whom you say it is intended will be returned tenfold to you. You have a parched and withered look. May the sap of gratitude and reciprocated friendship rise in you. We were not put on earth to be forever sad."

Before retiring, he called in on Kay and found Beatrice sitting with her. Neither woman made any demonstration of affection.

"When did you get back?" he asked Beatrice.

"Not long ago."

"Are you well?"

She looked at her mother as though for confirmation. Was there a nod, a smile?

This is hard on her, Strulovitch thought—meaning everything. This is too cruel. She's a child. "You look well," he lied.

"I doubt that," she said. "But thanks, anyway. I'm unharmed, if that's what you mean. And unbetrothed, if that's what you really want to know."

"It's enough you're here."

"It's enough for me too."

It was enough she was here. It was everything she was here. But some unquiet, unappeasable sprite of fatherly fault-finding nudged aside the joy he wanted to express. "If you'd told me you were coming home today," he said, "you'd have saved everybody a lot of trouble."

"Maybe I didn't want to save everybody a lot of trouble."

In her stony unforgivingness she resembles Shylock, Strulovitch thought. Were he to ask her what she was thinking he had little doubt how she would answer.

I will be revenged on the whole pack of you.

He was not of an age, but for all time.
—*Ben Jonson*

For more than four hundred years, Shakespeare's works have been performed, read, and loved throughout the world. They have been reinterpreted for each new generation, whether as teen films, musicals, science-fiction flicks, Japanese warrior tales, or literary transformations. The Hogarth Press was founded by Virginia and Leonard Woolf in 1917 with a mission to publish the best new writing of the age. In 2012, Hogarth was launched in London and New York to continue the tradition. The Hogarth Shakespeare project sees Shakespeare's works retold by acclaimed and bestselling novelists of today.